Die Coast Bye Cecilia

Die Coast Bye Cecilia

also featuring

Permanence Reviewed

Andrew Malcolm

Die Coast Bye Cecilia by Andrew Malcolm Copyright: 2023
Updated Edition: 2024
Andrew Malcolm, Pressure of Light Books, Hamilton ON
Permanence Reviewed by Andrew Malcolm Copyright: 2024
Andrew Malcolm, Pressure of Light Books, Hamilton ON
AndrewRichardMalcolm.com
ISBN: 978-0-9952152-4-5

In Memory of Alix and Flo

Contents

Die Coast Bye Cecilia

Part One: East Hamilton, to Toronto Harbour Lighthouse, to Toronto Islands' Ward's Beach, through the Eastern Gap into Toronto's Inner Harbour, and scenic paddle along the inner harbour's industrialised East Shore.

"'He says the weather's horrendous. And getting worse. Perfect! Just what you wanted!'"

—Redmond O'Hanlon, *Trawler*

Chapter One

2008 – East Hamilton (Friday before the Dragonboat Races)

We step outside and see no sign of her. We walk around to the backyard and see no sign of her. Then we plop down on the edge of their back deck, which overlooks Lake Ontario, Toronto's skyline just visible through the hot, humid air.

Sam says, "She's probably feeling really awkward about all this, particularly without your parents here. We have our whole family here and we feel awkward."

Kate says, "What? I don't feel awkward."

"Okay, whatever, I'm just trying to show some understanding."

"Coast, what the fuck's up with your sister, is she always like this?"

Since I haven't spoken to Cecilia in three years, not since she graduated and started university two years ago, I don't know if she always acts like this. I'm feeling a bit embarrassed about not knowing my twin sister that well, so instead of answering Kate's question I ask her why she called me Coast.

"Coast, because you're a fisherman, and you moved from one coast to the other. So now I'm calling you Coast. Be happy, I could call you worse things."

We continue looking for Cecilia, walking along the sides of the yard down towards the water, where I spot her. She's sleeping in a canoe-catamaran – two aluminium canoes lashed together with old wood paddles and polypropylene rope. It has a tarp sail that's held up with tent poles, and one of the canoes has a heavy green nylon sheet clamped to the gunwales of the front half so that the sheet forms the hammock bed that Cecilia is sprawled out in.

She looks so peaceful when I come down to the dock, I can't help but get a flash back to the last time we were really close, when we actually talked and spent time together – right before high school.

Sam says, "Holy crap, is she okay?"

"She's fine," I say. "I guess she was really tired, maybe hasn't slept for a while."

Kate says, "What the hell is she sleeping in?"

Sam says, "Isn't this set-up great? I'm test rigging for a trip next week. It's going to save us two days of paddling if we start with a tail wind, which there always is on this la— "

"Okay, I don't care about your fucking hippy-trip-innovations when you could just as easily bring a trawling motor."

"So why do you think she's here?" Sam asks me.

I'm happy to have a piece of information to relay about my sister with confidence. "She can fall asleep instantly in any boat and stay asleep through anything. I think it was the only way to get her to sleep when she was a baby. My parents would bring her down to our dingy anytime she was crying."

"Aw, that's adorable. Is that the same with you?"

"Me? No, I hardly sleep at all. I think it's been a couple days actually. That's why I'm the best deckhand to have on a crew. Nobody sleeps on fishing boats, at least not ones with serious captains, and I never sleep anyway."

Kate says, "Jesus fuck, did I ever get your name right then."

"You know what? If I'm not out on a fishing boat, I'm on a beach around a bonfire, so yeah, I guess you did."

Kate says, "I think your parents are here."

Up the hill and through the trees on the left we can see part of the driveway, and coming up it is a cab.

I say, "All right, guess we should head up there."

"Don't sound so fucking excited."

"Ah, I'm not to be honest."

We stay around and talk about what to do with Cecilia, eventually deciding it's best to leave her where she is. Obviously she's exhausted, and it would be better if she was rested before joining a full family reunion.

We walk up the hill, but drag our feet. I don't think any of us are excited about mingling with the older generation while they awkwardly reacquaint themselves.

IT'S UNBELIEVABLE. OUR PARENTS ARE UNBELIEVABLE. The reunion fell apart so quickly, so terribly. We go down to the boat, then stand there in shocked silence for a while, Sam snivelling and Kate rubbing her back. I think a million thoughts, make a million decisions, while looking at the still peacefully sleeping Cecilia.

Kate, after Sam relaxes a little, says, "Jesus fuck what a shit show. First time the two halves of our family get together in twenty years and it turns into a brawl."

Sam says, "Oh my God, look, a cop car is coming up the driveway."

Kate says, "We shouldn't have to deal with this shit."

Sam says, "I'm so sorry about your mum, Coast."

"No, it's fine. It's my parents too, they're horrible towards people. Seriously, that fight is nothing to do with us. Let's just forget it."

"How? It's still happening."

At that moment I feel a warm wind roll down the hill and out to the water. Away from the shore I see ripples, ripples that will eventually build into waves crashing against the shore of that city across the lake.

I say, "Hey, why don't we jump in this canoe-catamaran and sail to Toronto?"

Sam laughs a bit and blinks at me through dried tears. "Coast, you're funny…you're alright. Kate, what do you think of this guy?"

"Well if you're okay with him then I know he's fucked."

"Seriously though, the wind's blowing directly away from here and towards the skyline. Would we have to paddle at all to get to the other side of the lake?"

"No, I'd just have to rudder us."

"Okay listen: before I came here I bought eleven bottles of expensive liquors, as gifts for everyone. They're in my duffle bag. I don't feel like giving them to our parents anymore, so let's go land wherever the wind takes us and have our own reunion."

Kate says, "What about your sister, and how the fuck— "

"We'll figure it all out later."

Sam grabs Kate's shoulders and looks at her with a sudden intensity. "Seriously, I'm into this. I want to get as far away from here as possible right now."

"Fuck, fine. I'll go grab our stuff."

Kate leaves, and after a moment of thought I ask Sam if there's a phone inside I can use.

"Here, use my cell, I've got long-distance if you have to call someone out West."

"Thanks." I make two calls: one to my landlord, to tell him I'm moving out immediately, and to keep my last month's rent because I won't be there to clean out my stuff (basically just a couch); and another to the captain of the fishing boat I'm supposed to go out on in a few days, to tell him I'm not out West anymore and probably won't be coming back.

After I hang up, Sam says, "What was that all about?"

"I don't know, I don't know what I'm doing, but I want to have nothing planned, I don't want to live anywhere, I might even just drift for a while. You probably think I'm messed."

"Definitely, but I love it."

When she comes back, Kate says, "Holy shit are they ever screaming at each other. The two cops look like they want to quit on the spot. Our folks didn't even register my presence so I told the cops to kindly let them know their kids are getting the fuck out of this circus in Sam's canoes. The guy actually shook his head saying 'take me with you'."

Sam says, "That's nothing, Coast just quit his job and told his landlord he's not coming back."

Kate looks at me like I'm insane. "You're really one for rash decisions, fuck."

We throw our stuff inside, climb in and leave while Cecilia sleeps sound and oblivious.

WE SAIL FOR ABOUT AN HOUR. Jake's house is already indecipherable from the rest of the shoreline. It would take the whole day to paddle back, so we're committed at this point. Realising this, I open a fresh notebook and start writing about how we ended up in the middle of the lake.

I've still written a lot since graduating high school, but not to finish pieces or publish anything. I either write on fishing boats – essentially expanded log books – or in notebooks around bonfires. I love writing descriptions of whatever's around me and noting down lines or bits of dialogues from conversations I have.

As I'm writing descriptions of the canoe and the lake, and Cecilia sleeping in the hammock bed, I think maybe this could be something serious, a tale from my life that I could turn into a book.

This isn't the first time I've made a rash decision, but it's an impulsive move that's suddenly woken me up to the fact that a lot of change has been stewing beneath my skin for a while. I'm not going back out West, not ever, and I'm never going back East either, not after what happened at Jake's, which is fine – Cecilia's the only one I wanted to reconnect with anyway.

This is the start of a new life for me; not just me, me and Cecilia, and it's all going to start with this…ah, this… "Hey Sam, would you call this a canoe trip?"

Kate says, "I wouldn't, because I don't go on canoe trips."

Sam says, "And we're going to a city. Canoe trips aren't really meant for cities."

Kate says, "Hmm, I didn't think I'd ever go to Toronto either. I guess if you put Toronto and canoe trip together, then I'm okay with it. As long as there's whisky."

"You know what? Forget what I said, this is absolutely a canoe trip. Why, are you writing about it?"

"Yeah, I'm writing this trip into a bo— "

"Woh, there's a bump," says Sam.

A wave picks us up and carries us before getting ahead. I look around – and I'm looking backwards, leaning against the bow seat with the notebook on my knees, facing Sam ruddering the boat (Kate's sitting in the stern of the boat Cecilia's sleeping in the bow of) – and I see that the waves have really started building.

The shoreline we're following – lined with houses and the occasional marina and condo building – is too far to gauge our speed, but the wind and the waves must have us moving pretty quick. I'm getting a bit nervous thinking about how big the waves will be by the time we get to the city. "Sam, we're not going to go over, are we?"

Kate says, "Oh, the big fisherman from the torrential coastal waters is scared of a little lake."

Sam laughs, "Don't worry, Coast, I got this. The wind is right at our tail, so no problem keeping us straight with the waves, and we're a catamaran! I hope the waves get huge, it'll be fun."

Even if we go over I figure we'd get rescued easily enough. There are sailboats and yachts scattered everywhere. I see a few kayaks too, and a six-person outrigger, which I'd usually only expect to see on an ocean, but this great lake is obviously ocean enough.

It's definitely a gorgeous day to be on the water. There isn't a cloud in the sky and the sun is glittering everywhere I look.

Kate says, "Coast, drop the book, you're scribbling in it like a madman."

"In a sec. I'm describing the lake."

"Why don't you describe yourself cracking open a bottle of whisky and passing it around."

"I can't do that and write at the same time."

"Right, so again, drop the book."

Sam says, "Kate, you're such a jerk. Coast, you're so good about it though. I hope you know Kate's a softie at heart."

"Yeah, I can tell. Let's drink some whisky."

Chapter Two

2006 – Vancouver Island (last story written by Alex about Cecilia)

Title: Nematocyst

"LOOK, THERE'S A LIGHT ON THE WATER, CLOSE TO THE MAINLAND."

"It's the sun's reflection." How could he not tell, he isn't making sense anymore.

"It's not moving?"

"No."

His eyes droop down to his feat, realising I'm right.

"My ass hurts on this log."

"Stand up and walk around a bit."

Or sit there and shuffle pebbles with your feet. A breeze filled with salt and rotting seaweed draws my attention back to the shore. I must look for anemones. There's one in a tide pool closer to the water. Tentacles surround its soft slimy mouth waiting patiently for the crashing waves to reach the tide pool and bring a fresh batch of prey. Stroking them causes the anemone to contract.

"Why do you always do that?"

"I like the feeling of a million spikes firing into my finger."

"What does it feel like?"

My eyes squint in the sunlight as I look at Alex over my shoulder, "Sticky." He smiles back, uneasily.

Think of me as a tiny cell on the surface of an anemone tentacle. Think of Alex as a microscopic larva. An unborn, immature larva floating by, looking for a piece of ground that will allow him to start his life.

"How long since we beached on this island?" Alex asks.

"You say that every day." He's shuffling more pebbles. "43 days, 45 since the boat sank, 10 since we stopped walking."

"Do you still—"

"—No, I don't want to stay here anymore."

Picture Alex the microscopic larva coming to close to me, not realising that I'm no ordinary cell. Beneath a hatch on my surface is an inverted spike, a nematocyst, with a poisonous tail at its tip, waiting to fire.

He's looking at me with the eyes of a child, "Cecilia?"

"Yes Alex."

"Are you sure we'll get rescued?"

"Yes Alex, I know the Great Bear Rainforest very well. This is a remote part, but I'm positive this channel is a route for cruise ships sailing to Alaska."

He looks down the beach, trying to locate an eagle call.

"How long could you survive here?"

"As long as I wanted."

Picture me, the anemone cell, and the hatch on my surface opening, firing the spike into Alex, the passing larva. Picture the barbed points that spiral up the spike like the lines on a candy cane shredding Alex's surface layer, and the three downward pointing blades at the base of the spike locking inside him just as an arrow head would.

He's walking away, down the beach, head hanging low, black shirt hanging of his thin shoulders, black bangs hanging over his eyes, hands in his pocket. People think Alex looks calm and mysterious, I think he looks useless. I hate useless, I hate the world he comes from. Anemones have purpose, nematocysts have function. Like this rock, in hands that have purpose it has function. One end is large and round, giving it weight; the other end is pointed, like the spike fired from me, the Anemone's cell.

He lies down against the giant tee-pee of fire wood, our beacon, the only place he can sleep. There, he rests on the beach that can bring escape. But this beach is so much more, the border between land and water, where life has found a thousand ways to survive. I can survive here too, Alex can't. He doesn't have the skills or the desire. To live in this environment every action must have purpose. Here, I live in a trance, gathering wood, building shelter, catching fish, digging roots, setting traps, wasting no energy. That is why I dress for function; I cut my hair short for function. But function is rejected by Alex, just as the cruise ship will reject it with steam rooms and dessert buffets. Function is laughed at.

He's asleep, unaware. I walk towards him. Picture the poisonous tail at the tip of my spike spreading its toxin inside Alex. The struggling larva goes quiet. It was never meant to live. It failed its function.

My shadow creeps onto his body. I stand at his feet, rock raised over his head. On the rock, I notice another small anemone. Beside it, I see my reflection in a tiny drop of water. Red hair, green eyes, thin face, thin lips. The anemone, pink oesophagus surrounded by tentacles on a soft green body. I pull the rock closer. We look nothing alike.

Alex wakes up, "Cecilia, what the hell are you doing?"

Tears in my eyes, I collapse beside him. Confused, he puts his arm around my shoulder and pulls me closer. His body is warm, I forgot about the warmth.

Chapter Three

2008 – East Hamilton (Friday before the Dragonboat Races)

We pass the bottle around, making a drinking game out of the waves. Every time one picks us up and gives us a boost of speed we drink and cheer.

Sam says, "I can't believe Cecilia's sleeping through all this. I hope she doesn't hate me when she hears what my dad did to your mum."

I say, "We don't have to get into details."

Kate says, "She's going to be pissed when she finds out what city we're going to. Look at it – Toronto – what a shit hole. The place is stuck up, selfish, boring, and…um…I don't know, just stupid. I don't even want to go there, just this once because we'll be drunk and it's going to be hilarious. But all we're doing is going to that big fucking tower then turning around and going back to Hamilton."

Sam says to me, "You have to explain all this to her. You guys must be really close. She'll understand when she hears it from her twin."

I take a big swig of whisky, looking back at Toronto, which is a lot closer now, close enough that I can distinguish the buildings in the skyline. "I haven't spoken to Cecilia in three years, not since I left for out West. I haven't spoken to her since she graduated high school. I graduated a year early, took off immediately and didn't call home for a year. I left her with my parents...alone...and I have a feeling she hates me for it."

Sam stares at Cecilia with terror in her eyes.

Kate says, "Nice fucking apology, buddy. She's going to be pissed."

"Coast, what is, what will, she's...do you have any idea how she's going to react to this? I mean, does she go on canoe trips?"

"Honestly, your guess is as good as mine. Our family doesn't really talk much, and all I know about her is that she's been living and going to school in Montreal for two years, and now she dresses like that."

"She dresses in a pencil skirt, a white blouse, a necklace of emeralds and shells, a gold watch and fancy sandals."

"Um...yeah."

"While we dress in shorts, jeans, tank tops and t-shirts."

"Yeah."

"And drink whisky in a make-shift-catamaran with a tarp-sail while she's unknowingly passed out inside it."

Kate, putting her fishing rod together, says, "What are you getting at?"

Sam yells, "She looks like she's been captured by pirates."

"Arggg...Me be catching some fish now."

"Seriously, what if she calls the cops on us?"

I say, "Take it easy, that would never happen."

Kate laughs, "Oh yeah, because your side of the family would never call the cops on our side of the family. That's never happened. Oh, hold on a sec, that's *all* that's happened."

"Oh no, this is all my dad's fault. I hate him so much," says Sam.

I say, "Sam, settle down, I'll take the heat, okay?"

"You overdramatic fuckers," says Kate. "Drink some whisky and pull yourselves together. Sam you've got to ease up on your dad."

"I hate him."

"And unless you got some fucking heroin with your booze in that duffle bag there's going to be no heat. Cecilia's going to wake up and realize she's in exactly the kind of fucking city she should be in, realize she gets to hang out with us instead of those old pricks on the other side of the lake, drink a shot and have a good time. Trust me, she'll love this."

Sam says, "I'm pretty sure you didn't talk to Cecilia once today."

"No, but I was watching her when she walked in, and…whatever, she can have fun because this is fucking happening and it's fine."

I spin around and look beneath the sail to survey what's ahead, then huddle down into the hull in front of the bow seat to write.

The city looks like it's inland, even though I know from pictures it's right on the water and has a big inner harbour. There are two shorelines ahead of it. The one closest to the city is forested. The only structure I can make out is a peer. The shoreline closer to us is the south side of a peninsula that comes out from the mainland east of the city, then curves far ahead of the shoreline with the peer, and ends at a lighthouse, which is ahead. There are no trees or any other buildings, just the lighthouse. "Sam, where are we going?"

"Straight, I don't want to go in any other direction until I get this sail down."

"So that shoreline with the lighthouse on it."

"Yeah, we have to land there first."

And it's on that lifeless shoreline that Cecilia will wake up.

WHILE KATE STANDS UP AT THE BACK OF HER CANOE, casting her rod, and drinking a can of beer from a six pack she brought, I pass the bottle back and forth with Sam some more. The canoe must have passed into shallower water, because the waves, which have grown into ocean-like swells, suddenly get steeper. Sam has the bottle to her mouth when one picks up the stern of the catamaran and tilts us forward so far that her paddle leaves the water. The boat starts to rotate, but before it can turn broadside to the waves Sam throws the bottle back to me, reaches down and out with the paddle, and draws blades full of water in to correct our course. Kate laughs as she almost falls overboard and Sam screams, "Kate, help me out, or at least sit down so we don't have to rescue you." But she keeps on fishing, even as a second and third wave picks us up and pushes us with nerve-racking speed towards the shore. Then Kate gets a catch.

Sam says, "We're letting it go as soon as it comes up."

Kate says, "Fuck you, we're feasting on this thing second we get to land, maybe sooner if I feel like sushi."

"That's fine, but you're eating every single part, even the bones, out of respect."

Kate gets the fish to the surface. "Respect I have, cousin. We've got a Northern Pike here, and I don't think it's the alcohol talking when I say it's the biggest one I've ever seen. Give me a hand, hippy."

"Don't call me hippy. And I'm kind of busy here. Coast, there's a net under your seat."

"On it." I grab the net and get it under the pike.

Kate wasn't kidding, the thing is huge and vicious. I'm just about to suggest we let it go when the biggest wave yet picks up the boat.

The momentum is what we need to get the fish up and into the canoe, but it's too much. Kate falls back and I practically throw the net and pike at her. They fall to the hull of the canoe together. Kate freaks out and jumps into our canoe. The extra weight and tilt on our side pushes the boat into the wave carrying us and we really start surfing – this one isn't passing us by.

Sam, eyes fixed on the fast-approaching beach, paddle held strong in the water, screams, "Oh my God."

Kate says, "Coast, the fish, it's going for Cecilia. Go fisher-man-handle that thing out of there."

But I can't stand up. The thing flops around knocking itself off the gunwales and tightening the tangle of the net until it catapults into the hammock bed and lands, mummified in green string, beside Cecilia. It stops flopping, but its gills are still pulsing just inches away from Cecilia's still sleeping eyes.

Kate says, "Sam, you've got this right?"

"I've got the canoes holding straight, that's about the only thing I can do right now."

"Well, shit, we're fucking surfing!"

And just like that we forget about the fish and Cecilia, getting sucked into a pretty thrilling moment – the catamaran tilted, but perfectly sunken into the downslope of the wave; the water crashing, the stone beach fast-approaching, and the curl of our wave charging at us from the left.

We all scream as the wave breaks and throws us on the beach (the beach's grade is really steep, so the crash happens right at its edge). And when we are sure we are thrown far enough that we won't get sucked back into the water, we cheer and high-five each other – Sam says, "Was that a perfect landing or what?" Kate says, "For a drunk driver you're all right" – but we freeze the second we hear a loud and alarmed intake of air from a now very awake Cecilia.

SEEING HER STARE INTO THE PIKE'S EYE in much the same way the Pike is staring into hers, I'm expecting Cecilia to scream, though now that I think about it I can't remember ever hearing Cecilia scream. Instead she grabs the handle of the net, shoots up straight, and lets out a martial arts "hraa" as she rotates the net over herself and slams the pike's head on the stern seat killing that fish dead.

Cecilia and I are twins, but while I look passive and unassuming, Cecilia looks fierce like a dragon – she has red hair (I have black), green eyes (I have blue) and she's wearing a necklace with strings of green things wrapped repetitively around her neck so that they look like scales running down her chest. With predatory eyes and a long slow-moving neck, she surveys the shore and the people that stare at her from the opposing half of the absurd boat she's woken up in.

Slowly, quietly, she says, "Is this some kind of joke?"

I say, "Cecilia, listen, I've made a stupid mistake, I brought you with—"

And screaming "Is this supposed to be funny?" She charges like a Komodo dragon on her knuckles and knees off the bed and onto the rocks. Kate, Sam and I jump out of the canoe and back away from her. I see red on her knuckles. She doesn't notice, but there's definitely skin tearing.

I say, "Cecilia, easy, there's an explanation here, and trust me, you're going to be happy you're here with us instead of back in Hamilton."

She springs up and shoulders past me and Kate, looks up at the lighthouse, out over the water, at the bank (that's too high to see over), and then she stands face to face with me. "Where am I?"

"It may not seem like it from here, but we're in Toronto."

"Toronto? How do we get back?"

"Well, we can't right now. We sailed this thing straight across the lake with the wind and waves, because our parents got in this huge, gross fight with theirs the moment they—"

"I don't care why you're here, why am I here?"

Kate, irritably, says, "Simmer down, you're here because we're on a trip to Toronto so we don't have to be in Hamilton where—"

"Where I shouldn't have been in the first place, and if I knew what a dump of a town this mysterious other side of the family lived in I never would have come down."

She shoulders through us again, grabs her bag from the canoe and storms off. I yell, "Where are you going?"

"Downtown, then Montreal."

I catch up to her. "You won't get to the downtown that way. We're on a peninsula that goes miles out from the city. Even if you walk all the way you'll only come to a bunch of houses and apartments way east of the downtown." She's trying to speed up with every word I say, and I'm having trouble keeping up. "You're acting crazy, Cecilia. We have to paddle to get to the city. It's the only way. I'm sorry, but you're stuck with us at this point."

She stops and throws her backpack to the ground. "You want to know why I'm acting crazy? I don't know those people, and you don't know me. We're not practical-joking-siblings who kidnap each other onto trips. You're just a goddamn weirdo, and I've suddenly woken up trapped on a beach with you and two strangers and no other people around."

"Ah Christ Cecilia, it's not as bad as that. And Kate and Sam aren't so bad, just come back and have a drink with them."

I look back as I say this, hearing Kate, holding an empty beer can, yell, "Oh I'll fucking do it, I'll fucking do it and you will fucking see me."

Sam says, "Kate, it's bad for your head."

She crushes the can against her head – "Why did you cover your eyes? Well shit" – and tosses the can into the lake.

"Kate, you jerk, that's pollution, that's going to kill fish, go get that."

Kate laughs, "You can't tell me what to do you fucking hippy."

"I'm serious, I'm not talking to you until you grab three pieces of garbage from the lake."

"Oh fuck…"

Cecilia says, "Not my kind of people, Alex"

"Oh come on, they're a little rough around the edges, but so are a lot of girls back East."

"Yes, they are like girls back East – crazy, unkempt and weird – but I don't live out East anymore. I live in Montreal, with other people who live in Montreal – the type of people who live in big cities like Montreal. And now that you've stolen me away from visiting our parents, I have to get back to Montreal and away from anyone who lives back East, out West, or in goddamn Hamilton. How is that going to happen?"

I look back at Kate and Sam again. They're lugging the fish up onto a flat chunk of rock. They probably want to gut it and cook it up on a fire – at least that's what I want to do. "Okay, we'll get back in the boat and paddle to the city. From there I'll pay for you to get to an airport and fly out of here."

"Fine, let's go."

We're walking back towards them. As we walk I'm noticing that the entire bank is made of concrete, brick, rebar, tiles and all sorts of other junk, and the beach, wave-worn bricks. There's nothing natural in sight. In some spots along the bank there are piles of stuff – a cylindrical pile of big marble slabs against the bank down towards the lighthouse, and behind me one of what looks like windshields. Kate and Sam are talking about all this as we walk up to them.

Kate says, "I know exactly what this place is. I'm surprised you don't, Sam, because we have the same beaches right in our hometown. Guess you don't know your own local landscape."

"Don't be a jerk, I know everything about our local landscape. I've paddled all the shorelines and been up all the rivers."

"So you've seen the beach I'm talking about? The new one?"

"There's no such thing as a new beach, they're not like dirt bike tracks, nobody builds them, beaches are from forever."

"Then explain what we're standing on, because I'm pretty sure bricks and rebar have not been around forever."

"Well crap, what is this then?"

"It's fill from demolition sites. A beach near us is used for the same thing, fenced off but we busted through to check out spots and found it. There's a whole peninsula built out into the lake, just like this."

"But that's so bad for the lake."

"Take it easy, hippy, it's just concrete and rebar. Rock that once came from nature and now returns to nature."

"Listen, I want you to get some terminology straight: I'm not a hippy, I'm a canoe tripper, and just because I like paddling canoes and not stinking up the world with gas powered toys doesn't mean you can label me. Ugh, Kate, my brain hurts and I have to sleep. Can I have a bit of the vodka first though, Coast?"

I grab the bottle from the canoe and come back. "After we have a drink, guys, we have to go, Cecilia—"

I stop, my voice overtaken by the crashing of a particularly large wave. Because the waves crash right at the water's edge, and onto the steep grade of wave worn bricks, the wave sounds like thunder, exactly like thunder. As the curl nears us, a distant crackle builds into a collective rumble. Awesome.

There's another sound, one that becomes more apparent as the crashing wave fades. It's a beeping, like when a truck is backing up, and another sound I can't quite place. Is that hydraulics?

Then I look down the beach at the half cone piles of windshields and marble, the ones that appear freshly dumped, and then I look up.

CHRIST, WHAT THE HELL WAS THAT? We all nearly got crushed. I looked up and saw the bin of a dump truck tilting right above us. I screamed run, grabbing Cecilia's arm and charging towards the lake with Kate and Sam right behind. The boulders of concrete crashed down where we were and an explosion of concrete dust enveloped us. That freaked us out even more so we just kept running into the water until waves were crashing at our chest.

We turn and look at the pile that almost killed us and the dump truck it came from, the bin still tilted high.

I say, "Everyone alright? Cecilia, you good?"

She snaps her dragon eyes at me. "Am I what, Alex?"

"Good, like not hurt."

"I'm not good or hurt. You on the other hand are fatally injured."

"No, I'm good, I'm fine."

But that's not what she means.

Kate stomps out of the water. "What the fucking fuck, I knew I hated this city for a reason. Our first landing on its shores and it tries to dump fucking garbage on us."

A fat guy with a goatee and a beet red face appears beside the truck on the bank. "Hey! Hey, hey, hey! Don't you understand open and closed times? The park is closed. Not open to paddlers. Shut down so we can work. Get it? Private property. You're trespassing, get out of here!" Kate charges up the pile of concrete blocks right at him. "You want to get yourself killed? This is a work site, you've got to go." She grunts and struggles to get to him faster, and he looks worried. "You better get down off those blocks, you get killed I'm not responsible." Kate practically screams in a final sprint up to him. He jumps back a few steps. "This ain't my fault. You're not supposed to be in this park."

Kate, sticking her finger into his chest, says, "You just buried my fish." There's a stand off silence between them. "I caught the biggest Northern Pike I've ever caught. We were just about to gut it on a concrete slab that you just buried with your dump truck."

The guy looks down at his hands and the red disappears. "Well shit lady, I didn't mean to bury your catch. I was just dumping fill like we do when the park's closed."

Kate laughs, "Um…what fucking park are you talking about? All I see is some shitty shoreline. You should be grateful we're gracing this crap pit with our presence. I suppose you're going to say you're the park warden."

"Hey! What a mouth on you. I'm a truck driver and I'm just doing my job like we do when the park's closed."

Sam, stomping out of the water, yells, "You just dumped a bunch of trash into my lake. That's not work, that's disrespecting natural waters."

"This ain't trash, it's fill from demolition sites. It don't pollute nothing."

Kate says, "I already told you that, Sam. See? I'm always right."

"And don't think you can camp or start a fire anywhere around here. All you're doing is getting in your canoes and leaving."

Kate says, "Do you live here? Does anyone you know live here? Does anybody live here at all?"

"Of course not, it's a work site and a park."

"Then what the hell are you acting like the fucking trespass police for? Just get in your truck and get the fuck out of here."

Sam says, "And be happy you didn't hurt anyone."

The guy storms off to the cab of the truck yelling that he's going to tell the authorities. Kate, facing us from the bank, makes faces in imitation of him.

Cecilia hasn't moved an inch. She stands in the water, frozen, her arms raised up scarecrow-like. When she finally starts walking to the shore, I follow. A big wave comes and knocks us both down. She's grunting out tears when she comes up. I don't do anything but follow, I can't imagine how to damage-control this train wreck.

When she gets to the shore I yell "are you all right?" as loud as I can. It doesn't matter because the waves crashing combined with the diesel engine lowering the bin of the truck cancels out any sound. I feel I have to do something, so I grab a bottle of liquor from my bag – Scotch, the most expensive bottle I bought – open it and offer it to her. I don't know if it's the water or what, but I see eyes of solid red when she looks at me and takes the bottle. For a moment I think all will be fine, that she'll take a sip, feel better and maybe see some humour in all this. Instead I end up on the ground, bleeding from the head.

Sam (she didn't actually see or hear what happened – the diesel engine blocked out the sound of Cecilia's "hraa" and my "ahh" when the bottle hit my head – she just saw Cecilia storming off) says, "Cecilia, come back. I have a towel in the canoe."

"I'm going to dry my clothes off up at that lighthouse. We're leaving when I come back down. Maybe you should give the towel to your new idiot-cousin."

Then Sam sees me, bleeding on the rocks, laughing at myself.

While she's cleaning me up with a first aid kit she had in the canoe, I say, "Did the Scotch bottle break?"

"No."

"Did it all spill out?"

"A lot did, but no."

"Can I have some?"

"Sure, but I need to do something first, gotta protect you from any Lake Ontario pollution."

Before I can ask what she means, she pours Scotch over my head wound. While she bandages me up we pass the bottle back and forth and watch Kate. She's climbing around the pile of freshly dumped concrete. Then she gets her head and arms between two big slabs, looking like she's about to fall in.

Sam says, "Be careful, you could get crushed."

She keeps rummaging until she backs out dragging the fish by the tail. "Caught you again you sucker."

Sam says, "Gross, it's covered in garbage now."

"Demo-fill, it's fine. Coast, time to build a fire. I'm starving."

I say, "Might as well. There's no telling how long Cecilia's going to be up there."

Sam says, "I guess there's no way she'll want to stay in touch after this."

"I don't know, she might come around once the shock from everything has worn off."

Sam laughs at me. "You can take a hit and not give up hope, that's a good quality in a person."

I fall back onto the rocks, "Thanks, I might just be stupid though."

WHILE KATE AND SAM TAKE DOWN THE SAIL AND SECURE THE CANOES, I climb up the concrete pile to find some wood. A mudflat stretches all along the top of the bank, and behind it grass-and-shrub-land runs for as far as I can see. Not the best territory for finding wood, so I walk towards the lighthouse.

A road descends the back of the lighthouse hill and continues, presumably, to the base of the peninsula. The rest of the hill faces the water and drops sharply to a rock and gravel base, a couple road-lanes wide. The base is flat and provides a perfect platform for viewing 270 degrees of horizon, from the open water to the distant smoke stacks of Hamilton's steel mills, and around the lake-shore to Toronto's skyline. I walk around the platform, past boulders, piles of fill and a whole bunch of crazy art pieces built from the bricks, rebar and concrete slabs. I walk until I can see the city, its office towers popping up from behind the tree line of the next strip of land. I can see a gap in that strip – our way to the inner harbour. I store that landmark in my memory and walk towards a forest between the road and the city-facing shore to find firewood.

So: I have a head injury, a price to pay for a flight, consequences to suffer for abandoning my parents and kidnapping Cecilia, no job and nowhere to live, but all in all a good start for a story. Cecilia's going to hate that I'm writing about this trip. In high school I wrote a lot about the two of us, but only because I had to. To accelerate my education in writing, my English teachers gave me lots of extra credit assignments – short stories and essays to write and publish in local newspapers and journals. They're what got me out a year early (and what were meant to get me into a prestigious writing program a year early) so of course I did them, but every teacher and workshop leader told me I had to dig into my personal history, to find those significant moments in my life and use them in my writing. Personally, I think all that 20th-century-build-your-character-through-Freudian-pschyoanalysis-crap is crap, but I went along with it for the credits. My teachers knew I had a twin-sister, so I based most of the stories on our mutual childhood.

They were made up though, I only acted like they were true in class. Like this family road trip story where Cecilia and I huddled together while our parents screamed at each other (our parents hardly talked, let alone screamed), or the story of my confrontation with her over an abusive boyfriend (she dated a chain of horrible guys, but, as demonstrated on the beach, she's good with weapons and can hold her own), or the story about her first period – she smacked me with a shovel over that one.

My writing took a more unorthodox form out West than in high school. In high school it was about getting into a good writing program, publishing and winning awards. When I broke free from all that expectation I turned writing into a gift I could give.

I scribbled away in notebooks either around a bonfire on a beach in Victoria or in the crew cabins of fishing boats. Whoever was hanging around me at the time would eventually ask "What are you writing?" – "Descriptions, notes from conversations; a lot from ours." And most people would get uncomfortable, maybe stop talking to me so much, until I'd rip out a page, something that I got down really well – "Hey, you might like this."

I never write anything personal or over-analytical about someone. The dialogues I handed to people didn't contain some unnerving representation of themselves, they contained characters that were alive and crazy because the dialogues were written from a whole bunch of crazy, funny or passionate words that came from the receivers. It was just the best parts of their minds in the form of a character.

People always loved those dialogues, and those gifts were important to me too, because people don't stay in my life very long – bonfire friends come and go, or I change places where I build fires; fishing crews change, and I rarely stay with the same boat for more than a few trips. I guess I make it difficult more than anyone. I don't own a phone, except a landline at my apartment, where I almost never am. And I don't check my mail or use email.

Sitting here and writing about this crazy beach-park and demo-fill-dump, and my rather unsuccessful attempt to reconnect with

Cecilia, I'm sitting with what I considered the most consistent, and really best, company I can count on – a bonfire. I'm looking up from my notebook every so often to watch the fire change in colour and opacity as the sun sets behind it. I'm up on the flat at the base of the lighthouse hill. Kate and Sam are still down with the canoes – they took down the sail (the air and waves are perfectly still) and they're gutting the pike – and Cecilia's up at the lighthouse, so it's just me and the fire.

Those gifts, if it weren't for them, all those people would just be transients in my life, and I'd be a transient in theirs. But I'm sure a lot of people still have those dialogues – some even said they'd frame them. I like that. It's a connection. And the writing that I never give to anyone is still a gift, a gift to my best friend. I've thrown every notebook I've filled into a bonfire, except for the first one, and maybe not this one. I'll see.

Chapter Four

2006 – Vancouver Island (first beach-bonfire-dialogues recorded by Alex, which followed two conversations at once)

"TWO DAYS TO GET FROM ALBERTA TO VANCOUVER ISLAND?"

"Because we hitchhiked here, hoping to arrive yesterday, but it got dark while we were still on the road outside of Vancouver. We thought we were going to have to sleep in the ditch, but this purple Cadillac pulled over—"

"—It was bizarre, there were dark-lights glowing inside on these three tough looking guys."

"The driver, the alpha in the group, yells at us as we run up to the window, 'Yo, you got any weed guy?'"

"We smoked him and his two friends a few joints, then he says we can stay at his mother's house; they were driving there to bring her some Kraft Dinner. I don't remember the name of the farm town where she lived, it was about an hour before Abbotsford."

…

"It's understandable that you're feeling anxious, this is a big change, but it's so thrilling to me that you're moving to Toronto, to Kensington Market, to search for the soul of a big city. I'm reading this book right now, *Venice is a Fish: a sensual guide* by Tiziano Scarpa, a Venetian poet. If there ever was a book about the soul of a city, this is it. I'm tempted to quote the whole book to you now, but I'll just give you the highlights:

"You're walking on a vast upside-down forest, strolling above an incredible inverted wood. It's like something dreamed up by a mediocre science-fiction writer, and yet it's true. Let me tell you what happens to your body in Venice, starting with your feet."

…

"Do you remember what else he said? 'You can stay at my house, but don't touch my sister guy, she's only sixteen!"

"Oh yeah, Ha—Ha, we're like, no problem man."

…

"Where are you going? Throw away your map!

"By the way, you have to tell me if this isn't helping. I've been living on Advil Gel caps, which make my thoughts about as crisp as mashed potatoes. My wisdom teeth have been shifting the last two months and I refuse to have them removed because a) why would they be there if they don't serve a purpose, and b) dentists are weasels."

"It's helping. Read me everything."

…

"At his mom's house, alpha showed us his fighting dogs, two rottweilers. They were in a cage, angry as fuck when he rattled the cage with a stick.

"We went to a party where his sister was, but didn't stay long. I had lots of weed, and that kept us all happy as we walked around this dinky little farm town.

"Back at his mom's place alpha says, 'Yo, you fight guy?', just kind of casual. I'm like, 'no, not really.' 'I fight all the time,' he says. He was really sweet though. He made his two friends sleep on the floor, he took the couch, and since we were the guests in the group we got to share the only bed."

…

"You spontaneously feel like touching it. You brush it with your fingers, caress it, pat it, pinch it, feel it, you put your hands on Venice."

...

"The next day, before alpha would drive us back to the highway, he said we had to help rob a crop of pot plants he knew about on an Indian reserve. We went searching early in the morning and eventually found a big crop of plants. It was infested with seeds, but we started filling our pockets anyway. Then alpha's friend pointed out a white car driving down the road. Alpha freaked out and said run for the car. We did and managed to peel off before the white car got there. Alpha ordered us all to dump the weed out the window. We turned off the dirt side road onto the paved main road, leaving the reserve, but the white car followed. It sped up and came side by side with us, in the oncoming lane, and a middle-aged Indian couple looked at us while apparently in a state of hilarity. They passed us, laughing, and disappeared down a side road.

"After that they dropped us off on the highway. Our next ride got us to the ferry and we made it here by late afternoon."

...

"The first and only itinerary I suggest to you has a name, it's called: at random. Subtitle: aimlessly."

"I suggest this spiritual exercise: become a foot."

...

"That's insane, I would never hitchhike or do anything like that. What do you guys do?"

"I work at a liquor store in Canmore. Mountain Dew Liquors, it's part of the Canmore Hotel. Nick works there too, in the kitchen…shit where'd he go? Anyway, It's a pub, music venue, but not really a hotel. The rooms are mostly used to house bands and a few ageing alcoholics."

"Fun place to work?"

"Every shift I pre-pint in the liquor store, then go get hammered at the bar and watch whatever band is playing. It's fun but not good for you. I spend my whole pay check on weed and alcohol, and because of that I trade mini bottles for food. I steal them from the liquor store while I'm working and trade them with the kitchen, mostly with Nick. He's my best bud at The Hotel for sure. Hold on…

"Hey Nick! Nick!!"

"Yo."

"What're you doin'?!"

"Drinkin', stinkin', never thinkin'."

"Haha, nice!…That's his line. He's so cool. When I met him I was blown away because he had a Propagandhi shirt on, one of my favourite punk bands, but one of their really hard to find shirts. It has an upside down American flag with 'Fuck Right Off' written underneath."

…

"You should learn to make the sign of the devil with your toes, to discharge the gesture into the earth, letting it run the whole length of your body."

…

"Nick, you're back, what's going on over there?"

"A girl's reading to another girl from a book about Venice, mesmerising stuff actually."

"Nice…during slower nights, when the kitchen is dead, I'll leave the liquor store in the hands of my co-worker and go play pool with Nick."

"Yeah, ever since I started working there, I've gotten a lot better at playing pool than I have at cooking."

…

"A blind writer said that for him a fine day is a day of wind, a day of rain. You can hear the trees crumpling the air in the background. The density of the pelting rain, its impact with objects, allows you to guess

*the shape of the city: here there's a very tall 'palazzo', over there the
awning of a bar."*

…

"The craziest night I had at The Hotel was Canada Day, when
my favourite Canadian punk band Dayglo Abortions played.
They're old now, but still so raw and aggressive. Funny thing was
I got hired as a temporary bouncer by the head bouncer, to work
the stage, and I've never done anything like that. There were three
other guys, but within ten minutes two of the bouncers bailed.
The mosh pit became a title wave against the band. I'd brace my
foot against the stage, put my hands out, and block the crowd
from tumbling into the instruments.

"Between songs Dayglo said to the crowd, 'We love your energy,
but stay the fuck off the drums.' When people jumped onto the
stage, I would grab them and toss them into the crowd as a block
against the wave.

"Things got messy. At one point someone ripped the power cord
for the lights off the roof and the whole place went pitch black.
Dayglo kept playing and we kept defending, and I was paid an
extra 150 bucks for lasting the whole night."

"Yeah buddy, you're a wild-man that's for sure."

…

*"…the philosopher Martin Heidegger explained that coming into the
world is like being thrown, it is a fall of being, diving into time. Life is a
cat asleep on the windowsill suddenly waking as it falls from the third
floor."*

"That line really gets me, like a cat 'suddenly waking as it falls
from the third floor'."

"Wow. Thanks for that, I feel excited again, but still anxious.
I'm just so sad to leave Vancouver Island. It's weird, I actually feel
guilty about leaving the island itself."

"That's not weird. I believe very strongly that as much as people need to love the place they're in, places need people to love them. Really. So here's what I'll do. I'll dedicate all my love to the island while you're gone. I have all my love to give anyway because I don't do relationships with people anymore. I've become a monk. I've all but taken a vow. And no, not a nun. A monk. Monks are cooler and they wear better clothes. And they spend all their time with books rather than orphans. The nun thing has nothing going for it. You might think I'm kidding, but I'm actually not. I've given myself to God. And the library. And I don't mean white-bearded-guy-in-the-sky-God, I mean Nature, the Universe, and whatever it wants me to do for it. And as far as I can tell, it really likes to be appreciated."

Chapter Five

2008 – Tommy Thompson Park, Lighthouse (Friday before the Dragonboat Races)

Kate and Sam come up to the fire.

Kate says, "Hey buddy, ready to eat some fish?"

Sam says, "Ew, you're not actually going to eat that are you?"

"I already told you, it was only covered in demo-fill, it's fine."

"But it was sitting in the sun for so long."

"Let's get cooking it then. Bartender, spare some liquor for a little marinade? Actually, if you have limes in there that would be amazing."

"Holy crap, look at all these sculptures."

"Uh huh, that's great Sam…limes?"

"No, just liquor. Here's some vodka."

"I think they're all figures or something."

"Or just a bunch of weird voodoo crap."

"Don't put this stuff down, someone put a huge amount of work into this."

"We need to put a huge amount of work into this fish. And I can't see what you're talking about anyway, I don't have your forest-elf night-vision."

I say, "I saw all that stuff in the daylight. They're just random stacks of cinder blocks and bricks on rebar. Some of those Inuksuk things are cool."

Sam says, "Oh my God, that's it. You saw them in the daylight, but that's not how you're supposed to see them."

Kate says, "Oh fuck, Sam's gone to fairy land."

Sam grabs the entire stack of wood I gathered and drops the whole thing on the fire. Both Kate and I jump up and back.

Kate says, "Cousin, I was going to cook on that."

"Well when it dies down you'll have great cooking coals. You can put bricks on them as a cooking surface."

"Smart, okay, bonfire time I guess. But what's the deal?"

"Just watch."

The flames creep through the pile of wood until they ignited a tower of fire. It's a good fire, but even better is what Sam has, quite literally, illuminated for us. The tall bending columns of brick on rebar polls, stacks of cinder blocks with long narrow marble arms holding beer bottles, and Inuksuk characters are not the scene themselves, but are built to create a bonfire party scene in shadows – shadows cheersing, hugging, laying against rocks and even standing with a poker stick.

One sitting figure is leaning back against a rock with knees propped up and arms curved into the pelvis. A flat piece of marble lays in the lap looking roughly like a book. I find a cylinder of concrete nearby and modify this figure so that a shadow of a pen is in hand over the book.

We take our seats and wait for the flames to die down.

I say, "Good call Sam, this stuff is really interesting."

Kate says, "This stuff is crap. You know what kind of art I appreciate? A good dirt bike track, with nicely sculpted bank turns and hits with nice landings following. Guys who can make that shit real, and do it well, and make it look good, now that's art."

Sam says, "That's not art, that's practical creation, that's utilitarian form, it's not there to look good or do anything artistic, it's just there so your bikes have a place to ride around."

"No, bullshit, I call bullshit, because I don't need to take my bike on a good trail to get the effect. If a track is made really well I can spend days and days just sitting in a lawn chair beside it with beer and maybe some smoke and just stare at it, imagining what it would be like to bike around. That's fucking art, more art than this shit."

"Dirt bike track? Pollock wouldn't think that's art."

"Who gives a fuck what fish think?"

Sam chuckles to herself, then continues: "There's something so mythical about these figures, so symbolic. I keep thinking that this place is exactly what a city that's been abandoned for centuries would look like, rubble growing grasslands and forests. These sculptures are in a place that represents the death of a city, the rubble of a city. And when were they made? There's no telling really."

Kate says, "You're making no sense. They were made probably not that long ago by a bunch of artsy street kids. They just took piles of scrap and turned them into slightly more organised piles of scrap, so what?"

"You don't know that. There's no reason to assume they're built by street kids. They look old and mysterious. Like, who's expected to see them, to understand them? It's not obvious. There's a message in them from the dead cities, from the past, or there's a puzzle in them, one meant for us."

"Oh my fucking God. You think something magical created these sculptures. You think a committee of wizards from another planet is trying to tell us something. This is what happens when you think too much about the universe and energy and all that weird hippy shit, Sam, you start to believe in magic and signs and

Christ I worry about you. You're vulnerable and weird and delusional and I'm going to have to spend my life watching over you and making sure you don't get sold magic beans…Magic beans!"

Sam, exasperated, says, "Let's talk about something else then. Coast, you were writing in your book when we came up. You looked so happy, like it put you in a better mood after the scene down on the beach."

"Honestly, nothing makes me feel better than writing in a notebook around a bonfire."

"Are you still writing about this trip?"

"Yup."

"Are you going to turn this into a book and publish it after?"

"I don't know. I'm not big on thinking about writing as something to publish or make money off of. I got a way of making an income that I like, and I have writing in my downtime. It all makes me happy as it is."

"That's cool. I'm the same way with guitar. I play classical, but I taught myself, so I won't be playing in any orchestras, and I'm never going to make a living as a popular musician. But my canoe trip friends love my playing, and sometimes I do shows at the library, and once I got paid to play at an art opening, but that's all I need from it too. I could use a better day job though, Kate and I work at the same restaurant. I'm a server and she's a line cook."

Kate says, "And I've definitely got the better job."

"No way, you have to hang out with all those greasy kitchen guys."

"They're fine as long as you keep them in their place. Better than your job anyway. I'd get fired so fast if I had to deal with all the assholes you serve."

"Wow, so you guys spend a lot of time together, eh?"

Sam says, "Yeah, even though she gets on my nerves."

"Fucking right, we're best friends!" Says Kate. "We're moving in together too, next month. It's going to be fucking rad."

Sam laughs, "Yeah, I'm looking forward to it too. It wasn't always this way though. We ran with completely different crowds in high school."

"But they were all douchebags."

"Yup, we both cut our groups off after we graduated. And then we were loners."

"Until we went for a beer together one night – the first time we ever hung out not at a family affair. When we discovered we both ditched our old crews it was an immediate holy fuck we just became best friends."

"That's great." They look at me awkwardly, and I suddenly get the feeling that Sam is about to ask why Cecilia and I aren't close. Before she can I say, "So Kate, you're into dirt biking?"

"Fucking right I'm into dirt biking. I was third in a contest just last week. Don't worry about what contest, it wasn't huge or anything, but I was the only girl in the whole thing and I kicked fucking ass. I was going hands free and shooting my legs out right off the launch. You guys should come watch me sometime. Not anytime soon though, my bike is fucked after that shit. Got to buy new brake discs, and probably spend the next month working on it. My dad could do it in a week, but he's so stoned he never gets to shit. It's fun though, I get all zen and the art of dirt bike maintenance about it, not that I've ever read that book, but my dad goes on about it forever when he gets stoned.

"Anyway, I get pretty into the zone when I'm fixing my bike. Engines are fun to fix and they're awesome – loud, mini-explosions; the greatest thing humans have ever invented. They're so important and wicked that I fully believe canoes should die out of respect for them. If we run out of oil and gas then fine, they can be revived, but paddling should just die while engines exist out of respect for their epic awesomeness, like when samurais commit suicide to save face and shit."

Sam, bottle of vodka in her hand, jumps to her feet: "I am so, so, so mad at you. That was the worst thing you have ever said to me, that seriously…but, but, I don't care. Actually Kate I feel sorry for you, because you're missing out on so much. It's great that you're into sleds and bikes, but that you've blown them up into these things that you think are the whole universe, like, that's just blinding. That's just closing yourself off."

"Easy bestie, I'm just joking. We should cook that fish, the coals are perfect."

While they gather up bricks, I write descriptions of the art scene and a few lines from our conversation about it. Just as they're about to put the fish on the fire we hear Cecilia coming down the hill. Crap. She's probably going to say it's time to go, and Kate's going to argue with her because she hasn't eaten yet. There goes the nice bonfire we were having.

She sits down beside me without a word and leans against a flat of concrete. I look at her. She's expressionless, but staring into the fire like the rest of us (Kate and Sam paused putting the fish on). She says, "Lights are coming."

Hmm…maybe she just needed to be alone for a bit. Maybe she's calmed down and can get into all this now, and we can have the bonfire, and cook the fish, and drink. I should pass her a…wait. "What did you say?"

CECILIA, CASUALLY AND CRYPTICALLY, was telling us that head-lights were coming this way along the road.

"That jerk ratted us out," says Sam.

"Fuck Cecilia," says Kate, "you could have been a bit more alarming."

Standing on a rubble pile, I see a halo of siren-light above the grass and shrub-land only a couple minutes away. "Okay, everyone to the canoes."

We all start grabbing our stuff, but Cecilia doesn't move.

I say, "Cecilia, let's go, that's security."

"Why? They'll give me a ride out of here."

"No, they're going to give you a trespassing ticket."

"I think they'll know that I'm not a trespasser, that I'm a pretty respectable person who's clearly been kidnapped by a bunch of skids."

"Fuck it, leave her," says Kate.

Kate leaves, but thankfully Sam stays. "Cecilia, I understand how much this sucks for you. But think about it, they're not going to believe you were kidnapped by family from a family reunion."

I say, "And I'm buying you a flight ticket when we get to the city, so let's go."

Finally she gets up. "Fine, but don't rush me, Alex, or I'll stick a piece of rebar through your skull."

We go down the bank just as two vehicles skid to a stop at the fire pit. Kate is already trying to push the canoes into the water. "A little help here?"

We throw our stuff in.

Sam says, "Ew, Kate, why did you bring the fish?"

"Listen, I'm eating that pike even if I have to drag it into a restaurant kitchen."

We start pushing the canoes in, everyone but Cecilia – she climbs back into the hammock bed.

"Or maybe I should serve it as a pre-flight meal to our first-class passenger here," says Kate.

We shove in and return to our original spots – I climb into the bow of the canoe Sam is at the stern of, and Kate sits at the stern of the canoe Cecilia climbed into.

I say, "We have to get around the lighthouse."

Sam says, "But that's the direction the security are in."

"So what?" says Kate. "They can't swim after us."

We paddle towards the lighthouse, but keep our distance from the bank. I should say Kate and Sam paddle, I'm just a passenger like Cecilia.

Kate says, "I can't believe that trespass cop of a truck driver told those jack-ass-trespass-police on us."

We hear security say, "I can hear their voices over there."

"Well done, Kate," says Cecilia. "Remind me never to attempt a prison break with you. Oh, that's right, your side of the family are the only ones who would end up in prison."

"Piss off. Listen to how overdramatic you're being about some trespass police who have no way of getting to us. Oh shit, I was wrong" (sarcasm) "they're driving their trucks over to us. Now we're done, and look, they even have their head-lights on; I suppose they're fucking tractor beams. Can—barely—paddle."

"Pull over and get out of the canoes."

Kate bursts out laughing, "You have to be fucking kidding me. Why the hell would we do that, who the fuck are you, and what are you going to do, high-speed-chase us?"

"If you get out you get a fine for the fire; if not, we'll radio the police marine unit."

"The police are not going to give a fuck about us and some fire we allegedly started."

Cecilia says, "Like you would know."

Sam says, "Actually she knows what she's talking about. Kate does a lot of trespassing on her dirt bike."

"That's right, I dirt bike and sled on private property all the time – not near people's houses or anything, like at schools. I've gotten ticketed before, but I've never paid, because it's never the cops.

Sometimes it's the cops, then you have to sit in the cruiser for a while."

"This is the most useless exclusive knowledge on a topic I've ever heard," says Cecilia.

I say, "Guys, let's get in front of those trees up ahead so we're at least concealed, then start crossing to the city and pretend we were never anywhere near this place."

Kate says, "For fuck's sakes let's, I mean what the fuck is this? We're getting hassled for stopping on a beach. These idiots should be happy we even bothered to stop anywhere in their stupid city of trespass police."

"She's right," says Sam. "No wonder we've never come to Toronto if this is the kind of welcome we get. The place has got to be lame to protect a beach made of garbage."

Cecilia says, "I love trespass police. They keep scuzzy people out of nice places, and therefore make those places nicer. See? That's what trespass police are for, making nice places nicer by keeping the scuz out."

Kate says, "Something tells me you're going to fit right in here, Cecilia."

Sam says, "I take it we're heading for that gap."

"Yup, that's our way in," I say.

Everyone goes silent. It feels awkward, because the stillness of the water we're crossing, the warm air we're moving through, and the view we're paddling towards is beautiful and worth commenting on, but nobody's bothering, at least not yet. I pull out my notebook and try some descriptions of the view.

The night time scene is dramatically different from what I saw in the daylight. We aren't the only boat out here. A lot of sailboats and yachts are moving around. Red, green and white boat-lights drag reflections across the black surface of the lake like lures on a fishing line. They're mostly heading towards the gap like us, funnelling into a cluster of lights that's about to join the bright shine beyond.

The eastern wall of the gap runs straight to the mainland, forming the eastern wall of the inner harbour. Seeing it through the gap, I can't make out exactly what's along it, but it's all industrial. I can see the stern of a freighter moored to the wall, and large buildings without windows. Behind them there are smoke stacks flashing aircraft warning lights.

The shore on our side runs both ways from the gap. To the east it's almost completely dark, and I can see the silhouettes of trees. There are some lights down where it curves back around and out to the lighthouse – the lights of a marina, with masts like pencil marks rocking back and forth in them.

Now that it's night, I can see that the shoreline running west from the gap has a boardwalk with dim orange lights that ends at a peer far west of us, but that's all the lights I see. Well there's a glow too. Where the boardwalk begins, almost at the gap, the shoreline curves out towards us and a bank of boulders encloses a small bay. Over the boulders I think I might see the flicker of fire light.

The biggest landmark in view is of course the skyline. It's burning bright white and fiery orange behind the silhouetted trees and dimly lit boardwalk of the west-running shoreline.

Sam says, "Are you describing this scene, Coast? It's so beautiful, for a city."

"You describe it and I'll write it down."

"Okay, can I have some more of that vodka first?...Yum, thanks. Okay, the mystical tree line is dark with mystery—"

Kate says, "Wo, wo, wo, no. Mystical means magical, and my sweet lost friend you need to learn how to describe the real world. The trees are black."

"The trees are silhouetted, I can say that, and because we don't even know what that shoreline is, it's..um...mysteriously black and silhouetted and...um...full of fairies probably. Oh, I'm no good at this, but yum, I love this vodka."

Kate says, "You have to describe what's silhouetting the trees. The city. The lights glowing from the skyline of Toronto behind the trees. Most notably its big fucking tower, which peacocks a light show up and down its shaft, as if it's stroking itself."

I say, "You know, my description was actually pretty good. You guys are messing it up."

Sam says, "Read us your description."

"Well…okay…they're calming, the way the lights are set in black, because there's no stars here. What you see from a fishing boat, when you can see every star there is, it's like this. As dense as the city lights in some places, and as scattered as the sailboat lights in others."

Sam says, "That's nice, Coast."

Then something appears along the tips of the trees – a plane. And its lights are a nice part of the picture.

Cecilia says, "There, see that? That's a passenger plane. There's an airport on the other side of the trees. I was watching from the lighthouse. That's where we're going. You're paddling me to that airport, and Alex you're buying me a ticket."

"Yeah, okay," I say.

She's right, it's a passenger plane. A twin propeller one. Taking off from…but I don't feel like describing anything anymore. Everyone goes quiet; Sam passes the bottle back. We're just crossing the water, going to the city so Cecilia can fly back to Montreal. That's it.

Kate says, "You're such a fucking buzz kill, Cecilia."

Chapter Six

2008 – Toronto Island's Ward's Beach (Friday before the Dragonboat Races)

I'm happy, happy as hell. That flicker of what I thought might be fire light was fire light. Once we were closer to the shoreline we saw a beach running out from it and ending at the long breakwater of rocks, enclosing a little bay. We saw shrub-land behind it, between the beach and the gap into the city. We landed at the end farthest from the boardwalk, near the breakwater rocks, and we joined a fire with five other people, and now we're finally going to cook the pike.

An older couple from Hawaii, Jonathan and Mary, are helping Kate cook the fish. They flew in for a dragonboat festival that's happening on the island – and that's what we're on, an island, separated by the Eastern Gap that we're heading for, and the Western Gap, which runs between the airport and a section of the mainland just west of the downtown.

The circle was really welcoming. We didn't even have to ask if we could join the pit – they waved us up before we landed, and Jonathan came and helped drag the boat up. "Wow, look at this rig, it's great. You guys paddle from the mainland?"

Kate said, "Yeah, but not the mainland you're thinking of. Actually, it's a bit of a tale."

"The greatest tale of idiots in canoes you ever heard," said Cecilia.

Kate ignored Cecilia and told Jonathan about our great crossing of Lake Ontario and showed him the fish (we also ignored Cecilia when she complained about stopping; we're ignoring her now).

Jonathan got really excited about the pike. "My wife Mary and I have cooked a lot of fish on a lot of beaches, but never in Toronto. When did you catch this thing? It smells a little fishy."

"Oh, it's good. I caught it a few hours ago."

Sam said, "Like eight hours ago, and it was buried in concrete. We can't eat that thing."

"Buried in concrete?"

"My cousin Sam's a bit of a hippy. She thinks we're all getting buried in concrete."

"I hope that fish kills you."

Jonathan brings the fish up while Kate grabs a hunting knife that Sam has stored beside the first aid kit (Christ, that girl stays prepared). Mary gets just as excited about the fish as her husband is. The other three – Damiond, Kelly and Rory – are talking about their dragonboat team as we walk up.

Rory, mockingly, says, "But Damiond, your practice sessions, you're happy about them, yeah?"

"I think our team is perfectly prepared."

Kelly says, "All we did was get drunk at every practice session."

"We talked about theoretical situations. We went out in the boat a couple times."

Rory says, "But Damiond, how much did we practise before the race?"

Damiond, flailing his hand at Rory, says, "Ah what do you know you Irish bastard."

Kelly says, "You guys practised none at all. We're going to lose tomorrow, like we do every year. You drunken bastards."

Rory holds up a guitar that's sitting in his lap: "Can anyone play this thing? I brought it all the way from Ireland and I can't play for shit."

Sam walks over and sits beside him on a cooler, "I can play, but I'm too shy right now."

"Oh come on, play an Irish folk song and I'll sing the words."

"I don't know any Irish folk songs."

"Good, because I can't sing for shit either."

I sit down beside the cooler Damiond and Kelly are sitting on. "You guys are in some races?"

Kelly says, "Yeah, International Dragonboat Festival, here on the islands. You don't know? Where did you come from?"

"Hamilton, we all just escaped a disaster of a family reunion in that canoe-catamaran. Sam rigged up a tarp sail and ruddered the boat all the way here in the wind and some nice sized waves."

Rory looks impressed. "Play me a sailing song."

Sam giggles, "I'm a paddler, usually, not a sailor."

I say to Damiond and Kelly, "I've seen dragonboats – the long canoes with a pacing drummer at the front and a guy standing with a steering paddle at the back, right?"

Kelly says, "And ten paddlers along each side."

"I've never seen a race though."

Damiond says, "They're sprints, heats of five boats at a time. There's sixty boats here so it's a huge festival." His attention gets diverted by the pike. "That's a nice sized fish."

"It is, wish I had some seasoning for these steaks though," says Kate. She has the pike on a picnic table and she's cutting steaks from it with the hunting knife. Jonathan went to find more rocks to prop up a grill with.

Mary says, "I've got an idea, it might sound crazy though."

Kate says, "This fish has already gone down the rabbit hole of crazy; what are you thinking?"

"We could crush this bag of potato chips into crumbs to use as breading. They would add salt and oil."

When Jonathan comes back he finds Mary and Kate crushing potato chips and coating pike steaks in them.

"Your wife's idea," says Kate.

"Now you know why I married her," says Johnathan.

Once the steaks are on the grill, the chip grease sizzles and the smell of salty fried fish stops all our conversations, we can only stare and drool.

After the meal I pass around a bottle of whisky and we all get quite mellow. Jonathan and Mary tell Kate more tales of animals they've cooked on beaches, Rory and Sam keep talking music and trying to convince each other to play, and Damiond and Kelly talk quietly, in a couple's conversation. I go and grab some more wood for the fire, come back and add some logs, stoke the flames, sit in the glow and start writing in my notebook.

A GUY WITH LONG ROCKER-TYPE HAIR, a muscle shirt (but he isn't muscular) and a big camper back-pack shows up. To everyone, in a Québécois French accent, he says, "Hello, I am Jean-Sebastien, but you can call me JS. I'm not a dragonboater, but I'm a friendly traveller. May I join your fire?"

And of course he's welcome in this circle of friendlies. He sits down beside me. "Hello Mr. Writer, you work all day while everyone else plays." I pick up the bottle, take a swig, then pass it to him. "Ah, you write and drink, so it's not work, it's art."

"I like that line, I'm going to put that down."

"All yours, free of charge. Almost. You must tell me who that is over there."

It's Cecilia. He's pointing at Cecilia. I didn't even see her, but there she is. Alone. Too far to say she's part of the circle, but close enough to hear everyone. I say, "That's Cecilia. That's my sister.

She doesn't want to be here. I made her come. I kidnapped her when she was passed out in those boats at a family reunion. She was really pissed at me." She doesn't look pissed. She looks bored and vaguely sad. "Now she just wants to go back to Montreal."

"That's sad. She should come around the fire."

"Yeah, she should enjoy this. But I don't know. What do I know? I haven't talked to her in years. She likes the city now. Maybe this just isn't her thing."

"I think she needs to smoke weed, I think that's her thing."

"Really? I wouldn't know."

JS lights a joint, walks over, sits down beside her and asks if she would like some. She isn't sitting, but crouching on the balls of her feet, like she's trying to touch as little sand as possible. She looks as if a joint, particularly one that someone else had smoked on, would offend her. But JS has one of those smiles that gets away with saying anything.

In an interrogating voice, she says, "Is that pot?"

JS loses his smile. "Uh…"

"Is it just pot, no tobacco or anything else in it?"

The smile comes back. "Oh yeah, all natural my friend."

"Oh thank fuck, pardon my language."

"Not a problem, somehow I knew you would need this."

"I don't have any because I flew here. I've been going crazy. Well more for other reasons, that idiot with the notebook to be specific, but this really helps." She takes a couple big drags off the joint. "Ugh, I could smoke myself languor right now."

JS says, "Languor, what does this word mean?"

"Extremely relaxed, lethargic even, but in a pleasurable way. I try not to smoke so much that I become a burnout, but it's inevitable sometimes."

JS receives the joint back from her. "You're very beautiful you know."

"Yes, I know. Well it's all relative, and as far as I'm concerned beach neanderthal isn't an attractive look. I'm the only one here dressed with some class, so…"

"Yes. Beach neanderthal, I think that's what I am. Why don't you come sit with the other beach neanderthals?"

"Over there?"

"Yes."

"I'm not sitting over there."

"Why not?"

"There's a fire."

"Yes, there's a fire. You don't want to sit around it?"

"No, I do what evolved people do. I move away from fires. I'm not a beach neanderthal, remember?"

Damiond says, "You know, we can all hear you."

When she got onto that beach neanderthal stuff everyone stopped talking to listen to her. Jonathan jumps up and says, "I think I'm more of a beach gorilla." And then he starts making gorilla sounds, hopping around the fire, and Mary laughs ("Stop it you big ape"). Rory joins him: "I'm a beach caveman." And he grabs a log of driftwood and starts beating the sand and grunting.

Cecilia says, "Jean-Sebastien, would you be so lovely as to smoke me another joint at the circle of primitivity? I need to explain exactly what fire represents to the beach neanderthal."

"Guys, you don't have to entertain her," says Kate. "We're her family and we just ignore her now."

Damiond says, "No, please, join the bonfire of neanderthals and explain to our primitive minds why we are the way we are."

"I'll try, if it's too much for you just recharge your mind by staring into the fire light you love so much. First, let me explain my expertise on the matter. This man is my twin, and I watched him waste years around bonfires, not only avoiding social contact or any real integration with society throughout high school, but generally freaking people out.

"Now look there." She turns and points down the beach, over the string of bonfires, over the boardwalk lights, over the trees, and up to the skyline in the backdrop. "I bet not one of you has looked at that skyline in the last hour, I bet nobody at any of these fires has. And how is that possible? The only real symbol of human progress in view? Because you want to de-evolve. I don't blame you for your choice, but you have to admit you're running away from something by sitting here."

Damiond says, "So you're saying that staring at a glowing screen in a coffee shop somewhere is more evolved?"

"It might not be better, but using gadgets that were invented sometime in the last two thousand years is, yes, slightly more evolved than this."

Mary says, "And I suppose paddling is an outdated technology, and that dragonboating is an attempt to de-evolve."

Cecilia, who hasn't sat down yet, instead pacing, like she's trying to find the place least in the range of the fire's de-evolving powers, receives the joint and says, "Actually your lizardboating is perfectly fine."

"Dragonboating," says Mary.

"Everything new has roots in something old. The point is the old needs to update and change if it's going to stay of value to people who are, hopefully, updating and changing. Your lizardboats—"

"Dragonboats," says Johnathan.

"Are probably made of some high-tech materials. And now something sporty and fun has come of it, a lizardboat festival."

"Dragonboat festival, Jesus woman," says Rory.

But everyone laughs, everyone has come to like her and everyone laughs except me, Kate and Sam; we ignore her rant and stare into the fire. I go back to my notebook.

Chapter Seven

2009 – Toronto Central (first freelance article written by Alex, one year after the Dragonboat Races)

Title: The Soul of the City

I sent a resignation email to the bakery at 9pm. That was that and I wouldn't be showing up to my 1am shift, but I wouldn't be going to bed either (sleeping schedules don't return that quickly). So I loaded up on coffee and set out to walk Toronto's streets, not knowing, at first, that on this particular night I would have lots of company.

It was on a residential street in Little Italy that I first noticed something strange. Walking by the usual garbage cans placed on the sidewalk for morning's pick-up, my eye caught something soft, orange and fury – a stuffed Siberian tiger. I stopped, walked back, and inspected the find. After a moment of consideration, I picked up the tiger, hugged it close to my body, and started walking home.

Along the way I noticed other objects on the side of the street – couches, love seats, mattresses, microwaves, television sets, book shelves and boxes full of old junk. In front of one house was a coffee table made of thick, red wood – a perfect replacement for the ironing board me, Sam and Rory had been using as a TV table.

So after dropping off the tiger I returned for the table. It was heavy; it took more than an hour to travel the fifteen blocks back. While I rested between blocks, I noticed flashlights scanning the sides of streets everywhere. Tonight was a scavenger's paradise, and Toronto obviously had many scavengers to enjoy it.

THE NEXT NIGHT I WENT TO THE PRESS CLUB. Sam's friend, who works for the newspaper *Toronto Star*, organised a Wednesday night get-together for any press-related people. I gave her some resistance at first – "It sounds intimidating, like there'll be lots of people with jobs, and lots of people asking what I do."

"You're a freelancer!"

"I'm not, I've just been saying that because I don't have a job."

"Someone there might be able to get you a job."

"I hate feeling opportunistic, that's the main reason I don't want to be a freelancer."

So I went, after convincing Rory to go with me. I wore a shirt that read "I make my living manipulating DNA".

Someone said, "I'm with the Toronto Star, who are you with?"

"My friend Rory, he's over there."

We didn't stay long.

Chapter Eight

2008 – Toronto Island's Ward's Beach (Friday before the Dragonboat Races)

Four people show up: two girls, Spry and Heather, and two guys, Martyn and Alemu.

Heather says, "Can we play cards at your fire? A bunch of annoying guys in golf shirts took over the last one we were at, and kept telling lame jokes and shaking hands. We left before we had to talk to them."

Jonathan says, "Of course, you're very welcome."

Martyn, softly and politely, says, "Thank you, thank you. We won't disturb you, please keep talking."

They throw their blanket down and start playing Asshole. Kate joins in and immediately takes to Heather. They both have broad shoulders, giving them tough-girl looks, although Heather looks more like an athlete because her arm muscles are well-defined.

They say they're on the Scarborough Bluffs Collegiate's Dragonboat Team – The Scarborough Buffs. The four of them graduated and turned eighteen this year, so they can roam the beach while the rest of the team has to stay in. I ask if Scarborough is in Toronto and Martyn said yes, but east of Toronto proper, and it wasn't part of the city twenty years ago.

Kelly says, "Damiond and I live in Etobicoke on the West side of Toronto Proper, and same thing, wasn't part of the city until amalgamation."

Kate says, "Good, so I can call Toronto stuck up and selfish and it won't offend you guys."

Heather says, "Go for it."

Sam finally plays a song, the only song she knows that has vocals she can sing – *Peace on the Rise* by her favourite Canadian musician Chad VanGaalen. Her strumming chugs through a dreamy chord sequence, and she looks at me as she sings the first verse: "We can sit around this fire / and let our spirits ride on out / Watching as the flame gets higher / I can see it in your eyes / peace was on the rise."

Rory likes the song so much she makes her teach him.

"There's only a few hand positions you need to know, and the melodic part is easy to add on top," says Sam, illustrating on the neck of the guitar.

Rory, sliding behind the neck, says, "Still, teach me like I'm a child."

Cecilia starts speaking to JS in French (I forgot she studied French and French Literature in high school, I guess that's why she chose Montreal for university) even though he's sticking with English; they both want to practise.

Damiond and Kelly are talking with Mary and Jonathan, and I can tell they've all mutually reached that point when the alcohol has removed any conversation inhibitions. Kelly, loud and animated, says, "Every year Damiond says we should rent our own place so there's not all our friends and Rory's friends from Ireland everywhere, but I say why? You get so drunk every night it's not like we could do anything anyway."

I'm sitting here listening to Kelly and Damiond's conversation. I'm listening to a couple's conversation. More than that, I'm listening to a couple's conversation with another couple. A newish one with an oldish one. I can't imagine what that's like. I've never had a girlfriend, never had someone that would sit beside me and tell another older couple lots of embarrassing stories about herself and me even if I got angry about it because who cares? We're going to be together for the foreseeable future, and as long as we're good who cares what other people think? At least that's what I imagine a relationship is like.

Now I'm listening in on the Scarborough Buffs' conversation, and Spry in particular. She says, "That was close. That was so close last week it was a bit of a thrill – *I got an eight*."

Heather says, "Tell Kate the story."

"Shit dude, I almost got dragged off a train yard downtown by security for painting this old beat up train car. There's a guy there that moves trains around with this remote controller, just like the ones for model cars and planes." She gets up, springs to her feet and holds an imaginary controller. "And the guy moves all the trains across fifty tracks back and forth like he's organising them." She sits back down, but spins as she does. Her movements are amazing: they're silent, somehow don't mess up the blanket or throw sand around, and appear to consume not a calorie of energy, like they're really just inflections in her story telling. "That guy's great. He's cool, lets me stay and paint anything that's basically junk. But a truck showed up!"

Kate says, "Fucking trespass police."

Spry, popping up on her knees and throwing her palms up, her bony wrists sitting loose, as if her hands and forearms were two ends of a pair of nunchucks, says, "Yes, exactly, fucking tress—pass—police. Trespasspolice. But I rolled between cars, over their connectors, and lucky the guys in the truck were lazy fucks so they just kept driving to circle around the end of the train to drive after me." She stands up, looks at her cards, *"Three Jacks, anyone?*

Three queens." And then she does another spin on the ball of her foot without messing up the blanket or cards.

Kate says, "Fuck, I'm going to be asshole again – *pass.*"

Spry sits with a knee up near her chin and holds her cards in front of it, "I signalled my guy, waved at him up on his platform, and he sees what's going on and he pretends not to see the truck and he's like, mrnnn…" – sitting on her knees, holding the imaginary controller and laughing, and she has a Joker like grin full of teeth, but wrinkles in the corners of her eyes that soften it (like an old man's). "The train's moving forward and the truck speeds up and he speeds the train up and the truck's honking trying to get his attention but he's pretending to look the opposite…" She falls over laughing.

Martyn gets up on his knees – not like it's an inflection on his speech, the way it is with Spry, but like he's trying to find the right position for what he's about to say. "Spry, go to art school. Stop with the street art. You're eighteen now. The cops know you, they will give you no leeway. You'll go to jail. Is that what you want? You want to go to jail with those girls at school that get in fights and go to juvie because they assault other girls – helpless people?"

Spry falls backward and says, "Easy my friend, my beautiful, protective, concerned, and how did we not see that he was going to enrol in nursing school" (she kicks her legs in the air) "because he's so sensible, friend. It's okay, I'm a cat."

She jumps up and crouches behind Martyn. Every time he tries to look at her over his shoulder, she dodges his eyes. He says, "I'm concerned SP. Just go to school. Alemu, our voice of reason." He really pleads with him, after Spry falls down laughing. "Tell her to go to art school."

Heather says, "First play your cards, let's keep this moving."

"Someone's eager to become asshole," says Kate.

"That's strong language to use with your President."

"Outgoing…"

"*Two 3s,*" says Alemu. "Martyn, our friend Spry is a different kind of girl. You say she should take advantage of the fact that her teachers and guidance counsellor support her so much that they applied to art and design college for her, but you don't see that she's taking full advantage of the situation in the way that she precisely wants to. A street artist of no skill or recognition is just some punk vandalist, but a woman who has acknowledged skill and professional opportunities and has rejected art school for street art, that woman elevates what she believes in."

Kelly, interrupting my eavesdropping, says, "Do you have a girlfriend, Coast?"

"No, I'm too non-committal."

"That's too bad. You're cute, a little short, but cute and strong."

Damiond says, "I'm going to have to cut you off in a minute."

"You cut me off? I don't think so."

I got back to listening to the Scarborough Buffs. I want to know if Martyn and Spry are involved at all. In a really tight group like theirs it's hard to tell the couples. They're one of those groups that's as tight as couples. That's something I've missed out on; not that I'm complaining, I prefer meeting random people all the time, rather than feeling stuck with the same few people. But still, watching this group play cards, I'm wondering what that kind of closeness is like.

Martyn says, "I just don't get it. Graffiti is what you believe in? Of all the ideas you could elevate, of all the beliefs you could advocate, you choose graffiti?"

Spry gets onto her knees and shifts, digging them into the sand. She puts her hands on her lap and then enters a state of perfect stillness, which, for this fractal of movement, speaks loudly enough that all have quieted for the speech. "I'm not elevating a belief in street art, I'm elevating a belief in the soul."

Martyn guffaws, "Oh, it's religious then, from the girl that says 'don't talk to me about that crap' anytime someone else talks about religion."

"It's not about religion, and please don't talk to me about that crap, because it confuses what we're all meant to do with our souls."

"Then tell me, what am I supposed to do with my soul and please don't leave out how it all comes back to graffiti–*three 5s, anyone? Three queens - I'm VP.*"

Spry, sitting cross-legged again, chin in her hand, elbow on her knee, says, "I don't know what you're supposed to do with your soul. That's my point: each person's soul is their own piece of the whole, their own bit of the universe to tend to."

"Fine, but what does that have to do with graffiti, and how is this not a religious conversation?"

Spry falls flat on her back, "*Pass*–because it's a mistake to think there's a God to tell you how to tend to your soul, a heaven to reward you for doing it right, or a church that you have to go inside to get it done. It's a mistake to think it's a collective responsibility at all." On the last point she pops back up cross-legged and falls into a deep study of her cards.

Martyn says, "And this is why you're going to let yourself drift into a life of jail, no income, and probably homelessness, because your soul requires full dedication to graffiti?"

Spry, daintily, says, "I prefer the term street art, but yes."

Cecilia crouches down beside me and speaks *sotto voce*, "You're drooling."

"What?"

"I bet she's far more attractive than the girls who are already street kids, I'm assuming that's your usual stock."

"I don't know what you're talking about."

"She's like your version of a virgin. Better, a virgin bursting with eagerness."

"Cecilia, I really don't know what you're talking about."

"Oh come, yes you do. Were you not just pulling out your notebook?"

"Yeah, because I feel like writing."

"Mmhmm, and when the homeless street artist" (she says artist with sharp syllables–ArT-IssT) "asks you about your writing, I'm sure you'll be quick to point out you don't like to 'think of writing in terms of publishing or making money'. I believe that's what I overheard you say at your last bonfire. Oh, and your bonfires, your great social de-evolution, I'm sure she'll love that."

"That was quite the little speech you had on de-evolving," I say, to change the subject away from Spry.

"It was only little because you stopped listening. You were featured quite a bit by the way. In fact little Spry would have appreciated hearing all I had to say about you. It was all meant as criticism of course, but she would have seen it as compliments. Just imagine, graduating high school into the arms of a bohemian, it's every girl's dream. Not mine, of course, but then I'm a university student."

I look at Spry through the flames, both Cecilia and I do. She says, "*Two Jacks, anyone? Two Kings I'm Pres.*" She gets up and does a backward cartwheel. It isn't tight like someone who takes gymnastics would execute, but she does it with this mysterious movement; she reminds me of how the arm of an excavator moves, how something about the bounciness of the hydraulics gives away that the force is coming from somewhere indirectly connected to the arm.

Cecilia says, "Adorable, but sad too." She sits back down beside JS.

Despite Cecilia's misguided perception of my reasons, I pull my notebook out and write down lines from the conversations around the fire. Spry glances over a couple times as I write, and I catch myself mentally rehearsing answers to questions. Dammit, Cecilia.

Chapter Nine

2009 – Toronto Central (first freelance article written by Alex, one year after the Dragonboat Races)

Title: The Soul of the City

In 2009 the Feds called an election. I was rather unconcerned about whatever changes it meant for the country, but excited because it meant a J-O-B for Coast (and Rory, because I filled out an application for him too, before he could say no). I was told on the phone that we would have employment from 5:00 to 9:00 every evening until the ballots were cast, but that we had to show up for a night of Revising Agent training right away (a revising agent, we eventually learned, was someone who went door-to-door and checked that people were properly registered to vote).

The training took place in the basement of Elections Canada's Trinity Bellwood's Office. Their temporary office, actually. Previously it was a portrait studio that had a 'closed for vacation' sign on the window for more than a couple years (someone told me).

Joy, the Training Officer, gave me and Rory the facts: "Trinity Bellwood's District has the highest number of revisions in the country – it includes University of Toronto along with most of the new condo buildings in the downtown. It's one of the most ethnically diverse districts in the country."

We were given yellow cards that explained, in English and French, "I don't speak your language". There was a phone number in large print on the card. Joy said, "Point to it, make a phone call signal, and hand them the card. Either that or ask their six year old to translate – they're usually happy to have the job. Some people will be happy to see you, but some people will be furious, deciding that at that moment you represent the federal government and its full history…" – Rather than Elections Canada for the three weeks they're pretty much willing to give anyone a job (our applications listed our names and SIN numbers – nothing more) – "Some people will want to talk politics, but for the next three weeks you are not allowed to have any political opinion."

The point Joy reiterated the most: "there's one lesson this job is going to teach you, there are all kinds of people in this city."

*"I suggest this spiritual exercise: become a foot."**

*Italicised quotes are from *Venice is a Fish: a sensual guide* by Tiziano Scarpa.

Chapter Ten

2008 – Toronto Island's Ward's Beach (Friday before the Dragonboat Races)

Two guys show up to the fire. The Scarborough Buffs go quiet and flash quick looks at each other, and then I notice the two guys are wearing golf shirts. They don't say hello or ask if they can join, they just walk up talking with each other as if it's their fire and they haven't noticed that other people are around it yet. Then two more come, also in golf shirts. They stand at a different spot and, without acknowledging anyone, chat with each other. Then two more show up, also in golf shirts, and these two stand between the fire and the spot in the sand I've reclined on so that their shadow casts across my face.

Our chatter quiets to the point where theirs is the louder. And then we go completely quiet. Another guy in a golf shirt – him built the biggest, and the side part in his hair the straightest – walks up to the fire and stands there, big arms on his hips, a smile of intense confidence, and surveys the crowd while all his golf-shirted-compatriots go quiet too.

Then he walks straight over to Rory with his hand out. (Sam drops her head and plucks a few random notes, pre-emptively avoiding having to shake his hand.) "Ronny Tailweather, and you are?"

Rory eyes him up, and seeing that he's just going to stand there, smiling that entitled smile until he receives his introduction, says through gritted teeth and a thickened accent, "Ronald Tailweather, I'm Rory O'Collin."

Ronny, seeming a bit thrown off by the accent, moves to Jonathan and gives him the same introduction. Jonathan and Damiond shake his hand coldly and introduce Mary and Kelly, saving them from the handshake. Just as he sees me in the sand behind his friends – his friends are still silent, looking smugly happy to be Ronny Tailweather's friends – I get up, walk past him and sit beside Cecilia and JS.

Then he walks over to Alemu. "Ronny Tailweather, I live on King Street right downtown, and you?"

Alemu, a guy well over six feet and with a warrior's build, beams the kind of large friendly smile that's meant to put people at ease. "Alemu, from Scarborough."

"Scarborough, that's too bad. We have some guys from Scarborough we gave mailroom jobs to. Tough place to grow up I bet."

Martyn says, "Actually we all love where we're from, and it's a big place that you can't really…"

But Ronny moves on to shake hands with JS. How weak is that? Drop a thinly veiled insult and don't even wait for the rebuttal. This whole situation is really bothering me. I love this bonfire, the crowd, the conversations, and I've seen guys like Ronny and his crew show up at a fire; guys who do just what these golf shirts must have done at the last fire the Scarborough Buffs were playing cards around – act friendly, but drop veiled insults, ignore that they're killing a buzz and probably feel proud of themselves when the good people disperse, because it only proves their sense of entitlement. Christ! I could get in their faces of course, there's enough guys to help head-butt them out of the circle, but a good bonfire circle doesn't recover from the anxiety everyone feels when groups of guys start butting heads.

He sticks his hand out to JS, "Ronny Tailweather, broker with RH Customs, our office is right downtown on Bay Street, what do you do for work?"

"Ah…hi, Jean-Sebastien, I guess I'm between jobs right now?"

Usually someone like JS would have no lack of pride in living the drifter lifestyle, but to be asked point blank in front of a crowd, quiet except for Sam's erratic plucking of her strings and murmurings from the golf shirt clan about work and whatever, it makes him visibly uncomfortable. Now I'm getting a really bad feeling that Ronny Tailweather is going to shake Cecilia's hand and she's going to dive right in and start chatting with this guy. Who knows, he could be her type. I can think of at least one of her boyfriends from high school that I hated as much as I immediately hate these guys. If that happens they'll never leave and I won't tell Ronny to fuck off which more and more I want to do.

"Hello there, I'm—"

Cecilia, not shaking his hand, says, "Yes, who the fuck are you? Are you running for an election? Are you the president of this beach? Why don't you go stand over there with your friends and throw me a dainty little wave like the Queen of goddamn England."

Ronny says, "Pardon?"

"Seriously, you guys are so official, and so alike. Although the parts in your haircuts are starting to fall out of sync. I'm assuming that's for aerodynamics in your…um…lizardboat races or whatever."

"Dragonboat races. Wait, you're not even part of the festival? What are you doing here?"

Kate yells over from the other side of the fire: "Not giving a fuck whether you think we should be here or not. It's a fucking beach and we landed in front of the bonfire."

Cecilia says, "Yes, but if this is a restricted access douchebag only zone then I'll have to apologise on behalf of myself and everybody here except your golf-shirted friends."

"Wait, you came in that thing? Ha—ha. Fellas, look at their boat, it's a joke. Is that two canoes tied together with paddles?" The whole lot of them start laughing. "That's so sad. It looks like junk from some trash heap. I feel sorry for you guys now."

Sam says, "Those are not junk, those are Grummans, and they're probably tougher than whatever you paddle. Those things got us here from Hamilton."

"Oh no, you're from Hamilton." Then to his snickering friends, "They're from Hamilton. Well I stand corrected. You obviously didn't get them from a trash heap. Why would you when you live in one."

Kate says, "Don't call Hamilton a trash heap you turd. Where the fuck are you from?"

"Oh, where am I from? You can see it. See that beautiful, brand new condo building right next to the tower? I just bought a huge place in there. We all live downtown."

Sam says, "That explains a lot."

"Yeah, explains why we're better than everyone here."

Kate says, "No, it just proves how fucking delusional someone can get living and working in the most pathetically selfish and stuck up city ever."

"It also proves how refined one's taste in golf shirts and khaki shorts can become," says Cecilia. "Near 1985 levels of expertise, apparently."

Ronny tries a few more jokes about Hamilton, but they're lame and Kate and Cecilia shoot him down with each one. He starts in on criminals from Scarborough, but the jokes are worse and borderline racist.

Heather says, "Do you even know where Scarborough is? Point to it, point in the direction of Scarborough."

When Ronny looks around like he might see where it is, but without finding somewhere to point, Spry laughs a beautiful Buddha-like laugh, "Oh my God, these guys are so dumb it's funny."

"We don't need to know where, ah, criminals are from anyway. Buddy, give me a sip of that," Ronny says to me. I'm drinking from a bottle of whisky, and I'm so very happy he's turned his attention to me in this moment.

I stand up slowly and face him, "You mean this bottle here?"

"Yeah, give me a drink."

"I'm sorry, I can't," and I make my way over to the Scarborough Buffs, talking over my shoulder, "You see, this is really good quality whisky. It's meant only for decent people from good places." I hold the bottle out to Spry. "Can I offer you a drink?" It's the first time we lock eyes for a good long time, and she smiles with all the wrinkles in her's.

As I walk back to where I was sitting I wondered what will happen next. The golf shirts initiated the hometown slamming after Cecilia put them to shame, and they lost that game to all the girls here. They can't escalate with the girls, so they either have to leave with their heads down or challenge the guys in the group. I sit down next to where Ronny is standing, sit up straight and solid, and survey Rory, Damiond, Jonathan, Alemu and Martyn – all of them are sitting up straight and solid too, waiting to see what old Ronny will do next.

Before Ronny can say anything, a guy named Eddie yells out to the Scarborough Buffs as he walks up to where they're sitting: "Guys, it's late. I've sent the rest of the team to bed. I know you can do what you want this year, but keep in mind you could throw away months of training by getting no sleep."

Heather yells to him, "I tried to tell them, coach, but you know these guys, all they want to do is play Asshole."

"Oh I'm sure you did, Heather. But seriously, you're the captain of this team; you should at least set an example."

Eddie's voice and demeanour completely diffuses the tension. He yells the entire time he talks, but with calm eyes and a voice that never gets that loud in volume.

Heather says, "He's right, we should get some rest, guys. We've got some ass to kick tomorrow."

Spry says, "Let's play a few more games first."

Ronny, seemingly thrilled to have a chance to return to his comfort zone, walks to Eddie, hand out, "Ronny Tail—"

"Tailweather, you live downtown and work at RH customs brokerage, and you introduce yourself to me every year. I'm Eddie, teacher at Scarborough Bluffs Collegiate and coach for their dragonboat team. You guys raised a lot of fuss last year, you planning on giving Les such a hard time again?"

"Ah…"

"In fact there's two people you were complaining about, but maybe you don't remember them either. Jonathan and Mary, how are you? Glad you made it for another year."

Mary says, "We wouldn't miss it, Eddie, how's your team this year?"

"Good, except all these four want to do is play cards, hour after hour. I don't know how you guys can do it."

Heather says, "We're leaving, Eddie, let's go guys."

"Just a few more games," says Spry, "I'm not tired yet."

"Then stay for a bit. Kate, keep this girl company, would ya? And get your butt to the races tomorrow, cheer us on."

Kate says, "I'll be there, but I'll have to see how good you are before I cheer you on."

Old Ronny and his friends walk back to the other fire. They were defeated by the girls, then Eddie put them more on the outside of the circle then any of us could. I'm so joyed by the win that I pull out my notebook right away to write down some of what was said. I'm still sitting beside Cecilia, who's deep in conversation with JS about marijuana, predominantly about the quality of weed in different places – JS has explored more places, but Cecilia's resolute that she lives in the best city for weed, if not as growers, then as importers from BC and elsewhere. Rory is playing what Sam has taught him, and Sam is eyeing him up with a glow while Rory is too focused to notice her staring at him. Jonathan and Mary left with Eddie, and the Scarborough Buffs left shortly after, all but Spry, who's talking with Kate, reinforcing that we have to get to the races tomorrow. Damiond and Kelly are convincing us too – "We'll find you places to sleep, it might be on a floor, but it will be indoors."

I hope that Spry has stayed behind for me. Cecilia asked if I could give her a bottle of liquor to exchange with JS for joints. I'll try talking with Spry after I grab one from the canoes.

OUR CHATTER'S GETTING A LITTLE TOO DRUNKEN. Rory passed out beer and said we should all come back to their place – his friends from Ireland will still be going for a few hours. "And you will sleep in my bed," he says to Sam.

Kate says, "I don't think so, pal, you'll see her tomorrow." And she goes and sits beside Sam.

Sam says, "She's my pit bull, don't mess with her."

Rory says, "I believe it, and I was just being a drunk."

Damiond yells across the fire at him, "And an Irish bastard."

"You're a Canuck bastard, keep it shut."

Spry, Kate's empty spot beside her, yells over to me: "Hey, I like your name, it's the only name I've heard that's as weird as mine."

I'm about to get up and sit beside her, but she does that first, coming to sit beside me using a kind of triple jump sequence. So we're sitting close to Cecilia. JS left after they made their exchange; without him she'll have nothing to do but listen in on our conversation. If I talk about bonfires, writing or anything bohemian-sounding, the subjects I know I can hit it off with a girl like Spry on, I'll immediately feel self-conscious. "It's a nickname, my cousins gave it to me when they met me earlier today, because they live in Hamilton and I suppose I'm the first person from the coast they've met."

"I love it, don't tell me your real name, I don't want to know it."

She jumps up when she speaks to me and sits to listen. I say, "You're the first street artist from a big city I've met. I haven't even gone into the city yet, or any big city. I bet you could tell me all sorts of interesting stuff about this place."

Spry, enthusiastically, says, "Oh yeah, oh yeah. You'll get bored though, everybody does."

"Tell me, I bore people too, so I'll be sympathetic."

She covers her entire face with her hands to laugh, but she's still laughing when she puts them on her lap. "Everyone in Scarborough says we live in a boring place, and I get it. It's like a grid of roads, ones that are almost highways. Inside the squares are apartments, plazas, community centres, schools and houses. So boring, right? Because it's not a grid of busy streets lined with bars and stores or whatever. But I think they're amazing. Those squares repeat themselves, like, endlessly. I mean there's Scarborough then this place then this place, but really it's just this landscape of squares closed in by highways, roads really, but highways sort-of, and they go in a big arc around downtown."

"You find this interesting?"

"I drive around those places all the time just for fun. I bought a car just for that reason. Honestly, I don't own a laptop, my phone is just a crappy flip phone, but I've got a beater. It's a Toyota Tercel, stick shift! You know Tercel's?"

"Yeah, sure. I've owned one too. This was years ago, but I did. I bought one back East, then drove it across Canada when I moved out West. I couldn't get it safetied out there, so I had to give it up."

"That's so sad." (She covers my hand with hers, and looks at me like I'm telling her about a friend who's died) "I'm going to make this car last forever, but I drive a lot. Everywhere I want to explore, I don't care if it's just the same plaza and apartment complex. I found an abandoned car a few days ago! It's at a plaza, and I swear the loading docks and dumpster area in the back is bigger than a parking lot, so there's all this stuff illegally dumped. And a car! I have no idea what kind it's so rusted. So I'm going to go back and paint something stellar. Tell me that's just the same plaza over and over.

"Oh! And the warehouses in Mississauga, beside Pearson International, but covering like three times as much space as the airport. It's…" She jumps up, puts her hands on her hips, and looks around like she's trying to locate a prop to use. "The warehouses…are just…I mean." She can't find the prop she's looking for. She throws up her hands, "There's just so many. My friend works at an auto-shop in one. He took me to check them out once and we drove for four hours." She holds up four fingers and pushes them towards me, palm out, thumb folded across. "Four hours and it's just a maze of warehouses, all near the airport. I want to, and you could join me on this." She sits back close to me and smacks my knee with her hand. "Write about it, because I want to do a camping trip. I've never been camping before and I want to do a five day hiking trip through them."

"Through warehouses?"

"Yeah."

"What would we eat?"

"We'd have to pack our food in, there's no stores. Oh! But there's coffee and sandwich trucks that drive around." She gets up on the log, crouching down and balancing on the balls of her feet, using my shoulder, though I don't think she needs it. "You think I'm crazy, right?"

Even though her head is turned away from us, I know Cecilia is laughing like this is a goofball comedy. I don't care anymore: "I spend every day and night I can around a bonfire. I do it on the coast, and I don't go to a park or anything. I live in Victoria and I just walk to wherever there's water, spots just like this, and spend days at a time there. No, I don't think you're crazy. I love it. I've never had the urge to drive around a city just to explore it, I mean I'm an ocean guy, if I'm not working on a fishing boat, I'm on a beach around a fire, so I just never thought I'd get into it. But the way you describe the city it sounds like an ocean – something endless in every direction."

"Yeah, yeah, you got it. That's the way. So you work as a fisherman?"

"Yeah, well I don't have a job lined up anymore, I quit right before we left Hamilton, but usually."

"And you have a place on the coast?"

"Yeah, well not anymore. I gave my place up right before I came here too."

She gets up and stomps her foot in the sand, "You're homeless. You're a homeless writer."

Cecilia's laughter is bursting at the seams.

Spry jumps up and warrior-stances in front of the fire, "So this is you, for days and nights at a time. But wait, how do you sleep?" She asks standing up straight and looking at me.

"I don't, not for days. I've always been like that, since I was a kid. My whole family has obscure sleeping issues – this one can't stay awake in boats."

Cecilia says, "Because they bore me."

Cecilia's cold serious in her tone, but Spry falls laughing through her grin full of teeth. Cecilia looks at her queerly. Spry jumps to her feet into warrior pose again, facing the fire. She says, "So like this for days at a time." She goes quiet, thoughtful. Then she turns, "I get it. The fire, the centre, it's, it's…"

I want to say "My best friend", but I'm self-conscious, and with Cecilia sitting cynically beside me it sounds stupid anyway. I say, "There's other people a lot of times too. I talk to lots of randoms on the beach, and sometimes I end up with a big group sitting around and chatting, like tonight!"

"And that's what your writing's about!"

"Yeah, but I want to do something different now. I'm not going back out West." I look at her and smile. "Driving around a big city would be something different."

Spry goes back to her place on the log. "Yes – but not just drive."

Almost immediately she jumps up again. She yells, "come here," as she runs down to the water's edge. I get up and Cecilia laughs at me and says, quietly, "Hey, if I ever see you guys on the streets, don't worry, big change only."

I walk down and see that she's pointing at the biggest smoke stack in view – to the east, and from here, probably because it's closer, it looks as big as any of the downtown towers.

Spry says, "That smoke stack is from an abandoned coal power plant. The building is so big, and it looks like a brick office building on its side." She faces me. "I've gone in. I'll show you sometime." She grabs my hand. At just that moment a plane descends above the smoke stack, and it's nice seeing the flashing lights of both. I kiss her. We kiss briefly, with a little passion. We hold eyes in the flashing smoke stack lights, then walk back to the fire.

When we get to the fire, Sam, looking distracted, asks me to pass her a bottle of something, and when Rory asks if she wants a beer she says "no, whisky". She takes a hard swig and says, "Coast, I want you to write something in your book later. If you've got stuff about me in there, then you should know why I hate my dad so much."

"If you really want me to, then sure, but back-stories aren't typically my thing. My philosophy in writing is if the present's not interesting enough on its own, then it's not worth writing about."

Kate laughs, "I like that. Like fuck back-story. The whole reason we're here is to get the fuck away from back-story. Let's drink a shot to now-story."

I run to the canoes and grab a bottle, a special bottle I wasn't planning on gifting to anyone. I give it to Sam. "Let's do a shot of this, I bought it off a guy who bought it in Paris. Apparently it's writer's booze."

"Absinthe, never heard of it." She takes a swig and makes a crazy face. We all laugh, watching her regain her composure, staring into the fire. Then her face turns serious, the kind of serious face so many writers throughout history have had on as they sat in front of a typewriter or screen, writing their own epic, tragic, whatever back-story.

"I'm going to tell you why I hate my dad, you don't have to write it down."

"Go ahead, I'll write it down later."

"My dad and my mom were really young when they had me. I knew it even as a toddler, like I remember seeing him with other men around and he always looked so much younger, but never immature."

She takes another swig of absinthe and, while cringing from the burn, passes it to Kate. Kate says, "Never immature. He was a serious guy back then, I remember from family parties – you couldn't joke around with him or anything."

"Okay, but I'm telling the story. My back-story. So he's a canoe trip guy. And that's what he leads me and my mom to do every weekend if he can, longer when he gets vacations from the mill—"

Cecilia says, "Mill?"

Kate says, "Steel mills, you know, in Hamilton? Steel town?"

"Yeah, so anyway, he brings field guides and challenges me to identify stuff. We go on big long trips where we have to paddle and portage for ten hours a day, and for weeks in places like French River and Algonquin. The trips were amazing because Jake, my dad, made them so easy. He did everything: set-up the tents, collected the firewood, and in the rain set-up tarp ceilings and ground sheets, so even those nights were fun."

Kate says, "This story's slow and I already know the ending."

Cecilia says, "I don't yet, and this is interesting. Sam keep going."

"Yeah, well here's the ending: it turns out up until I was born Jake was this punk-scrapper, spending all his time getting drunk with his friends and getting in fights."

Kate says, "He was a teenager, so what?"

"Exactly! So why does he turn into the same asshole now when he's thirty-five? The moment I turn eighteen he stops the trips, tells me I'll have to organise my own if I want to keep tripping, then two months after that he's moving out of our house and into his own apartment. Mom tells me it's because he wants to spend more time with his friends at the bar, and that she's fine with it. A month after that and I'm hearing stories about him getting into fights and pissing people off. It makes me sick to think about him now. He's nothing like what I thought he was."

Kate says, "You know, you could see this as he changed completely just to raise you, that he did something *for* you."

"Ugh, I don't know how you can defend him."

"Because my dad's an annoying hippy like you, so I know what it's like to have one on your case."

"Your dad is a mechanic and I'm a canoeist, get it right."

Sam looks morose. She grabs the bottle back from Kate and takes another swig. Cecilia reaches out for the bottle and Sam hands it to her. Cecilia says, "I think you're completely in the right to be pissed. When I meet someone, then find out weeks later that they're not the person they presented themselves as, I never talk to them again. It infuriates me. Your dad is that, but on the largest scale possible. I sympathise with you."

"Thanks, Cecilia, thanks for your understanding. And I hope you're still understanding when I tell you what I'm about to tell you: my dad…um…right before we left, when they were fighting…the last thing that happened…"

"Jake threw a drink in your mom's face," says Kate.

The understanding expression drains from Cecilia and she shoots up off the log, "What?"

Sam says, "That's why we left, because it got so ugly."

"That's *why* you left?"

"Your dad called the cops," says Kate. "Jake's probably in jail for assault, your mom can charge him and it sounded like she would."

"Good! And what did you do?"

She looks straight at me with dragon eyes. "I had to help Sam, get her out of there."

"And what about our mother, did you do anything to help her? Did you say anything? Did you at least get her a goddamn towel?"

Her voice is sobering. And when it ends the whole beach seems to go silent, waiting for my answer. "No, I...left."

"You just left? To help Sam? Spry, tender-of-the-soul, what do you think the soul has to say about a man who, after seeing his mother have a drink thrown in her face by an unknown side of the family, joins that side of the family and with them kidnaps his sister so even she can't stay and perhaps make their parents feel like someone's on their side, like their kids."

Spry shoots up, energetic and up-beat, not tense at all by the moment (as if she weren't even listening up to that point). "Um...I'd say that's pretty weak and the soul would think so too."

She isn't even trying to criticise me, she was led to say it by Cecilia – Cecilia's good at that. I look at Kate and Sam. They aren't saying anything. Of course not. They're the runts of that rant, the sad mutts that I've chosen to play with instead of taking a serious position on "my side". I'm feeling bad for Sam again, and then I'm angry, and I yell at both Cecilia and Spry, "Neither of you were there, so what the hell do know." Cecilia abruptly turns and marches to the canoes. "Where are you—"

"Airport. I'll paddle myself if I have to."

Kate and Sam follow, their heads hanging morosely, neither of them in the mood for a rebellion.

Rory, as they leave, says, "Make it to the races tomorrow little lady."

I look at Spry; she's taking steps backward with her palms up. Before I can say anything, she says, "I didn't want to get involved in your argument, dude." With a couple skips she turns then runs down the beach with light, silent steps.

I bend to grab my bag, sighing in frustration.

Rory says, "You put your arm around Sam in that moment, Coast, that's good for the soul."

I say bye to Rory, Kelly and Damiond, and look over my shoulder as I walk to the canoe, but Spry has disappeared.

Chapter Eleven

2009 – Toronto Central (first freelance article written by Alex, one year after the Dragonboat Races)

Title: The Soul of the City

Over the first two days I did four hours of actual work for the government – they paid me for eight. Rory and I arrived at the office at noon, and waited while streams of people moved around us. At 12:30 they told us to come back at 2:00. At 3:00 they finally gave us an assignment – starting at 5:00.

We were scheduled to sit at a desk and check passing resident's names with the voter registration list. The building manager buzzed us into the lobby – a high ceiling room with lounge chairs, a chair-less desk, and coffee tables, all made from cheap fake wood. We stood in the lobby, waited, waited, discussed the situation, and finally asked someone who looked official where the building manager was. He pointed to a set of elevators outside the lobby, but said he didn't really know because he was from the fire department. We went up the elevators and found ourselves in an office, which, after talking to someone there, we found out was the reception area for the office floors, and nothing to do with the condo.

The building manager sounded annoyed when we buzzed her again. She said, "You were supposed to bring your own desk."

I called Joy at the elections office: "She says we're supposed to bring our own desk."

"Use their desk," was all I got from her.

The building manager sounded even more annoyed when we buzzed her again. "Our manager says we have to use your desk."

"You can't use our desk, it's too expensive and you might ruin it."

After buzzing her twice more we were finally granted permission to use two lounge chairs and a decorative side table.

Rory was the first to try, and fail, at grabbing people's attention. As it turns out, most people don't care to "spare a few moments of their time for Elections Canada".

So I changed the script to something a little more aggressive. "Excuse me, do you mind if I verify your name on the voter registration list?" That seemed to work, perhaps because it was polite but informal, intrusive but in an obscure kind of way. Even the response of most condo-Canadians to any elections question – "I don't vote" – didn't really work. "I didn't ask if you vote, I just need to verify your name on the voter registration list."

Rory would get quite worked up over the non-voters, saying he couldn't wait until he was a citizen so he could vote. I said, "Or is it because you can't wait to finally pledge allegiance to the Queen?"

"Take that back or I'll murder you right here right now," he said.

On the second day we showed up at 2:30. We sat down with Joy at 3:00. She immediately said, "Can you guys wait at the front while I find you an assignment?"

At the front the receptionist said, "Can you guys wait downstairs, it's getting quite busy with the public and they need the chairs."

We went downstairs, then I said to Rory, "I should go tell Joy we're down here and not at the front anymore."

Back upstairs in the tornado of people, I found Joy. "Hey, we're waiting downstairs now."

She said, "Okay," until I started walking away: "Hold on, what are you waiting for?"

"You," I said, "to give us assignments."

"Wait a second...who are you?"

They didn't have an assignment for us that night, but we left in high spirits because hey, an hours pay is an hours pay, no big deal.

WE WEREN'T SCHEDULED FOR ANY ASSIGNMENTS THE NEXT DAY EITHER, but I woke up at 7am anyway. After a half hour laying in bed, and a half hour meditation, I got up and put on yesterday's clothes. My thermos-mug needed coffee, so I checked my online banking to see what was left of my overdraft. Good news! The bakery had finally deposited my last two weeks pay. I walked to the bank machine, to the coffee shop across the street from my place, then back home. But I didn't just sit on the stoop to waste the morning away watching Kensington's morning traffic; I made my bed, ate an apple, sent an email, took a shower, and put on deodorant, lip balm and tee-tree oil for my feet. I put on clean clothes, jeans and a white t-shirt; decided on sandals for the day; and put aside a grey button-up shirt with white stripes and a hoodie, my favourite hoodie, later to be packed in my backpack.

I finished packing my backpack at the same time I finished my coffee. So I washed my mug, brushed my teeth, flossed, and started charging my mp3. While my mp3 charged I walked to Augusta Avenue with a clean thermo-mug and bought a peppermint tea.

Back at the place I double-checked my backpack and put some new music on my mp3 at the same moment the little orange battery-light turned green. There was a fifteen minute wait for the streetcar on Queen Street heading East. I let the first one pass (it was packed), got onto the next car, sat down and put my headphones on. The car inched its way through downtown, rumbling and swaying along metal tracks, but sped up as it crossed the Don Valley to the east side.

"The first and only itinerary I suggest to you has a name, it's called: at random. Subtitle: aimlessly."

Chapter Twelve

2008 — Toronto Harbour's East Shore (Friday before the Dragonboat Races)

Kate and Sam paddle out of the bay and around the rock bank at a good pace, quietly, perhaps now as eager to get Cecilia to the airport as she is, but we get held up at the gap. Two tugs are pushing a freighter through. We hover behind its propeller, half sticking out of the water, seeming to advertise its ability to crush us, dice us, destroy us in an instant, or maybe it's just my mood. The freighter doesn't even look like a ship. I glare up at the tower of crew decks above its many storied hull. It looks like a warehouse, the lights half working because the warehouse owner is too cheap to replace the bulbs, the walls flaking red paint, and the red paint mixing with rust to look like puke, and to complete its neglect, the base has been allowed to break off from land and it's now floating like flotsam. I feel sick.

Cecilia suddenly shouts at me, "Why didn't you punch Jake in the face?"

"What would that have accomplished?"

"It would have evened the score quickly, then dad wouldn't have had to call the cops on him."

Kate says, "That's a good fucking point actually."

I say, "Christ, Cecilia, I was looking out for Sam. Mum was fine, she was thrilled, don't you get it? Having a drink thrown in her face was the best thing she could have hoped for. You could see the happy-anger in her eyes, even in dad's, the sick pleasure of it. Believe me, you didn't want to be there, I sure as hell didn't."

"I just remembered something," says Sam, changing the subject. From a pouch clipped to the gunwales she pulls out two red bike lights for the stern and two headlamps for the bow. She passes them to each of us with clips to fasten them. "There, now we're legal." Then she focuses her attention, or pretends to, on the tug that's positioned to starboard of the freighter's stern-end, pushing it at an angle that's counterbalanced by a tug to port of the bow-end. We can see a guy on the brightly lit deck. He waves at us. "I'm going to stay in view of him, in case he signals us anything."

We follow the freighter through the gap. As we're passing through, a zodiac speeds up alongside us and spotlights our canoes so that we can't see their boat. The light is so bright even the reflection off the aluminium of the canoes is blinding.

From the boat we hear, "Where are your life jackets?"

Sam says, "Under the seats," and she pulls out hers to demonstrate.

"Tow rope?"

"Same place," and she shows it.

Kate says, "I'm sorry, but who the fuck are you?"

They switch off the light so we can see the zodiac. Three cops stand up in it, looking at us like stone figures. The zodiac is made of heavy-duty black and red rubber and has a steel base. It has twin 300s, a stand-up cockpit and a chrome trellis that arches over the back and holds, in a metal mount beside one of the cops, a rifle with a scope.

After a tense moment of silence, the zodiac speeds off to port of the freighter.

Cecilia says to me, softly, "What did you mean you had to get Sam out of there?"

"She looked like she was suffering from that scene worse than anyone."

Cecilia looks down at her feet, holds her pinkie toe between her fingers, lets it go and looks at the East Shore.

The tugs shift the freighter away from the shore then hold it fast. The guy on deck signals us to overtake her to starboard. We haven't actually decided which way to go from the gap, but since we can't see any of the harbour yet, following the East Shore is as good an idea as any. Sam and Kate paddled us between the freighter and the East Shore, and I start to write.

Even though the freighter is a good distance away, its hull still feels ominous. When I look up at it, it fills my vision like an IMAX screen. When I look way up to the railings my gut reaction is to picture myself falling from there – I'm not great with heights, so I'm focusing my writing on the East Shore.

The first lot after the gap is all cement trucks. They're lined up in military-like rows. They must operate all night; I saw one leave and right now one is driving around the rows looking for a gap to park in. We pass the trucks and paddle in front of a mountain range that lines a river going inland. Not really, but these huge black tarps cover piles that I'd guess are cement mix. I'm seeing them as we pass a channel that cuts into the shore beneath a drawbridge framed in green painted steel, a channel that's probably for freighters. The black-tarp mountains run for a long way along the channel, and behind them smoke stacks flash aircraft warning lights as high as office towers would – this industrial land covers a lot of ground. There's a crane hanging a bright work light over one of the mountains, and at the base a crew of guys in fluorescent vests and hard hats talk and laugh.

Now we're paddling alongside an island of adult fun in this sea of late shifts. I can hear the sounds of a bar behind a row of tall hedges we're passing, and before we got here I saw a drive-in theatre and a go-kart track on this side of the channel.

There's another channel cutting into shore ahead, and on the far side there's a recycling plant. I see a pick-up backed up to an open bay door of a long flat warehouse. There's garbage spilling out of the door. The pick-up left and a bulldozer came and it's pushing the pile back in. We get closer and I can see more open bay doors, and the brightly lit interior where people in one-pieces stand at conveyor belts. There's a ship – smaller than the freighter we're passing – moored beside the building, and forklifts are running back and forth between them.

We've passed the freighter and I can see the city right to the water. Finally. It's a good look from here. Really bright for kilometres of shoreline. And at the edges there's highways. Where the East Shore meets the mainland there's one that's raised. A train too. Far away, but I can see the lights. The train is green, it's bright enough that I can see that. The raised highway curves inland, so the stream of white head-lights from the cars turns into red tail-lights. It's good. It's a good looking shoreline.

I notice Cecilia staring at me while I write, looking mischievous. She says, "What are you doing?"

I say, "Writing."

"Are you writing down things that I say?"

"Yes."

"Stop it."

"No."

Woh! She sprung for my book, landing like a bridge between the canoes. I had to spring backward to the centre. "What are you doing?"

Cecilia yelps, "Help, I can't get back."

Kate says, "Jesus." She grabs her skirt and blouse and pulls her back onto the bed.

Cecilia huffs and puffs and laughs like a crazy person. She stops, looks around and says, "What's that?"

At the end of the channel, which goes not too far, there's a crowd of people up a grass hill with white-tarp-tented-roofs, the size of festival booths, above their heads. The booths are strung with lights – incandescent bulbs in yellow plastic cages, like they use on construction sites at night – and, because of the people passing in front of them, they're flashing like strobe lights. In the flashes I see smoke, and the smoke immediately makes me aware of the smell of BBQ in the air.

Cecilia, with surprising enthusiasm, says, "I think it's a night market, like an Asian night market. Let's go!"

Sam says, "I thought we were getting you to the airport."

Cecilia, jokingly, says, "Want to get rid of me now, huh?"

But Sam doesn't want to play along. She's sitting quietly with her paddle in hand, looking indifferent. Cecilia grabs her pinkie toe between her two fingers and starts examining it again. I spin around and face forward in this awkward moment, while we sit dead in the water, floating next to the recycling plant, where I can see fleets of green garbage trucks, and the full length of the warehouse – it runs the length of the channel – and I can see that it's made of red brick; floating in front of the raised highway, where head-lights morph into tail-lights, and follow the highway into the city, as if the highway is feeding a fire, a bonfire, burning bright white at the base, warmer orange a few stories up, and dissipating into sparks at the tops of the towers.

Cecilia says, "My mother's a horribly critical person, I mean she's a cunt."

Sam, with some confusion, says, "Um...okay."

"And I'm a lot like my mother, so..."

"Oh."

I look back and catch a look of satisfaction on Kate, but she, quite considerately of the moment, turns her head away from them. I turn back to the book.

Cecilia says, "But you seem like a really good person, Sam."

I didn't see Sam's reaction, but after a moment she paddles a stroke, then another, rotating the canoes so that we're pointing towards the night market. Kate joins in and then we're moving.

The moment creates a silence between the four of us, but not a bad one, a silence like a group might have on a Sunday afternoon, when everyone is sitting on couches hungover, and there's nothing on or happening, so usually conversation would be expected, but because of a mutual need for rest and recovery, mutually accepted silence is created for everyone to sink into. We fall into something like that as we move to the end of the channel, to tie up at a low wall at the bottom of the grass hill, then climb our way into the flashing, smoky lights.

Chapter Thirteen

2009 – Toronto Central (first freelance article written by Alex, one year after the Dragonboat Races)

Title: The Soul of the City

The next day, when I first arrived at the condo for revising agent duties, I stood out front on Young Street with Rory, talking about our respective job-hunts.

Rory said, "The weirdest job I ever had was fixing palettes. I got paid per-palette and beer was free. Every Monday we drove around in a rental moving-truck drinking beer and picking up discarded palettes from warehouses all around Dublin. Then we'd take them back to the yard, fix'em, and every Friday throw'em back in the truck, drive around to the same warehouses and negotiate prices."

Inside the condo, the work session was slow, uneventful. One of the residents let us know that there was another entrance that was probably used more often than the lobby. I went downstairs and posted a sign, indicating that people could register to vote in the lobby until eight. To our delight, it enticed one person to track us down.

I asked Rory what the worst job he ever had was:

"The worst job I ever had was here, for a construction company contracted to fix-up a sewage plant. It was outdoors in thirty-below weather. The only warmth was in the trailer we ate our lunch in, but even that was cold. I'll never forget the crunch of my sandwich bread after it froze sitting on the floor.

"The first day they showed us vats of sewage that were so aerated that if you fell in, you would sink straight to the bottom and drown before anyone could get you. The construction company was awful and dangerous; they never tied off their ladders, so I'd be 20 feet up a concrete wall, alone on this shaky ladder, using a hammer-drill to chip pipe out of a wall; worse than that, once their crane almost dropped a full dumpster on me. I told them it was going to happen too. They were trying to lift it out of the drained concrete pit I was working in, but there was only one strap around the thing. I moved all the way to the corner of the vat and that's the only reason I didn't die.

"Then one day my coworker got sprayed with sewage when our foreman accidentally kicked a pipe in the basement we were all working in. It was hilarious, but that night, when we drove home, we both agreed that was our last day."

Our last two days of revision work took place at University of Toronto, at two student-residence buildings for Trinity College. We talked to the college's bursar, who proved incredibly helpful. He told us about Strachan Hall, the dining room, where we could catch students at dinner and at lunch the next day. The residence had massive oak doors, vaulted ceilings, and stone blocks with inlay carvings of weird faces. The dining room had long oak tables and incredibly comfortable chairs. When students registered to vote we asked what house they lived in.

"But the houses don't have addresses?" Rory asked one of the students.

"They're just different wings in the same building."

I said, "Yeah Rory, haven't you seen Harry Potter before?"

The courtyard in the centre of the building was elegantly landscaped with carved stone benches; trees, too, and I thought when their colours changed it would be the best fall spot in the city.

We left the gothic-intellectual-sanctuary and returned to that old portrait studio that was now the elections office, and handed in a stack of voter registration forms (the students proved more eager to register than any of our other assignments). We asked to book our training for the actual election day. They forgot about us again. The positions we signed up for were all taken.

"What am I going to do with you guys?" Joy wondered out loud. "Well, how would you like to be central poll supervisors."

"Ok...what's that?"

"The highest paid job with the most responsibility."

"Perfect!"

They needed someone good, and Rory and I were...good? We left the building laughing about our rise to the top.

"...the philosopher Martin Heidegger explained that coming into the world is like being thrown, it is a fall of being, diving into time. Life is a cat asleep on the window sill suddenly waking as it falls from the third floor."

Part Two: The Night Market, to Toronto Portland's Black-Tarp Mountains, to The Island Cafe, and through the Canals of Toronto Islands.

"I began to head off through the snow, but then I remembered. I found a splintered two-by-four sticking up above the surface, returned to my front yard and started to dig. I got down on my knee by the birch tree, pulling out T-shirts, spoons and empty bottles. And finally I found what I was looking for, three spiral-bound notebooks: November, December, January—three cold chapters of a buried book. I tucked them inside my jacket and trudged through the snow once more, over the ice and away from the river."

—Shaughnessy Bishop-Stall, *Down to This*

Chapter Fourteen

2008 – Toronto's Portlands (Friday before the Dragonboat Races)

The night market is a maze of booths, a mess of booths really. They're all made of the same scaffold frames and white-tarp-roofs, and the same construction site lights hanging from extension cords, so it's really a lot like a construction site at night, except for the crowds and the food. The crowds are thick and every booth has a line-up, except the one booth that isn't Chinese or Indian – selling ribs and cornbread to practically no one. Sometimes the crowds form a glob, and others think it's a line, and mass-confusion is created until the mistake is mass-understood and the aisle moves again. There's a guy with a megaphone speaking in Mandarin, then English, "Stinky tofu line starts here, stinky tofu Hong Kong style over here." He isn't selling it, there's already enough interest, he's simply creating some order in the mess of people around the booth. Some people have deep-fried potatoes cut and stretched into long coils and skewered, and they have to keep directing others to where they can get them. Everywhere people speak through stuffed mouths about the next meal – "Let's get some noodle soup"; "No, let's go back to the dumpling hut".

As much variety in dishes as there are, I can't stop buying BBQ skewers. Every second booth has troughs of coals around their perimeter with skewers of meat across them. There's beef, lamb, fish, and I have a skewer of chicken meat, a skewer of chicken livers, and a skewer of chicken hearts. I walk up to a booth just as a guy dumps a garbage bag of purple, fist-sized squid on a chopping block and starts cutting pieces for skewers. The only calamari I've had is the breaded rings. I buy one, the tentacles and body parts looking like pieces of the baby alien in Alien, and eat the meat doused in Teriyaki sauce. It's so good I grab two more, then go to find the others.

I find them in the back row of seats for a stage where a band is playing – Kate eating BBQ pork, Sam eating steamed dumplings, and Cecilia eating glass noodle soup. However, Cecilia is frozen, a spoon full of noodles and broth hovering an inch from her mouth.

I sit down beside them. "Anyone want to try squid-on-a-stick?"

Sam says, "Gross", but Kate – "Fuck yeah." She grabs my other skewer. Cecilia is still frozen, her eyes locked on some point ahead of us, though not the stage.

I say, "Cecilia, what's going on?"

Sam answers for her: "I think we've found Cecilia's type."

Then I realise what she's looking at. In a booth beside the stage is a DJ, doing the sound for the band at the moment, but he has one of those turn-table sets that plugs into a laptop too.

Kate says, "DJs? That's your type?"

"Oh…yes."

"Fuck DJs, you can have him. He is a looker though."

I say, "He's short and scrawny, shorter than you, Cecilia. And he has a big scruffy fro."

"He's a DJ, let's not get bogged down with details. I need a good first line. How about 'There's some good meat around here, how's yours?'"

Sam laughs, "Wow, I didn't expect that from you."

Kate says, "That's a little raunchy even for me, Cecilia, well done."

"Oh, you can help, I'll tell him that my cousin over there likes you, and she sent me to fuck you and report back how good you are."

That was weird. Nobody laughs. We go quiet.

"Okay, I'll go with the first one. I think I need some new apparel though. Sam, come help me choose something at that clothing and jewellery booth in the corner."

"Cecilia, I get so bored in places like that, where it's all about buying stuff."

Kate says, "That's because you're a fucking socialist who needs to know that everyone owns exactly the same thing and eats exactly the same porridge."

"No, no, it's because I'm not so weak that I think the only way I can maintain happiness is by owning certain things that supposedly make me different, like a dirt bike or a sled."

"No, uh—ugh, it's because you hate when people have the freedom to do things that you think are…are…Christ, you're such a fucking hippy."

"And you're a…a…gear head. Or worse, you're like an American or something."

"You're a communist."

"Just because I don't get all excited about buying crap doesn't mean I'm a…Cecilia, actually yes, I'll come help you choose something."

"Whatever," says Kate.

And they leave.

Our squid on a stick done, we sit back and watch the band. It's really awkward, because we're one of only three groups sitting in the seats, and the other two are families organising themselves and not paying attention to the show, so every member of the band keeps making eye contact with us, the only eyes on them I suppose.

Kate says, "Why do you think nobody's into these guys? They're pretty good."

"Maybe because a roots band with a fiddle player is a bit out of context for an Asian night market."

"Ha—ha, yeah, no shit."

A song ends and we both clap. The singer laughs and says thank you directly to us.

Kate says, "That food was amazing, good call on the squid."

"Thanks, and thanks for that fish. This is turning out to be a tasty trip."

"Fuck yeah, that dragonboat festival better have some good food too."

The band plays their last song. Kate yells out "encore! encore!" and they all laugh while they keep wrapping up patch cords and putting instruments into cases. The DJ starts up some music, stuff with medium tempo beats and loops of instruments that sound more appropriate to an Asian night market.

Kate says, "I guess the next show is your sister hitting on that DJ. I hope she gets shot down, I'd rather see a comedy than a romance."

"I wonder what the guy's like. I've met a lot of people, but I bet I've never met someone like that guy."

"Go interview him. Bring your notebook and say you're doing a lifestyle piece or some shit."

"That's not a bad idea. It'll piss Cecilia off though, I think my writing annoys her already."

"Even better." Kate puts her feet on the chair in front of her and pushes herself deeper into her seat – poised for a show.

I gave the guy a spiel and he bought it, believed I'm a journalist with a lifestyle magazine out West, and he let me interview him. I asked him what other kinds of gigs he plays, what range of stuff he's into and how he got started. He ended up telling me his whole back-story, and I think because I wrote so much as he talked he was inspired to elaborate quite a bit. He seems like a cool guy, and he offered me a T-shirt with his name on it – Paul Brazer (no special DJ name).

For most of the time he talked I wrote about the night market and the food, but I got a summary of his story down: Paul started DJing when he was twelve, in a bar! His parents owned a bar in what was once a seedy part of the city. Historically it was a rock bar, and he grew up playing songs from his parents' large collection of 60s and 70s rock albums. Then the area gentrified and the bar was able to make more money booking shows. Paul got into electronic music and persuaded his parents to let him host some EDM nights. Then he branched out by playing gigs like the night market and producing some of his own music. One more interesting piece of information: he lives with his girlfriend.

Cecilia shows up just as he's telling me this. I'm sitting with Paul in the centre of the booth and Cecilia walks around us, slowly, looking not at us, but at the tables around the perimeter. She slows at the table with the two turntables, laptop and sound board, dragging her finger across them, and I notice she has a silver bracelet of many loops covering half her forearm.

Paul flashes a look of confused excitement at me just as he says "hi" to her.

She looks at him for the first time, steps towards him and places her hand, the one with the bracelets jingling up from it, on his shoulder. "What are you doing?"

Paul hesitates, then says, "I'm, ah, interviewing for a lifestyle magazine. This guy's a journalist."

"No, he's not. He's an idiot. He's a fisherman who likes to scribble in notebooks like a crazy person. I should know, he's my brother."

Paul looks at me, at first incredulous, then laughs, deciding I'm a joke and that's all. Cecilia's always had the ability to make me look like a joke. I was going to tell her about his girlfriend, save her the trouble, but I decide just to join Kate and watch the show.

IT'S SORT OF A WEIRD MEMORY. I was on the floor, three, or maybe four years old. My dad was watching the news. He must have been, that's how he would have found out. So he's watching the news and he starts to cry. I remember seeing that. That might have been my first really clear memory. He had his face in his hands. He wore jeans and a grey shirt. There were grey streaks in the sides of his hair. And his fingers went damp.

It was the fisheries closing of course. The government shutting down the Cod fisheries. He was a fisherman. I was too young at the time to know fisheries, but I remember his yellow oilskins, his boots and thick rubber gloves that smelled of the thousands of fish they gutted. Do I remember that? Stick with the facts, keep from embellishing, Christ.

Mum came in the room. Suddenly I got this pang of sympathy for my dad that was so strong I started to cry. Mum came and picked me up; that made it so much worse. If she'd gone to him I would have stopped crying.

I sit back down beside Kate and Sam. I don't tell them that the guy has a girlfriend – I want it to look like Cecilia simply gets turned down.

She's speaking to him lasciviously, pushing her hand flat against his chest, and keeping her eyes close to his. He has his hands up and he's shaking his head.

I'm thinking it's all over when Cecilia steps out of the booth and Paul goes to his laptop. But she stands in front of the booth and looks up to the sky, and when Paul puts something on – probably one of his own songs (it starts with a sitar and ambient street sounds, then a train blowing a horn, but punctuated and softened so that it sounds like an instrument, then the beat comes in and it really isn't a bad song) – Cecilia slowly reaches her hands in the air, and it's obvious she's still playing the seductress, because she dances slowly, moves her knees slowly, and slowly moves her wrists, pointed inward, in a seesaw motion, as if she's trying to get loose from a rope. What a glutton for punishment, he's a good guy and he's not going to cheat on his girlfriend.

Then he comes out. He stands behind her and wraps his arm around her belly. She pushes back into him. They kiss.

Kate says, "I was hoping for a comedy and instead I'm getting porn."

She's right, it's awkwardly hot and heavy, awkward for us anyway.

They walk past us. Cecilia says to me, "Watch DJ's stuff, he's going to show me his van."

As they walk away I hear "My name's Paul".

Cecilia says, "That's sweet DJ."

Kate says, "Fuck, she's like a guy."

Sam, who keeps staring at them, until they get to the van, says, "Your sister's personality keeps surprising me. She's kind of nuts."

Kate says, "Yeah, well, look at her brother, I mean you guys are *identical* twins if you just consider how fucking crazy you both are."

"I think you guys are both really smart, but you have the weirdest ways of applying your intelligence."

We go quiet.

Sam says, "I'm going to lay down on the grass by the canoes until Cecilia comes back."

"Me too," says Kate. "Have fun watching DJ's stuff while he shows your sister his van, Coast."

So I walk over to the booth and sit down with my notebook. The night market is over. The crowds have dispersed because nobody is selling food anymore. Some of the tents, the ones that weren't selling food, that provided information on a credit card or a travel company, are already gone, and the festival looks smaller. Then I can see the fluorescent green sign for T&T Supermarket.

I'm a bit disturbed by the fact that Cecilia has seduced a guy who lives with his girlfriend. The way he had his hands up, and shook his head – for sure he was telling her. She was in a handful of relationships with guys in high school, but never in what anyone would call a healthy relationship. She had a short temper, and it only got worse with guys she dated, so of course the guys had to be awful enough to justify her attacks. That was my take on it at least. I can't believe I'm writing about this stuff. This is not my style. But this, this disturbs me. I don't know enough about Cecilia, about what's going on in Montreal. Do I really want to know? Christ, if I'm really honest with myself, it's why I came here.

The food tents are mostly gone, and all the lights are off, so the lighting is all from the supermarket sign and the tall parking lot lights above us. I'm sitting in a parking lot, and with trucks pulling in to have grills and propane tanks and electric stoves loaded onto them, it looks like a parking lot. The festival covered a lot less ground than I thought it did when we first arrived.

Suddenly I want to leave. I could, what do I care if this guy's stuff gets stolen? I wouldn't even have to say bye to Kate and Sam. All I'd leave behind is the liquor and some clothes.

I calculate that I could be back on a rock beach beneath the stone banks of Beacon Hill Park in Victoria in less than twenty-four hours, staring across the strait at Port Angeles on the American side. It's not a view of the open ocean, but I love the rocks there, love having a bonfire in the centre of a pile of big flat rocks that I can circle all night jumping from one rock to the other – of course that's what I do only if there's no other people around, but there's always lots of randoms wandering the beaches in Victoria, so usually it's more like people sitting on different rocks around the fire, and yeah, it's not the open ocean, but a pod of orcas could pop up – I've seen it.

But there they are, the DJ and Cecilia, splitting in the middle of this dirty parking lot, the DJ walking towards me, and Cecilia going to the canoes. I guess I'm staying, I guess…

AS WE HEAD BACK TO THE CANOES I'M REMINDED OF SOMETHING. I'm reminded of how disgusting Cecilia was when we were growing up.

When she was a kid, friends of our parents thought she was the sweetest thing. She knew how to smile, and knew how to sing a song and do a dance at just the time that would make the adults laugh and come to adore her in a single, simple moment. What they didn't know was that never has there lived a child more obsessed with her own shit. And I'm not talking just when she was toddler, I mean age four, five, six. She'd throw it around her room, shit in the bathtub, shit her pants when she was mad at our parents, and she even shat on their bed one time, like an angry cat. Eventually it stopped, but something like that never really stops, it just transforms. I don't know what the hell I'm doing. I don't know what in the hell Cecilia, my cousins, my parents, or anybody on this fucking planet could possibly offer me.

I'm writing and Kate, Sam and Cecilia are yapping away, but I don't feel like noting down anything they're saying. Kate and Sam are fawning over her, praising her, and Kate even looks slightly intimidated by her. It's like she's a man, a player, talking about one night stands and how she only cares about a guy's looks and if he's a DJ or whatever, and Kate and Sam are laughing like she's a comedian. It's just her singing a song and doing a dance at just the right moment to win someone over in a few seconds flat. They don't even remember how much of a bitch she was being earlier.

Cecilia starts describing the van, the carpeted interior and how nervous Paul got on the inside. "I lit a joint and let the smoke curl around me. I took a big hull and blew it right in his face. Then, to fuck with him a bit, I asked, 'What did you bring me here for?'

"He immediately looked nervous. 'I don't want you to do anything you don't want to.'

"'But you brought me here already. So what are we doing?'

"He was completely lost. This poor man, so confident in his DJ booth, probably so confident with the dumb little club girls he's used to, was now lost for words. I leaned over, blew smoke right in his face again, and asked, 'Am I here because you want to fuck me?'

"He was almost shaking, 'I don't know, yes?'

"I got right up to him, sucked on the joint, almost burning his skin with the burner, blew smoke in his now unbelievably tense face, and shouted 'I'm just fucking with you, relax'."

She laughs hysterically.

Sam, eagerly, says, "So, did you sleep with him?"

"Yes, of course; and look, I got a t-shirt!"

We paddle out of the canal. It's still dark out, but the sky has a slight tinge of blue in the black. I'm at the front of Sam's canoe, facing forward, and Cecilia of course is sprawled in her hammock bed at the front of Kate's, with her Paul Brazer t-shirt. We pass a ship to our left, and the recycling plant to our right, which is closed now.

Sam says, "Cecilia, you're so different now. I know you're in a better mood, but I don't even recognize you from before you got out of that van."

"Oh, yes, yes, I see, that's before sex Cecilia you're talking about. An irritable bitch, I know, I hate her as much as you do. Here now is after sex Cecilia. Cecilia without irritation. Cecilia who sees the present moment in the most positive way possible. Cecilia without knots in her back."

We leave the channel.

I say, "Let's go straight across the harbour. Time to get you to the airport, Cecilia."

"I have a better idea."

"I thought getting you to the airport was the only idea that mattered. Let's go."

Kate says, "Woh, someone's fucking testy all of a sudden."

Sam says, "Be nice to Coast, Cecilia scored instead of him, and it's supposed to be his story."

"Hey, I got a scene for your book, a good one," says Cecilia. "Let's go back to those black-tarp-covered mountains we passed on the way here, climb one with a bottle of something right and watch the sunrise."

Kate and Sam are thrilled about the idea. A plane passes above us, nose diving towards a cluster of lights across the harbour. It lands and the cluster of lights suddenly forms the pattern of a runway – it took a plane landing to make sense of the lights from where we are. I say, "Yeah, okay. But Sam, I have a question: why would getting a girl make this my story? Why is having sex or falling in love or whatever always the most important element in a story?"

"That's a dumb question, because that's what people are interested in. Ask anyone what's the one thing they would want improved in their life, or to get better at, and they'll say love, or sex, or picking up, or whatever. It's what's on everyone's mind the most so it's what stories are always about."

"But I think that sucks. Stories are about experience, and yeah, that stuff is a big part of experience, but if you think about all the possible experiences you can have in an entire lifetime, it's such a small part of the whole. Like, are guys the most important part of your canoe trip memories? Is some hook-up you had on a trip your best memory?"

She's thinking. "No, it's not. No, not at all. It's when I discovered this waterfall and…yeah, it was when we went into it and…"

"Tell me the story."

"Okay, I was deep in Algonquin with this group of eight I go with sometimes. We stopped for lunch at the end of a portage, but didn't plan to stop long because we wanted to cover a lot of ground that day. I finished eating and went to pee up a river that emptied into the lake beside the portage path. As I walked up I saw that the banks quickly turned into cliffs, so I went farther. The banks got higher and rockier and eventually I came to a waterfall. It was perfect: fifteen feet high, heavy flow, but not so heavy that you wouldn't swim up to it, and an amazing pool at the base enclosed in granite. I ran back. Everyone was like 'where were you? We have to move', but I said 'never mind, follow me,' and they flipped when they saw it. Everyone shouted 'Shower' and we jumped into the pool.

"So we're swimming and trying to get as close to the falls as possible, but the cliffs make a narrow V, and the rush of water from the narrow section in front of the falls is too fast to swim against. Then this guy Scott dives under and pops up right in front of the waterfall, rushing back with the white water. He told us that if you swim far enough below the surface the water is completely still. So we played around swimming underneath the white water, popping up in front of the falls, then getting thrown back.

"Then! And this was my shining moment, I decide to try and swim as deep and as far back as I could go. So I'm under a rush of frothy white with this pillar piping down ahead of me. I push as hard as I can through the pillar and find a pool of still water beyond. When I surface I'm behind the waterfall. Not only that, there's a small cavern where the two cliffs meet. I pull myself up to it and sit on this ledge right behind the falls.

"I was in ecstasy man, kicking my legs and waving at the blurred images of people through the falls, and I can tell they can see the blurred image of me through the water, and soon my friends are surfacing below my feet, climbing up to sit with me on the ledge. That was the best. You're right, Coast, it's all about experience, and what's sex compared to finding a waterfall like that."

She isn't looking at me, she's so back in that moment, so there that I can see the waterfall in her expression. It looks grand.

Chapter Fifteen

2010 – Netherlands, Belgium and Germany (personal essay written by Alex, shared with no one)

It's all bots. That's what I'm learning about the modern world. We used to marvel at how "computers are in everything now." Now everything's a bot and I guess that's the new thing to marvel at.

What I want is a good conversation-bot. No more chat-bots – they're so low-brow, so predictable, obvious, so much like how I feel about myself. I need a smug chat-bot – I mean conversation-bot – that will make me feel smarter just by expressing her smugness.

But it will never happen. Conversation is untouchable, except by the greatest, greatest, bestest writers. I tried to be part of that group my whole life. Now I just drink like a writer.

Sam and Rory think I should move back in with them, but it's better I live alone.

"EVERYBODY JUST WANTS TO FUCK. I go over to my friends house to play games and do drugs but it always ends in sex. I just want to hang out with someone who isn't always interested in only that. I knew him for five years, you know? And as soon as I said I didn't want to fuck anymore he stops hanging out with me. Isn't that shitty?"

"That's really shitty, Elke, it sounds like you hang out with a lot of shitty people."

"Yeah," She laughed, but she was also starting to cry. "Why does everyone have to be such a fucking douche bag. I hate the fucking world."

"Hey, come on. You met me! I'm cool, and I'm not trying to make you do sexy things. Because you're cool and fun to drink with. So that's all right, yeah?"

I SAID, "ALRIGHT, IT'S WHISKY TIME."

"What are you pouring into the glass?"

"Soda."

"Huh, hey are guns legal in Canada?"

"It's nothing like America. But you can own a gun to go hunting."

"So there's lots of guns?"

"There's enough for hunting, I don't know."

"But are there enough to shoot all the Canadians who pour soda in their whisky?"

"Woh, okay. Funny, Elke, but no, I don't think there is."

"Oh hold on, I have to go blow my fish."

"Wait, what did you say?"

"Ha—ha, hold on, I'll be back."

When she came back she told me that the tank's aerator was broken, and she kept the fish alive by blowing bubbles in the water with a straw.

EINDHOVEN WAS THE FIRST CITY I DROVE IN. I really enjoyed driving in Holland – especially because Elke's grandmother's car is stick, which I missed – but I couldn't have enjoyed it without Elke telling me when to turn and when not to turn because the other car has the shark teeth, and telling me what's a bike path and what's a road (and when a bike path can also be a road). She's a great navigator, and she's a good driver too, but she can only see out of one eye, so she can't get a licence. Maybe that's why she's such a good navigator, all her other road-trip strengths are stronger.

We parked on a residential street and walked with Lola, Elke's lab-retriever, through the city toward a park. Holland is a place where the brickwork is always pleasing to the eye, the landscaping is always something interesting to look at, and the art is never kitschy – even the lawn ornaments are something abstract and thoughtful. When we crossed main roads that were also cobble roads, with the ever present rows of historical buildings and cafe patios, I pondered how Elke could grow up here, as if it were a normal thing to grow up on a set of a European movie. I said something like this to her, but she brushed it off and crossed the street.

The park was a more familiar landscape, although I was still getting used to the fact that all the streams didn't actually move, and were in fact canals.

AFTER AN EVENING OF DRINKING BEER AND EATING CROQUETTE at cafes in Maastricht, we walked back towards the car through groups of drunken university kids. We found a park where Lola could run around when we got outside the main blocks of the city (which in Holland always surround a church – in the case of Maastricht, a big one with old walls and gateways, large courtyards, and gothic sculptures of dead saints carved into archways).

In the park Elke wandered away with Lola, and I looked around in the darkness at the scattering of trees, and the stars above, and eventually the animal pit not far away with a giraffe lying down inside. Not just a giraffe, but a girl in what looked like a prom dress.

"What the..." I stepped closer. The giraffe looked sick, and the girl looked like she was caring for it. "Elke, do you see this..." I stepped closer and saw a gash in the giraffe's neck, right where the girl was sitting, the neck across her lap. "I think something really fucked up...or, wait..." Then I saw it. The stillness of the actors – the fact that they were sculptures.

I was freaked out, but at the same time thrilled by the experience. Elke, the devil, played the scene perfectly, apparently repeating for me the same experience she had when she first came here.

WE PARKED NEXT TO WHAT WAS A LARGE GREEN SPACE on the map of Brussels – we were only concerned with finding a place to walk Lola so she could piss and shit, then we could go find a patio somewhere in the city and order a beer. The park had a tall, ornamental cast iron gate around it. Just inside the gate were well manicured open spaces with trees that grew into connected, vertical terraces, and pathways of perfectly maintained grass for barefoot runners. We stepped through the gate and got lost in the pathways. We found our way back to the road we parked on, but at a point where armed guards stood outside a building's gated entranceway.

We didn't at first plan to spend the night car-sleeping in the middle of Brussels. Before deciding to stop in Belgium's capital on our way to Middleton, we first considered stopping at a highway-side park next to a conservation area. We were both creeped out by the spot. When Elke started describing figures she saw in the forest near where I was peeing, I jumped back into the car, and peeled out of the park and back onto the highway.

Elke said, "Why don't we stop in Brussels."

"I like it, just find somewhere in the city we can park, and sleep in the car 'til morning."

"Grab a beer on a patio somewhere."

"I'd much rather sleep in a city than anywhere out here right now."

"I think I'll feel safer in a city."

"Right now I agree."

Of course later we found ourselves sleeping in the car a few blocks down from a building that needed five armed guards out front to protect it.

IN MIDDLETON WE STAYED AT A CAMPSITE.

"I can't believe you found this party tent today. You're a superstar, Elke."

"Yup, but the water is piling up here where it sags."

"That's alright, if it gets full you just have to push it so the water falls over. Sometimes when we camp in Canada we dig trenches around the tent to divert the groundwater."

"Woh! There was a lot more water in there then I thought."

"Watch out, you're going to get the stoop wet."

"Push that section up there."

"Yeah, alright, but it's not even full yet."

"Perfect. The party tent is good."

"High five, superstar, we did it."

That night, while the rain pounded against the tent, we took off all our clothes and slept beneath the same blanket. What I remember most is Elke's sighs.

THE FIRST TRAIL WE TRIED IN THE *Naturpark Nord Eifel* was too rough on our ankles, so we turned back quickly. It was nice though. Lots of jagged rocks descending to a stream that zigzagged down the hill.

The second trail we tried was through grassland. Lola wasn't allowed on the boardwalks, so we stuck to the main gravel path. It was all we needed. Butterflies appeared that Elke had never seen. The first was small and neon green. I gave her my phone and she started taking pictures.

We came across a purple one as well, and Elke got more shots. Not long after the photoshoot we decided we were satisfied with our nature experience, and that it was time to go find a beer garden.

ON THE LAST DAY OF OUR ROAD TRIP, we parked on a street at a point where we thought we'd find a pathway towards windmills in grasslands we could see in the distance, but no such luck. We kept walking along the road, which had shipping yards beside a large canal to our left, and to our right old row houses with backyards descending to the grasslands and windmills.

We walked for a long time, Elke getting annoyed with Lola for tugging on the leash, me getting annoyed at her for getting annoyed with Lola. She stopped to roll a smoke and discovered she had no light. I borrowed one from a busboy at a cafe, and Elke ordered a coffee.

I SAT IN AMSTERDAM CENTRAAL, SIPPING COFFEE AND WRITING.

I thought about Elke, about the trip, about my first time – my first time! – and how none of it seemed to make me happy.

I spent a few extra days in the capital, with what was left of my stupid fucking credit cards. I stayed so I could interview this guy about an open-education system and pretend that the trip had some kind of career ambition behind it.

After the interview I finished writing up my notes, then just sat, and stared, sipping coffee, feeling sad.

Immediately thoughts of Elke. I wanted to check Skype to see if she tried to contact me, but I knew she wouldn't have. Our goodbye was friendly, no kiss, not even a hug. Maybe that's why I stayed longer, keeping myself busy with writing and coffee... so I didn't have to feel the ending.

Chapter Sixteen

2008 – Toronto's Portlands (Saturday, day of the Dragonboat Races)

We turn into the channel and pass beneath the green steel drawbridge. The bridge is brightly lit, and there are flood lights near the sides of the channel, enough to keep everything illuminated. Our voices echo off the corrugated steel walls, maybe just because it's so quiet. No cars are crossing the bridge. There are no other boats on the water. No wind, just a mild breeze. There are only a few boats parked along the walls of the channel – a large house boat, boarded up, and a sailboat that barely looks like it's keeping itself afloat.

We tie to the wall at a ladder, get up onto the concrete lot, then hide behind a backhoe briefly to make sure no fluorescent vests and hard hats are in sight. The mountains are all the same shape, long and narrow, with steep faces descending to the channel, and ridges gradually rising to the top.

At the base of a ridge Cecilia points to the summit and yells, "Engage".

Kate and I stare blankly at her.

Sam says, "I got that, Jean-Luc Picard of the enterprise, ha—ha."

We charge to the top and sit down facing the mainland, passing a bottle of gin, feet dangling down the steep face.

Cecilia says, "Captain's log: we've reached the summit of black-tarp mountain, from which we are able to scan the desolate, soulless, industrialised world of Toronto, a land full of hostiles in golf-shirts and fun-spoiling trespass police."

Everyone laughs. Kate says, "Fuck Cecilia, you're funny after a while."

"Aw, thanks Kate. Captain's log: the local crew has finally accepted my leadership."

"I hate to admit it, but let's face facts, who but the captain would be lying in a fucking hammock this entire time, giving us fucking orders."

"I don't like your flippancy pit bull. It's a good thing you're the only one who can deal with trespass police."

A passenger plane across the harbour rotates towards us from the far end of the runway. It fires up its twin propellers in a buzzing roar and takes off on a trajectory that looks destined to crash into us. Everybody yells, "Ya; fuck yeah; awesome" as it soars above our heads and banks a turn out towards the open water of the lake, and so close to the top of this black-tarp mountain that I see a couple faces in the windows – lit up by the reading lamps above their heads.

Kate says, "That was fucking awesome. Coast, buy us all tickets to Montreal. I want to fly in one of those."

Cecilia says, "Oh yes, what a classy entourage I'll have on my return trip."

The sun is just starting to come up, a thin red section peeking out from behind a landscape of tree canopies and large apartment complexes – a landscape that slowly rises up from the shoreline running east of the city – and streaks of red light beam at us through low-rise buildings, smokestacks and mountains of construction materials.

We spin around to face the islands, our backs to the mainland. We can see the geography of the islands from our height, the archipelago of small islands inside a large sickle that curves around from the Eastern Gap to the Western Gap, forested and sparkling with a cottage-country-like scattering of house lights and rows of lights for pathways that go through the houses – not roadways, but pathways – and a row of lights I can just make out through the trees at the outside of the sickle. The boardwalk! Of course. We are not much higher than the tree canopies and there are trees everywhere – except the canals and marina docks the canals link up. I love the way the marina and cottage lights look against the brightening sky.

Cecilia says, "Let's go to the islands. Let's go see those lizardboat races."

Kate says, "Wait, what the fuck? Now you want to trip with us?"

"More like watch the lizardboat races before Alex flies me out of here, but sure, say it your way."

I see two pick-ups speeding towards us from the rows of cement trucks. They're spinning yellow sirens. "Trespass police. Let's go!"

Kate says, "What? Fucking trespass police." And she's gone, sliding down the steep face of the mountain towards the channel. "Ahh," she yells all the way down, "shit," as she hits the dirt and somersaults onto the cement. Sam yells, "Kate, I'm coming," and screams as she also slides down and somersaults off the dirt pile onto the cement.

I say, "We better go," and we do, the trespass police closing in.

Chapter Seventeen

2011 – Toronto East (segments from Alex's present-tense-journal)

First I need to brainstorm some questions for Greg Proops: If you were a small country talking to your big country neighbour, how would you speak, what would you say? What do you think Marshall McLuhan's famous line, "the medium is the message", means in terms of podcasts, what's possible? Can you tell me more about notebook writing and comedians? That's a good question! I don't know why I'm so infatuated with this guy. Apparently he's too far-left-extreme for Rory, and he won't let Sam come see him with me. I think I just like how drunk he gets during his live-show-podcasts, how funny he is when he's raging against the right. Maybe he makes me feel like less of a chaotic person myself.

It's been a long time since I hung out with Rory and Sam. They never come to the East-side of the city anymore, and I never go West.

DRUNK. SHOULD KEEP THIS QUICK. Proops show was tonight. I ended the show! Didn't ask any questions I brainstormed. Mic came to me for the final one and I said: "Hi Greg, I'm Alex down the centre. First off I just want to say the black bird that attacked you on Toronto Island is actually called a cormorant."

"No it isn't," he interrupted. And then he launched into a long rant that ended in, "And that's my answer to your question you impertinent welk."

My question ended up being, "…the black bird that attacked you is actually called a cormorant…"

Chapter Eighteen

2008 – The Island Cafe (Saturday, day of the Dragonboat Races)

When the hell did I last sleep? I seriously can't remember. My head is such a haze. There's no way I'm going to sleep, not with the sun coming up. Sam and Kate are paddling very slowly. They are paddling very, very slowly. Up ahead I can see a ferry leaving. Must be the first ferry of the day. On the far side of the ferry dock is a canal cutting into the islands – I can't see it, but I see the masts of moored sailboats a little ways inland. I don't think we'll make it very far in. There's a thin beach on our side of the ferry dock. "Just go to the beach beside the ferry dock, guys."

Kate says, "Just mph the fucking heat my friend."

"Sense, you make none," says Sam.

I feel Kate and Sam have to get some sleep. They can't survive sleep deprivation like me. They can't stare into the fuzz and find the bits of streams of light poking through. That's what staying awake is, finding that one, narrow stream of consciousness that still represents sanity. Of course you have to know the difference between your sanity and your insanity, it's a tricky line to distinguish.

Kate says, "Stop telling me what to do."

Sam says, "No one's talking."

"Cecilia?"

"Asleep."

I say, "Let's just get to that beach beside the ferry dock, guys."

SLEEP CONTINUES TO ESCAPE ME. I'm watching the city, the sun getting higher in the sky, and anticipating the others getting up. Don't let them sleep. Wake them up. Don't wake them up. Let the sun wake them up.

The light fills the cloudless expanse. Crazy. I can already feel the heat of the day in the brightening blue. It's pure humidity and heat creeping into the sky. Don't think of the heat, think of the alcohol. Maybe a shot before they wake up, one just for me. Gin, that Plymouth stuff. Okay, that's my shot. A shot of Plymouth Gin to go with the sunrise.

There's that crazy shoreline highway. Beautiful idea, building a highway on the shoreline. Actually beautiful right now though, bits of light reflecting off scattered cars. Here's to shoreline highways, Christ this stuff is delicious. One more for the crazy industrial lands of night markets and black-tarp mountains. Holy shit that's the best bottle yet. Let the girls sleep, this feels too good. Got to pace though, pace and think. Here goes consciousness. Think about cities. I know nothing about them. Think as if you do, put yourself in their centres. Do they have centres? If so this ain't it. Starting to see the island and it's all parkland. Residential of some kind to the east of us, but all parkland otherwise. Big trees, huge trees, like this is Georgia or Virginia or some Mark Twain river country house flashback. That made no sense. Don't compare places to places you don't know, or authors you haven't read. It's this Plymouth stuff, makes it so I've been everywhere, read everyone.

CECILIA WAKES UP AND GETS OUT OF THE CANOE.

I say, "You should sleep. Kate and Sam are completely out."

"I know, but I'm fine. I don't really feel like it."

So she sits down beside me.

We sit staring at the water for about ten minutes, not saying anything. Cecilia pulls out one of her joints, then second-thoughts it, puts it away. We sit and stare at the water for maybe another ten minutes.

Cecilia says, "What's sleep deprivation like?"

"It's weird. Your head plays a lot of tricks on you. You start talking about a lot of strange things with people, things from your subconscious."

"Right, I see, I think I have that now."

"Didn't you just get some sleep?"

"I was pretending…I have these urges to tell you things, to talk about our childhood. But I know at the same time it's a bad idea. Maybe if we spent a little more time together, but not now."

"That sounds like sleep deprivation. And it's usually best to resist it."

I'm sitting on the sand. Sitting with Cecilia. I'm thinking. Cecilia's sitting. I think she's thinking too. Things are different. They're so different. Because we're both completely different people. I guess that's the truth about right now.

Cecilia says, "look at these two sleeping. There's something so adorable about them. Something so adorable." Her voice trails off.

"Yeah, they're all right, eh? I kind of wish we knew them growing up. It's so stupid how disconnected our family is from each other."

"It's really not a big deal, people are way more disconnected from their families than we are. I'd say we're better than average."

"Christ Cecilia, if we're better than average then average must be shit."

She laughs, but laughs like it's true. I know it's true. Be grateful for your sister. We drifted apart. We became so different in high school, but so what? I look at Kate and Sam. They never hung out in high school, and now they're best friends.

Cecilia says, "I think Mum hates me. She probably thinks I'm possessed by the devil and prays for me in church."

"From what I remember she thought that about everyone."

I can see the ferry leaving from the dock across the harbour. I write descriptions of it in my notebook. The ferry docks are close to the big fucking tower, but not that close. They're closer to where the raised highway curves inland, right about where the skyline drops to low rises. I read some of what I wrote, but I can't tell if any of it's interesting.

I say, "I'm kind of fascinated with this place right now, but probably only because it's so much bigger than Halifax and Victoria. I'm sure it's old news to you, since you live in Montreal."

"No. It's interesting. I've never seen Montreal's skyline from an angle like this. They do seem like similar cities from here though, except for the big fucking tower of course."

There are no other boats on the water except the ferry. The ferry doesn't seem to have a lot of people on it. I love watching ferries, even more so than watching freighters. I don't know why, maybe because they're linked to so much human activity.

"What are you writing about now?"

"I'm describing that ferry moving towards us."

"You have to be fucking kidding me. You should write something interesting, Alex, if you're going to spend all this time scribbling."

The ferry's docking. There's a guy on it whose job is to throw a lasso of heavy rope from the ferry to a post. A few passengers watch, and it takes him two tries. How do I get that job? It's so simple, yet bound to get an audience every time.

Cecilia says, "Please tell me you're not still writing about ferries."

"Yeah, because I love them."

"Why don't you just write about clouds, how they're magnificent puffy curves set picturesquely against the bright blue background, and how that reminds you of childhood in all its innocence."

"I just want to write about the ferry!"

There's a cafe behind us, between a sports field and the savannah-parkland that's all I can see to the west except the masts of sailboats where the canal must cut in. Cecilia practically runs for coffee when she sees it, but comes back with the unfortunate information that we have to wait another hour for it to open.

The need to kill time forces Cecilia to give into her sleep deprivation. She starts talking about me as a kid: "Holy shit, you were so intense as a kid, Alex. I know drive and focus are complimented qualities in a person, but the extent you took it was ridiculous. The first time you really scared me was when we were seven and you built your own sailboat. Seven! And you built it from scraps of fibreglass and wood and metal from our yard and our neighbour's. It wasn't that you used some genius, ingrained talent for engineering, you just used persistence. Piecing things together, testing, sinking, re-piecing, experimenting, testing, sinking, ha—ha. Mum and Dad just thought it was a game that would go on until you got bored. Then one day we all went down to the beach and there's no Alex, no Frankenstein sailboat. Dad flipped when he found you through the binoculars not ten metres from the mouth of the cove, almost in the open swells with this crazy mosaic-of-scrap sailboat you made. 'Kitty, let's go!' And we ran to the boat to tow you in."

"Kitty, I forgot he used to call you that."

"And we could see how scared he was, we all were, about what crazy goal you would accomplish after that. It was definitely the last time anyone failed to take you seriously."

After that she got into a serious discussion about our parents, but not an emotional one, a mechanical one. Cecilia described this completely set and fabricated relationship she wants us to have with them. She said by instinct we're both set to abandon them, and that that will just make us feel guilty later, so we have to proactively make sure we don't. She suggested one phone call every three months each, alternating so it seems like more, and one visit every year. She said we have to ask about their health, so they don't get cancer or something without us knowing.

It's such a depressing conversation. I say, "Cecilia, I'm never going back East. Not after what I saw yesterday, I mean I'm just going to drift for a while, or live somewhere new."

She grabs her pinkie toe. After examining it between her fingers for a moment, she says, "Why did you come here then?" I'm about to say to reconnect with her, not them, but before I can she says, "Fuck, never mind, that cafe is open." And she leaves.

Chapter Nineteen

2012 – Toronto East (segments from Alex's present-tense-journal)

Adventure day! I'm on the bus to Leslie Spit. It's raining, but there's 40 kilometre winds and apparently three-metre waves. I shall travel to see them at that historic lighthouse where me and the girls first landed. I'm reading Redmond O'Hanlon's first book of travels into Borneo to get into the mood. He drinks a lot to get into the mood, but it's morning and I can't be that uncivilised in a public park – not in the morning anyway. But I brought a bowl with bits of weed that was encrusted to my grinder. I have gum boots on in case I go into the water.

There's stuff I sort of want to write about – the cockroach problem in my apartment, and my mission to define satire in my writing, and possibly see myself as a satirist – but not now cause I'm in adventure mode!

WHAT A MISSION! But first, I'm listening to the beautiful voice of Toronto singer Rhye, the second song on the album, which starts with, "Oh, make love to me." Of course no one is asking me to make love to them, so that's kind of depressing.

What a mission! But, I was just reading *Spurious* by Lars Iyer. There was a part that had the protagonist W. reminiscing about his long walks on the moors, and he mentioned his walking partner, that he always had a walking partner, and never walked alone, because walking alone leads to enormous melancholy! I thought that was funny, but also laughed at myself. Possibly I want to be immersed in enormous melancholy, which is why I go on long walks in the rain over the most isolated place in Toronto – Leslie Spit. It's also perhaps why I keep looking for Spry, searching for info and pictures of her on the internet (there are none, no mention of her at all!).

Maybe I'm still in love with her, and I'm living regret, but I think it's more likely that I just crave enormous melancholy!

What a mission! I should write about it, but I can't feel enthused right now because of enormous melancholy. Anyway, I got photos.

Chapter Twenty

2008 – The Island Cafe (Saturday, day of the Dragonboat Races)

We're at the cafe, on a patio, underneath umbrellas, and also in the shade of a couple savannah-parkland trees.

Sam says, "It's really nice here. I love the trees. Trees can only grow big, spread-out canopies like this in parkland, you'd never see trees like this in a forest."

Kate says, "And what a cute fucking cafe, fuck. Island Cafe. I guess because it's on an island and they serve coffee, how fucking original."

Cecilia says, "Wow, are you always this chipper in the morning?"

A waitress with a name tag that reads Carolyn walks up. "So I'm just going to grab you guys four big glasses of water and four bigger mugs of coffee, sound good?"

"Thanks, honey," says Sam

We look like shit. We look and smell like shit. The girls look normal to me, but that's not saying much. Carolyn brings our drinks.

Cecilia says, "I'm assuming nobody wants to eat. Let's down these coffees and go find out where these lizardboat races are."

Kate says, "We're not going."

"Of course we're going. It's why I'm not at the airport right now, and Alex needs something interesting to happen in his book."

"Party's over, Cecilia, the fun is done."

"You're just going to have to turn that frown into looks of wonder, cousin, we're going."

"Fuck sakes, you were easier to hang out with when you were pissed at us."

"Alex, can you pour some sunshine into these coffees? I think some of us need a pick-me-up."

Kate says, "Seriously? We're just going to keep this going?"

Sam says, "If we don't we have to start thinking about how we're going to get these canoes back to Hamilton."

"Oh fuck that, bartender, sunshine for my coffee, let's go."

Carolyn walks up to the table. She looks like she saw us pouring brandy into our coffees. "Ah, guys, you can't pour booze in your coffees here, maybe you should take those to go."

Sam says, "She's right, we're going to get her in trouble."

"But you're the only one here," says Cecilia, smiling brightly.

Carolyn says, "My manager will be here in, like, twenty minutes though."

"Perfect, grab yourself a coffee and join us. My brother, the weird guy scribbling in a notebook like a crazy person," (I'm writing about the cafe and Carolyn) "is a huge, huge tipper."

"Uh huh, well, I am kind of hung-over, and some booze in my coffee would help with this headache. Okay, I'll be back."

Sam says, "You're such a charmer, Cecilia."

Carolyn's very sexy, and she has a Southern accent. She comes back and sits down beside me. I pour some brandy in her mug.

"Thanks. So what's this?"

"A bunch of writing about this weekend. Stuff people have said, descriptions of the harbour, and now this cafe and you."

"Sweet Jesus you've written a lot already. Hey, you should come down to West Virginia. That's where I come from, and it's a beautiful setting for a book."

"We're in canoes, so I can only go places accessible by water."

Cecilia says, "Speaking of such, how do we get to the lizardboat races?"

"You mean dragonboat? If you're in canoes then just paddle up the canal beside the ferry dock. It goes past all those sailboats over there. Just keep paddling that way. Eventually you'll come to a big white bridge. They race is on the other side of it."

I say, "Are you staying in the city?"

"No, here on the island. I've stayed with my friend for two months every summer since I was sixteen. Her family lives in one of those cottage houses over there. To be honest, I've barely gone into the city at all."

"That's really cool, those places look nice."

"Uh huh, they are. They're real cottagey, and instead of roads there's walkways, because it's car-free here. Actually they're more like garden paths, they kind of remind me of some places in West Virginia."

"Your friend is so lucky to live here."

Kate says, "Why? Because it's so fucking quaint and cute?"

"Yeah Kate," says Sam, "that's exactly what they're saying, because it's nice."

"I've seen nicer spots to own a cottage home than this. You only think it's something special because it's right next to that concrete shit hole. No offence to you though, nice place to visit."

Carolyn says, "Uh huh, it's nice, and it's nice to live here too, a lot of people think better than the city."

Kate says, "Yeah, that's my point though. The only reason people would live in a place like this and not in cottage country or outside the city is so they can look across the water and talk about how dirty and smelly the city is and how everybody should live on an island."

"Oh my God Kate," says Sam, "you don't know anything about this place or anyone that lives here."

Carolyn says, "Yeah, I've known my friend's parents my whole life and they're really cool people. They're artists and there's a really good arts community here."

Kate says, "Artists, that makes perfect sense. Everything's got to be quaint and fucking cute for an artist to work, and of course they need a big fucking ugly concrete tower next door to remind them how much better they are than everyone else."

Carolyn gets up. "Thanks for the brandy guys, but my manager's going to be here soon and I've got to do some prep stuff."

Sam says, "Thank you, we'll leave so you don't get into trouble. Good luck with the rest of the summer."

"Let's slam these coffees back, folks, and off to the canoes," says Cecilia.

Sam says, "Kate, why do you have to be such a jerk? She just left because of all that ignorant stuff you were saying about people here, and after she let us drink brandy in our coffee."

"She didn't let us, we were going to drink them anyway."

Cecilia says to me, "Um...bartender, perhaps now's the time to take order on the rising irritability that's really putting a damper on our morning."

"Right...yeah, so...what do I do?"

"More booze my good man, without the coffee this time."

"Okay, you know what? I have something a little softer at least: there's a bottle of wine in my bag."

"Well done bartender. Think I'll spark up another joint for that."

I look at Cecilia's glossy red eyes. "Yeah, let's get in the canoes first. That stuff's making you weirder and weirder."

Kate and Cecilia leave. I stay to pay, and Sam stays with me, looking glum.

"Hey, everything good?"

"No," and she kind of drawls that "no" out.

"Kate's buggin' you, eh?"

"Yeah, but it's not her fault. When she starts to get on my nerves she, I don't know, I guess she's kind of similar to my dad, or the way he is now. Just gets me thinking about him again."

"Wow, he really gets you down."

"It's stupid, when I'm here. I should be more like Cecilia. She wouldn't dwell on this kind of thing."

"I don't know if being more like Cecilia is the answer to anything."

"Do you like your parents, I mean, like who they are?"

"Oh Christ no. I'm actually in a similar situation to you, except I can't remember what my dad was like when he was someone I could respect. That was before the Cod fishery closed, before he decided to give up completely on life. And my Mum leads this religious life that's just filled with so much anger, I don't know, I just can't relate to her."

And silence again. We're all just philosophers here. Thinking about family. I wish I could philosophise on more than that, but honestly I can't think of what else to think of. Family, Christ.

Chapter Twenty-One

2012 – Toronto East (segments from Alex's present-tense-journal)

I'm still drinking. The whisky is very good, but I have to go to bed. My brain needs sleep. I crave emotion. It's after midnight. I know that introspection needs to be wordless. I'm looking forward to 2013.

My feelings about the trip are complex. I have these beautiful memories from Toronto Island, memories of the trees and savanna parkland, memories of the people I enjoyed the landscape with. They are broken because of broken connections with the people. But I can't leave my memories behind. That might be unhealthy for me. At any rate I have to stop searching for Spry on the internet. She's not on there, just like I'm not on there, and there's no reason for me to care. It's all just compulsion.

I HAVEN'T MOVED ON FROM SPRY. How can someone I spent such a short time with still plague my brain four years later? Because...because...because I was so hopeless then and I'm better now, except I'm not. Why is someone from four years ago plaguing my brain today? Is this just a ridiculously unhealthy obsession with one particular memory? Chad VanGaalen has just arrived to help me with these questions. Chad:

"We can sit around this fire / and let our spirits ride on out / Watching as the flame gets higher / I can see it in your eyes / peace was on the rise."

Nice lyrics. Does nothing to help me.

Chad: "If you see her let her know I made it. If you catch her, tell her that I'm in. We sit and wonder, if you're special by design."

I'm a satellite from the life that I should have had with Spry. I don't know if Chad's helping.

Chad: "Somewhere, I know you're somewhere, somewhere in the unsailed sea. Nothing, there's nothing..." —no, I'm not writing the line right. It means nothing anyway.

The oboes playing at the end of the song are where the answers are. They remind me of her smile.

I'M FULL ON LAMB, SQUASH AND ASPARAGUS – I love lamb – and listening to Greg Proops, expecting he's going to do a Nelson Mandela obit. He's reading an article about some pig protest in Italy. He's singing a lot in this episode. I'm drinking Guinness.

He's doing the Mandela Obit. The way Proops speaks is so emotionally driving. I'm Drinking whisky now. Proops is defending poetry in politics. Mandela the poet:

"If you talk to a man in a language he understands, that goes to his head; if you talk to him in his language, that goes to his heart."

"Resentment is like drinking poison, and hoping it will kill your enemies."

Proops keeps saying, "We're all lucky to have lived when he lived."

It's a good show, and the last one I'm ever going to listen to.

Chapter Twenty-Two

2008 – The Canals of Toronto Islands (Saturday, day of the Dragonboat Races)

We get into the canoes and paddled towards the cana…Jesus! The ferry blew its airhorn and scared the crap out of us all. We stop while it backs out in front of us. I write some more about the ferry, about the few people I see aboard. I get a closer look at the hull's—

"Alex," snaps Cecilia. "I know you're writing about that stupid ferry again."

"Well Christ, it's right here in front of us."

"That doesn't make it interesting."

Well it does, because this moment is cool. We're all just sitting in this canoe-catamaran, passing a bottle of wine around in the early morning, Cecilia with one of her joints going, and passing it to Sam, and even Kate is smoking from it, and there's a ferry pulling out in front of us. Why is this not interesting?

The ferry passes and I can see the canal. "Forward girls, there's the canal."

They don't move. Kate's hysterical. "Sam, look, I'm smoking weed. I'm a fucking hippy."

"I'm not talking to you."

We paddle into the canal, alongside sailboats moored parallel to the edge. On the grassland next to them are permanently installed

BBQs with people sitting around (presumably next to their boats) eating BBQed breakfasts and drinking coffee. There are boats with owners painting hulls, fixing trim, adjusting ropes and otherwise tending to their little bits of aquatic property. The boats must be to the owners like cottages and cabins are to so many others; I wonder how often they even leave the canal.

We pass under a pedestrian bridge and the boats vanish. There are forested islands and openings to the inner harbour to the right, and to the left the unbroken stretch of parkland with a road and more densely forested parkland beyond, and I'm just thinking a mile a minute, and it's all bubbling up, and I just have one point to make…

"I'm really just thinking a mile a minute here, guys. I think I have some really good ideas for myself. I mean really, I could do anything from this moment. Like consider this, I could live on this island. If I didn't spend much on food and slept in a tent I could do it for a year. And be a crazy bonfire builder. Or an artist. You guys saw all that stuff on Leslie Spit and how into it Sam was. I could do that. And Carolyn said there's an arts community here. I mean holy Christ, it's like serendipity, right Sam? Isn't that what this is?"

"Well, sure, why not? Yes Coast, I think you're meant to become an artist."

"Yeah, because it's just coming up with ideas, right? That's all art is. And what's an idea? It's just something that bubbles up to your mind, you don't have any control over it. So there's not even the matter of coming up with an idea. All that matters is having the patience for the right one to come. And maybe that's why canoeing is a really good thing. I mean paddling through this canal—"

"Hey, I've got an idea," says Cecilia. "Why don't you turn this dialogue into some awesome silent narrative to go with your ferry writing."

"Okay, okay, keep it interesting. That's what you always say, right, Cecilia? I have to be interesting. I have to talk about my feelings, what I think about the world and how it affects me, and what comes next?"

"Yes, well, once again, why don't you turn this awesome dialogue into an entry for your feelings journal."

"Guys, guys, forget it. Listen to me. I don't want to be an artist. Okay? But I want to tell you what I really want to be. I do, because this is big, it's really big. It's big because I've never told anyone. I wanted to, but I couldn't. I couldn't tell guys that I fished with because they'd make fun of me, but the randoms that hung around my bonfires knew I was a fisherman so I couldn't tell them, they'd never take me seriously. You guys see? But now I'm sitting here with the three of you, my family, and I can tell you guys anything, that's what family's for, right? So I'm going to tell you. And this is why I think we should hang out, like really be a family. Because these are the benefits, right? You have people you talk to in Montreal, I'm sure, Cecilia – university friends, who you talk about French Lit with, right? – but you can't tell them everything, not like Kate and Sam can, so think about what I'm saying."

Cecilia says, "Okay Alex, tell us, please just get it out. And after you're done, stop talking so fast and crazy; your tongue is going to fall out."

"Okay, okay, so here it is. Wait, sorry, I'm going to do this the long way. I read a book called *Trawler* by Redmond O'Hanlon. It's amazing. I mean it just went on and on with these long rants and crazy dialogues. It reminded me of *Crime and Punishment.*
Someone gave that to me at a bonfire, said I had to read it. I

started into it right there, and it was good at first. The murder, the gruesome double murder the main character commits, but then it just gets into talking and talking and talking."

Kate says, "Does anyone else want to shoot themselves in the fucking head right now?"

"Yeah, okay, get back on track. That's what you're saying. So *Trawler*, I kept reading it because of Luke Bullough."

"Okay, Coast," says Sam, "Luke Bullough, stick with him and tell us whatever it is you wanted to tell us."

"Right. On point. Okay. So Luke Bullough, and it's a non-fiction book by the way, so he's real, a real guy."

"Thanks for explaining what nonfiction means, you raving lunatic," says Kate.

"Yeah, ha—ha, of course. So he's a fisherman, and a great one. You can tell because this whole book is on a deep sea trawler, and it's just yammering fishermen."

Cecilia says, "Sounds horrible, does the book explain how to get the yammering fishermen to shut up?"

"But you can tell their respect for him. And he's a lifeboat guy too, risks his life all the time, way more than I do. But this is the thing, he's also a marine biologist. He's doing a doctorate on deep sea fish in the book. Epic! I couldn't believe it. In all the fishing I've done you have marine biologists and fisherman on opposite sides. The closest thing to the middle are inspectors, but they're just guys looking for a job, they're not passionate or anything."

This is crazy. I know why I'm yammering. It's the sleep deprivation. This is the point. Your brain goes crazy. Luke Bullough described it perfectly. It's like your brain is fighting a virus, so it goes into overdrive. Or what was it, the other thing he said? Your brain can't heal and sooth itself with dreams, so instead it talks, but not your usual verbal diarrhoea; it starts throwing stuff up straight from the subconscious. Of course on a fishing boat everyone's in on the same experience, everyone's crazy. It can be great sometimes, but these girls are going to turn me into an institution by the end of this day.

I say, "But you know what guys? That's not even an idea. It's stupid, not what Bullough's doing, but the idea that I would do that. I don't want to go to school."

Kate says, "Then what the Jesus fucking Christ are you telling us this stuff for?"

"Because Luke Bullough is this guy that really dominates, that's worked twice as many hours as I have, but as a biologist, a fisherman, and saving lives. I'm just wasting my time."

Sam says, "Coast, stop it. You've done so much more than most guys I know. You have an awesome life, you love fishing, writing and bonfires. Yesterday you impulsively quit your job and gave up your place to drift and write and do whatever; I don't know anyone else that would do that. Honestly, I'm happy to know I'm related to you."

"Thanks, Sam."

Chapter Twenty-Three

2013 – Toronto East (segments from Alex's present-tense-journal)

I'm out for a paddle with Kate and Heather's dragonboat team, seeing them again for the first time in a while. Their dragonboat is kept West of the Western gap, behind the breakwall. There's no other boats out practising anymore, because it's November! Kate and Heather like forcing the team to tough it out, that's their style. Also it's night, it's completely dark out on the water, but Heather already set up lights at the front and back. So beautiful to see the city at night, the street lights and cars, the lights in the windows of all the different buildings. I can see it all so clearly. It's such a better view from the summer, because the cold, crisp air makes the lights crisp and bright. It feels great paddling in a toque, experiencing it all and feeling so cold at the same time. I feel new.

Chapter Twenty-Four

2008 – The Canals of Toronto Islands (Saturday, day of the Dragonboat Races)

Hmm...this is nice. I'm writing with one hand, and I have a joint in the other. I kept yammering until Cecilia insisted I smoke. She hopes it will stop me from talking, but I'm on such a role and sleep deprivation is a tough force to fight.

I take a nice big hull, and cough a lot. I'm not used to smoke. Sam passes me the wine to help me stop coughing, and it helps. I take another big hull. I think I'm feeling something already. The girls are staring at me, laughing at my smoking. Cecilia in particular seems amused by this. I take my last hull, a big puff of smoke leaving my throat and diffusing into the sunbeams, obscuring everyone's faces. I pass the joint to Sam, take a swig of wine and pass the wine to Sam.

They're all laughing at me. Kate says, "Coast, the expression on your face is fucking priceless right now."

"Cool. Look at these trees. Look at the canopies. They're so green."

They look at the trees.

I drop down to the hull. I lay flat on my back, my head against a life jacket leaning against the bow seat, my feet sticking towards Sam. I hold the notebook up, and behind the notebook I can see a cathedral canopy from the massive oaks stretching their arms over the canal and it looks so high up and perfectly formed and just shady enough but sunny enough and there are birds flying in and out of tunnels formed by branches and leaves and I wish I lived in that canopy.

I inhale a deep breath of air. It smells so perfect. Clean, but with pollen and fresh cut grass. I want a drink, but I can hardly move. Don't need a drink, just the canopy. My eyes are focused on my writing so the canopy is passing in the background of my focus. It's perfect. The perfect wall paper. The perfect design for a lamp. The perfect pattern for a shirt.

I sit up again. There's frisbee golfers on the side of the canal. I feel all tuned into people. So I'm noticing these frisbee golfers. There are three of them, and they all have beards and hats. One is carrying a cooler on wheels, like one of those luggage bags on wheels. Another throws his frisbee and cheers when it hits the inverted tepee of chains that catches frisbees at the hole.

They remind me of a guy at a bonfire in Victoria who told me about a design he had for a frisbee. He got me to sketch it out in my notebook, something he was never able to do himself. He said I got it perfectly, he was kind of mesmerised by it. I offered to rip out the page and give it to him, because it was a design idea and all. He told me he was happy just to see it on paper, that he would never do anything with the design anyway.

Neither Kate or Sam take notice of the frisbee golfers. I guess frisbee golf isn't either of their things.

Sam stops paddling to wave. Kate doesn't wave, but she giggles at something. Neither I nor Cecilia turn to look, because we're like that, and anyway it's obvious there are kids waving at them.

All of a sudden the sun is blocked out and there's a wood bridge – not a big one – above me. We pass to the other side and I see three kids run to our side of the bridge, and then they're waving at me and Cecilia. We aren't the waving types. Eventually their parents tell them to stop. It might be my imagination, but both Kate and Sam look vaguely amused by us.

There are moored sailboats appearing from my left side, and more savannah-parkland to my right.

Cecilia's reading out the sailboat names: "Break Away, the Long and Winding Road, Starry Nights, Gone Fishing, I'd rather be sailing, the Cat's Ass, that one's okay, the Silver Lining…oh God. Okay, here's my impression of someone naming their boat the Silver Lining:" (in a lady's voice) "'so what are you going to name your boat, dear?'" (in a man's voice) "'Gosh, I don't know. All I can think about is how hard our lives are, how tragic really.' 'It's true, dear, but at least we have our health, and millions of dollars in the bank.' 'Yes, but not so many millions that our kids will have millions…or would if we had kids.' 'That's true dear, but we don't have kids, and perhaps that's a silver lining in our troubles.' 'What did you say?' 'The silver lining, dear, that we don't have kids.' 'Why you're right darling, we don't have kids, but we do have a boat; no kids, but a boat, a boat called Silver Lining.' 'Oh, well done, dear.'"

We laugh hysterically.

There are lots of people with dogs. There's a couple with two dogs that are very high energy. They keep running up to others in the park, and the couple keeps yelling at them to come back, and saying stuff like, "Lemon, what has gotten into you?"

Cecilia says, "I despise it when people treat dogs like kids. Really, it just gets me so much."

There's a family with two babies crawling around the grass in front of the parents' blanket. Sam awes at them and Kate says "Fuckin' cuties" and laughs.

Cecilia looks at the sail boats: "Maiden mist. Wave Trough. Ha, look at that one. Unsinkable II. That's funny, I'll have to remember that."

Sam and Kate aren't listening to her. They're watching the babies crawl around the grass.

We come to an intersection where the row of sailboats ends. To the right is another waterway into the harbour. Straight ahead the water leads into a mini theme-park. There's some kind of mock village to the left of it, a landscaped area with interlocking brick walkways to the right, and an in-water carousel of swan boats at the end of it.

To port, the way we turn, the savannah-parkland continues on our left side, and ahead on the theme-park-side I can see a farm-animal zoo. There's also a gondola above us. After the zoo we turn to head in the same direction we were going before. There's still savannah-parkland on our left, but the road is just beyond it, and a concrete barrier beyond the road, and then the lake.

Chapter Twenty-Five

2013 – Toronto East (segments from Alex's present-tense-journal)

I consolidated my debt earlier today, on the phone, while walking around Allen Gardens Green house, which went a long way in calming me. Actually discovered – discovered is the wrong word because you can't discover something in a public greenhouse – but stumbled on a wing that I hadn't noticed, and it's like the best one with a river and I think much more heat so crazier flowers. Such a great place to consolidate your debt into a fixed payment loan. My budget is going to be really tight for a while, but I worked-out the numbers today and I'm reasonably sure I can still afford to be a wino. Thank you cheap dry white wine.

In other news my boss did shitty stuff blah blah anger me and frustrated blah blah brain's all stressed out and crazy blah blah but then you see the horizon line on a cold but beautiful fall night paddling with Kate and Heather's awesome dragonboat team and shit I just got to keep it together. Maybe stop thinking of new ways of being difficult at work...who cares! Work sucks! For everybody! My boss just makes me one with the people. So do the cockroaches and the debt and the loneliness. So just be grateful for writing and paddling.

AT DRIFT, MY NEW FAVOURITE BAR, with Sam, Rory, Kate and Heather, drinking oatmeal stout and heavily engaged in conversation about the NSA, network encryption, Russian tragedy in World War I, *The Gulag Archipelago* (and what constitutes an archipelago, Toronto Islands? they think not), revolution, the coming fall of the Western World, HTML, Calvin and Hobbes, mountain biking, getting old before the revolution, and food. It's good to be with people again.

Chapter Twenty-Six

2008 – The Canals of Toronto Islands (Saturday, day of the Dragonboat Races)

I forgot to write in the book. Doesn't matter, write what happened now. What happened? I'm really high off that weed. It feels great. I couldn't write, or even talk for a while. I remember that, and more sailboats. Then, oh shit, then I remember there was a zoo and a gondola over the canal. No, I must have imagined that. I say, "Guys, did we pass a zoo and a gondola before?"

Sam laughs, "Coast, you're such a rookie stoner. Yeah, look behind us, there it is. It's part of this weird theme park village beside us. And look, gondola, above it all. And you know what? We just got you to shut up about it all five minutes ago."

Woh, there's people everywhere. The village thing is to the right, and to the left is a huge stretch of parkland, with so, so many people, and trees that are scattered around it but so, so, so big, with these huge canopies that are all shady and amazing. I say, "Guys, check out the trees, there so—"

Kate says, "Huge with big canopies and there's so many people everywhere and shut the fuck up for Christ's sakes you already said all this."

"But I didn't write it down. I forgot to write in the book."

Woh, up ahead is a huge, giant concrete pedestrian bridge. Okay, maybe I'm over-qualifying everything I see, but it all looks so big. Okay, there's a pedestrian bridge ahead made of concrete. On the right just before the bridge is this pub up a grass bank from the canal. On the left the bridge empties into this huge...don't write huge anymore...these impressive gardens. People are crowded on the bridge and around it and looking away from us and this is the part I wanted to get to. I can see beneath the bridge and see that beyond is where the Dragonboat Races are. There's an expanse of water, like I'm pretty sure through that space beneath the bridge everything opens up, and there's boats, and it's like a magical gateway to the most exciting thing that...this weed is amazing and...

I say, "Guys, I'm sorry if I sound like a stupid rookie stoner but I'm so excited about these races."

Kate says, "Fuck yeah, dude, I am too, I want to see the Scarborough Buffs kick some ass."

Part Three: Toronto International Dragonboat Race Festival, to Toronto Harbour's West Shore, to Ireland Park, and back to Hamilton.

"I wrote all night until the sun came up, page after page, and my wrist didn't hurt at all. I remember laughing, so amazed, like I was finally able to see it all, beautiful and wretched—how the air can be so pure here, on the edge of the city and the lake—and then the wind shifts and the stench comes up like bile. I could see angels of vengeance rising, pigeons diving, vagrants stumbling under the weight of their desperate freedom, my thoughts finally flying…"

—Shaughnessy Bishop-Stall, *Down to This*

Chapter Twenty-Seven

2013 – Toronto East (segments from Alex's present-tense-journal)

It's Saturday night. It's the night I should do something big, like make it to Toronto Island and sleep overnight. Bring the hammock. Bring the books and a head lamp. Obviously my backpack. Sleeping bag. Water. Just spend some time remembering when we paddled through the islands, and I smoked weed for the first time. How I felt during that paddle along the canals with Kate, Sam and Cecilia, in Sam's crazy catamaran, wow, it's still the best I've ever felt in my life. At least up until the end, when Cecilia...yeah, up until I felt *the worst* I've ever felt in my life.

I NEED TO GET COMFORTABLE WITH MY PROTAGONIST. What is he now? Young, long curly hair, big eyes, tall, lanky – okay, other ideas: he lives in the city, is from the city, but doesn't have family to stay with.

Maybe to get comfortable with him, I just have to think of him like a traveller. He's just a guy checking out the world. Grew up out West, maybe in a suburb. His family was, or is, well-off. They sent him to university and he got a biology degree. At the end of it he was primed to do something crazy, like anyone would be. And the craziest thing he could think of was leave the province (more importantly, the family). He left with Tess. Nobody wanted him to leave, especially not with Tess, but he was like, "hey, I'll be back in six months."

He's like me – isn't really into the back-packing thing. Instead, he wants to live in a far away city, really check it out. And all this mental-reminiscing is happening while he's up the tree. Maybe it's five months in, and he's worn out. That enthusiasm from when he first moved to the city is long gone. He feels like he's a different person. Someone jaded, someone dark, someone alone in the world.

WHAT'S INTERESTING ABOUT THIS SCENE ASIDE FROM THE STORY? Coast falling from the tree. So exactly how does that happen? Coast cuts the branch, the huge elbow shaped one with a devil face in the wood.

Maybe the scene should start with the accident. They're cutting the tree down, not just the branch – cutting the tree down is probably better than removing a branch.

How about Coast, who has climbed half-way up the trunk, cuts the V or wedge shape into the side of the tree, the side facing away from the house. Kidd says it will fall away from the house, even though the giant elbow shaped branch is hanging over the roof. To Coast's surprise the tree starts falling in the right direction, but it also twists. The devil-faced elbow of the branch comes right for him. It knocks him off the tree, breaking his harness.

Coast's agility helps him: flying with the elbow, he frantically flails his limbs – no, he's super agile: in mid-air he climbs around the elbow, and with a half-climb-half-jump he manages to get up to the canopy...okay I'll work on that part, but something super cool that lands him in the canopy as the tree crashes. He lands okay except he gets his wrist pretty bad.

Chapter Twenty-Eight

2008 – Toronto International Dragonboat Race Festival

We pass under the bridge and into the path of five attacking dragonboats. Each has ten heads hanging off each side that are wild eyed and frothy mouthed as they beat the water with violent, but perfectly synchronised, chops. They say "see what we're doing to this water? That's what we're going to do to you." The pacing drummers' backs and heads divide the rows of faces, bobbing down and up with every stroke – an illustration of the power each burst of force creates. Heads with sunglasses stand above the teams behind them, stable, hands holding the long rudder-paddles that maintain trajectory to us in our defenceless canoe-catamaran. The heads yell battle screams to get every ounce of efficiency out of the warriors before we get away: "Hard! Dig! Stroke! Hit! Hit! Hit!"

The sight frightens me, until I clue into the fact that we have simply entered the dragonboating arena at the end of the lanes, separated by buoys (red, orange, blue, green, orange, red), as a heat is finishing. Shaking off the initial shock, I get a sense of where we are, first by looking for the race announcer broadcasting the placement of the teams. He's broadcasting from a stadium about twenty rows of seats high, situated on the north side of the small lake the canal widens to around the lanes. Looking down the shore from the stadium I see white-tarped-booths – the festival part of the dragonboat festival, and people moving back and forth between the booths and the grassy shore. The dragonboats manoeuvre around us as they paddled to the south side. The attention of everyone on the stadium, of all the spectators along the shores and on the bridge behind us, and crowds sitting on the grass hill across the water from the stadium, go from them to us.

Kate says, "Ah…fuck."

All of a sudden a motorboat with a kid at the till and an old guy with a raspy bulldog voice (and somehow that voice tells me this is Les, the race organiser Eddie talked about at the bonfire) comes charging up to us, "Hold the boat! Hold the boat! Just what the hell do you think you're doing here?"

His boat putters around us with Les standing, hands on his hips, to starboard, so that he continues to face us as he orbits the canoes, and I wonder why this kid is doing that. It has a great effect, making Les look intimidating. Did he say to the kid before they got into the boat "If we have to talk to anyone that doesn't belong here, make sure to circle them for effect"?

"We've got a goddamn race going, you can't just pass through."

Cecilia, on her knees, spinning on the hammock bed to keep up with Les, says, "We're not passing through, and I would ask you to speak with a little more respect. Don't you know who this is?" She points at me. I stare at her, my expression as curious as Les's. "This is Alec Le-loc, the famous Montreal sports reporter."

"The hell he is, he looks like a street kid. You all do, except for you, but you're laying in a goddamn hammock. What is this?"

"I'm the classy looking one because I'm Alec's agent, and this, my friend, is immersion journalism, modelled after Hunter S. Thompson's *Hell's Angels*. Are there motorcycles here, by the way, or is it all just boats?"

"This sounds more like Hunter S. Thompson's *gonzo journalism*, and that's all I need. Write your story, but stay out of the way. Jr., let's go, to the docks."

They speed off along the South Shore, which bulges out and around a forested island. There are spectators on the grass where the shore curves away from us, and farther along I see a series of spaced-out, temporary docks, half on the grass and half floating in the water. The dragonboats that we saw race have each paddled to one of the docks. They're unloading four at a time, because that's how many the width of the docks can accommodate. There are teams waiting to get in, and people that are helping the returning racers out and moving the boat along, and I think that's the only reason the helpers are there, to keep the changes going fast, like a pit crew. Three other dragonboats loaded-up before the ones we saw race got there, and they, paddling around the bulge of the shore to the start of the course, are disappearing behind the island.

Back from the docks the savannah-parkland is dense with teams and tents – equally as crowded and loud as the festival side. We paddle towards the docks and team prep area to look for anyone from last night. Staying close to the shore, we pass beneath hardwoods that grow at an angle so they shade both us and the racers eating protein bars and drinking electrolytes on the grass. The racers all wear team shirts, and between the shirts and the announcer listing teams in the heats I get a good survey of who makes up the teams. Some are high schools, colleges and universities, some are professional associations (York Region Dental Association Paddle Demons), and many are paddle clubs. Most are from somewhere in Ontario, but many are from other provinces and the US (Florida, Chicago and New York). I hear the announcer speak of one team from Japan, and of course half of

Damiond, Kelly and Rory's team are Irish (called the Bastards – fitting).

We find the Bastards before we get to the docks, sitting on the grass shore in the shade of a hardwood, and they look in rough shape. Rory tries to brighten up for Sam, but you can tell he's struggling. "Dear, I hope I didn't bother you last night. And it's a good thing you didn't stay longer."

Kelly says, "Oh my God, you don't even want to know. They set a pizza box on fire in our kitchen. We're never going to rent from that place again, and I loved that place."

"You were laughing last night," says Damiond.

"I know, I know, well what am I going to do? I might as well get as drunk as you guys do. But look, I'm ready today, I can paddle. You guys look like death."

"We're going to do great, believe me."

I say, "Shouldn't you be warming up like that team?" In a field past a pathway behind them, a university team in circle is following their coach through toe touches and torso twists. As I speak, another team, all 50ish, jog pass on the pathway. Then two shout "hi" to us and I see that it's Jonathan and Mary, wearing team shirts that read Sunset Masters. Rory and Damiond turn to look and wave, lazily.

Damiond says, "We feel ready."

Rory says, "The fuck we do. I feel death coming, sweet Jesus."

I say, "You guys need a pick-me-up?"

"Yes, please," says Rory.

Kelly says, "That's not going to help us. I seriously don't give a fuck what you guys feel like, you better do well today. All five of us" (she gestures to herself and four other girls that are sitting near her) "went to the gym all winter specifically for paddling."

Damiond yells in a weak hangover yell, "You went three times." With great difficulty he pushes himself up from his recline in the grass. "What you don't understand, Kelly, is dragonboat races are won by fast thinking and spontaneous effort."

"Are they now?" Then she says to us, "Guess what our best placement is? Third."

Kate says, "That doesn't sound so bad."

"From last. Third from last. Usually, we're second from last or basically the slowest time here."

Sam and Rory get in a personal, and giggly, conversation. Sam tells Rory to sip some whisky, Rory tells Sam to sip with him. She's been turning down drink since the coffee shop.

Kate spots the Scarborough Buffs. They are about to start loading at the last dock along the bend. "Fuck yeah, they're about to race, let's go wish them luck."

Sam says, "I'm talking with Rory."

Sam's tense with Kate. She has been since the coffee shop. Kate seems to ignore it, or not understand it, but it's getting worse, even when they aren't saying anything to each other. They bicker about leaving. Rory finally says, "Go, we'll have a beer after the race, I'll be in better shape then."

We circle out around the docks until we get closer to the Scarborough Buffs. They're loading up. I see Spry, she looks at me nervously from the grass behind the dock, so I wave and look as harmless as possible. That seems the right thing because she relaxes and smiles.

Martyn and Alemu are getting in the dragonboat as I approach, and they pause at the sight of me. Alemu speaks to Martyn, but loud enough for us to hear, "Hey, look who it is: Coast, the man who kept us awake all night."

Martyn turns and looks at me, then smiles along with Alemu, "So it is, so it is. Interesting fellow, nice guy really, don't you think?"

Alemu says, "Oh sure. Sure, sure. A little inconsiderate, since he woke us up when we were trying to sleep for the race. And the conversation he woke us up with was quite one sided."

"That's true, that's true. I mean there's lots of topics we might have wanted to talk about all night, but we didn't because Coast really dominated the conversation."

I'm very confused. This is all a joke, obviously, but at the same time they really do look tired, and I want to know what the hell they're talking about.

Spry, who's getting in the boat now, says, "Guys, stop it. I told you I'm sorry."

Then I get the explanation. Last night, after we left, Spry went back and sneaked into the boys room that Martyn and Alemu were sleeping in and woke them up…to talk about me! I almost make the mistake of saying "It's okay", like I should tell her not to feel embarrassed, that I have this effect on lots of women, oh the sleepless nights I've caused. She doesn't have a trace of embarrassment on her face.

Alemu says, "Look, Martyn, look, he's happy. He doesn't know, you know."

"How could he? His presence was entirely manifested."

"That's the thing though, he doesn't know all the ways it was manifested."

"Word is, Coast, you got angry and yelled at our girl Spry here."

Spry's eyes widen like she's frozen in anticipation of a movie's murder scene. I don't have a good way of explaining; luckily, Cecilia chimes in: "Oh, that was because of me. I was pissed at Alex, so I said some stuff to get to him. It's easy to get under his skin and make him do something foolish, but he's not like that, you're probably the first girl he's raised his voice to aside from me, and it only happened because I was pissed at him."

Spry bolts to standing. "Because someone threw a drink in your mom's face and he left and kidnapped you so you couldn't help her either."

Heather says, "Spry, sit."

Martyn says, "You never told us about that last night." Now he looks angry with her.

Spry, sitting, shy, says, "So what? It's just his family stuff. And now I know you yelled only because you're easy to aggravate. That's great!"

Cecilia says, "Oh yeah, it's real amusing."

That seems to settle it. Spry's sitting in a seat that's on our side, and I grab their gunwale and pull the canoe-catamaran up so I'm next to her. Martyn sits in a seat beside Alemu and I catch an either derisive or suspicious look from him. There seems to be something like dislike in it, not severe, but there. I can't think about that. The sun is bouncing off Spry's hair. She smiles at me, and wrinkles the wrinkles in the corners of her eyes.

Heather says to Kate, "About time you got here."

"Better be a good show, why's your paddle made of plastic? I thought you were the example set-er on this team."

Heather, defensive, says, "It's carbon fibre."

"Looks like plastic. Feels like plastic. I think you got sold a plastic paddle."

Eddie, still standing on the dock, says, "That's what carbon fibre looks and feels like. Trust me, you couldn't break that if your life depended on it."

Martyn and Alemu are in a conversation with each other, Heather's talking to Kate, Sam's looking away distractedly, and Cecilia's talking to a couple of the younger guys in the boat. It's a moment when I can speak somewhat privately with Spry. As if not to ruin it, she sits remarkably still. "Honestly, I could care less about your family stuff." She looks subtly from side to side, then speaks more quietly, "I left home when I was sixteen, and I'm never going back. I make my own family and I would never judge someone for how they make theirs." I hold her eyes and nod. She brightens: "Anyway, you made a decision in the moment. You were decisive!"

I say, "It's funny how we make decisions in the moment, and then they're something so different later on."

"What do you mean?"

"We take action, and see ourselves and think 'this is right'. But then later, in memory, or in the point of view of someone who wasn't there, it's..."

"Like now you're talking about a different life, a parallel one, a parallel universe." She grabs the gunwale with both hands and leans way out and over.

Heather says, "Spry, stay in the boat."

I say to Spry, "You look tired, all of you, I hope it's not bad for the race."

"No, no. As soon as we get to the start we'll be pumped. I'm already getting excited; I get butterflies in my stomach before a race, but not from nervousness, just anticipating…um, I'm not sure how to say it."

"Like you're going into battle?"

"That's it!"

We smile at each other; the moment feels warm, like everything is set right again.

Eddie, who's in the boat now, standing at the back holding the long wooden rudder, pushing down on his end so the blade is leveraged out of the water, says, "Okay, everyone on the right give me a draw to shift us away from the dock."

Les putters by. He's in a very official looking position. While Jr. holds the till of the motor, Les, clipboard in one hand and radio in the other, leans against his knee, which is propped up by his foot on the bulkhead of the boat. He yells in his raspy, staccato, bulldog voice, "Getting some good stuff I hope." Then he disappears around the island.

Eddie says, "What's Les talking about?"

"My brother's pretending to be a journalist," says Cecilia. "That's how we got this contraption in here. I tried to talk him out of such a crazy stunt, but he doesn't listen."

I say, "This was your idea."

Les comes puttering back from around the island. He eyes me through his bushy grey eyebrows.

Eddie says, "Well, you better start looking like a journalist. Les will toss you out of here himself if he finds out you're lying."

Heather coaches the team through paddle technique, reminding everyone of what to focus on. She demonstrates and I can see why she's captain. Through her whole stroke neither of her arms bend at all to move the paddle. The stroke is completed by the twist of her torso, and a reach out and pull back that comes entirely from her shoulders and upper back.

Kate says to Heather, "Nice form, fucker."

"Better form than you, canoeist."

"Let's take our boats out to the open water and see who has the best form there."

Eddie says, "She's got you there, Heather, we'd go over in a second on the lake."

Alemu says, "Oh, bested by the canoer."

"Hey, nobody bests me. We're going to win this race, then Kate ya bitch I'm going to kick your ass at Asshole in the beer gardens."

Martyn says, "Ladies, please. Let's play a civilised card game for once, like Bridge."

Alemu says, "You know what card game we should play? Baseball."

Eddie says, "That's poker. You can't fool me, I know all the poker games. No gambling everyone, not on my watch."

At that moment Eddie catches sight of Ronny and his golf-shirted crew approaching from the dock closest to the lanes. There are a lot of girls in the boat, and I wonder why they weren't with them at the fire. Maybe they aren't brokers, but admin staff pressured into doing this through work, but damned if they're going to spend a night drinking with the brokers.

Ronny coaches the team from his place in the boat, roughly the same position Heather is sitting in. They have different styles. Heather says helpful stuff to the whole team – "Remember to breath, and stay in sync, no matter how tired you get never fall out of sync." But Ronny – "Stew, if I see you hold that paddle at an angle I'll smack you with it. Cynthia, eyes along the side of the boat. Dimitri, if you see her looking to the side during the race, toss her out, I'm serious."

"Oh no, please tell me I don't have to shake his hand again," says Alemu.

Kate says, "Those guys are in your heat? You have to kick their asses."

We all watch for a moment. Ronny and a few others keep screaming at individual people; everyone on the boat looks either angry or miserable. As they pass us Ronny yells out, "Might as well give up now, kids. Paddle out of here and take your Hamilton trash with you."

Eddie cuts in before anyone can shout back: "Ronny Tailweather of RH Customs, let's try to stay civil today, and keep the complaints to a minimum."

Ronny goes back to shouting at his team.

Eddie says, "Okay everyone, paddles up."

The kid on the drum says, "We going to beat them to the start, Eddie?"

"No, we're going to trail them to the start, then make sure we take a lane next to them. I want you guys to think of this race as a head to head with those guys. They're your fire. So take it away, nice and easy, but let's keep up."

I say to Spry as they paddled away, "Give'em hell." She's twisted around and smiling, but she passes her flat hand over her face to reveal a warrior's glare, and a damn good one, before turning away to paddle.

Chapter Twenty-Nine

2013 – Toronto East (last story written by Alex before leaving Toronto, first draft)

Title: To Be Determined

"GUESS WHAT! GUESS WHAT!" Kitty, hanging up her phone, yells to Cecilia, who has just finished chopping up carrots and onions. "That was the principal; Alex isn't going to have to repeat grade eight. Oh yes, we're celebrating tonight, celebrating with a big meal of, um, Cecilia, what are we eating?"

"Carrots and onions."

Kitty frowns. "Ugh, at least make some rice, and maybe some protein. Cook the chicken fingers in the freezer."

"Frozen food…gross."

"Not everybody can live off boiled carrots and onions, okay? Anyway, Doug, the principal, said he faced a bitter set of teachers who wanted Alex to stay behind, but he managed to push the trauma argument enough to account for a second academic year."

"A second year that was academically worse than the first."

"Yes, but the point is he's moving on to high school and in September he will go to class and do, um, do what Alex does."

"—sit at his desk and stare at either a piece of nature crap or some object he picked off a shelf at a store and walked out with.

He'll sit there and ignore the teacher. He won't make eye contact with any other kids. He'll freak everyone out by staring continuously at whatever is in his hands."

Kitty throws her hands up at Cecilia and turns away. "Ugh…"

"Dear God Kitty. Listen, I'm happy Alex is moving on; it's great that you pushed the principal to push the teachers. My point is you're not recognizing the real issues…are you listening to me? It's no wonder Doug's battle with the teachers was so bitter, you wouldn't even listen to them on parent teacher night. You drag me along and who ends up keeping the discussions going, asking all the questions? All the while his teachers are trying to explain his absent mindedness to the mother of the child, not me, but you won't even pay attention in those meetings. You're not even paying attention to me – right now."

Kitty, who has drifted over to the window that faces the front yard, says, "You know I've been watching these guys all afternoon. They've been our garden crew all summer, but I never really paid much attention to them until now. There's only three in the crew, the old guy, the boss I gather, and two kids, one who I can't get my eye off. He's so mopey and slow, yet so good looking."

"Dear God Kitty."

"The other one is pretty quick on his feet. Right now he's up a ladder, trimming the garden hedges, and when he first arrived he was up a tree pruning the branches off. Everything with some different gas powered machine. The mopey kid just cleans up after him. He follows him around with the rake and broom, piling stuff into garbage bags, and he's always getting showered with twigs, and right now with cedar branches. The quick kid and the boss yell at him constantly. It's no wonder he looks so depressed, his head hanging so low, dragging his feet. I really feel for this guy."

"He sounds like the worst employee ever, they should fire him immediately."

"He's not a bad worker, he's just demotivated, and what a surprise. His boss is doing absolutely nothing, just sitting in his truck, drinking coffee, reading a newspaper, and yelling at this poor kid. That's all he's done the entire morning, can you believe it? It's just such an odd crew."

Kitty walks over to the patio door just as the mopey kid is walking past. "Hey, I need you guys to take down that huge branch hanging over the driveway. Look at that thing, it has to be ten feet around where it sticks out from the tree, and it must weigh a ton where it curves up into that big canopy. Every time there's a windstorm I think it's going to crush the car."

"I'd love to say yes, but I'm just a labourer here. You probably looked at me and saw I was about twenty, that I've been an adult for about two years now, and thought 'hey, that guy must make important decisions.' But no; I'm a complete failure in adulthood, so I'll have to relay this question to my boss, or my co-worker, who has far more responsibility than me. They'll give you an answer and I'll get back to sweeping up the foliage left behind from the hedge trimming – which of course I'm not allowed to do."

"Ha! Listen to you, what's your name?"

"Coast."

"Coast, you don't look like you're feeling too well."

He looks up at the sky and sighs long and depressingly. "It's partly to do with my apartment. I live in squalor. There's rats and cockroaches everywhere. I told my landlord to get me another room in the building. He said there was a vacant one I could take, but it was deeper than the one I currently have. I said how could it be deeper? My apartment does have a window, but it faces a well sunken into a sidewalk on the Danforth that people always throw garbage into. He said the place wasn't deeper, but the ceiling was lower. There's no window, but there is a ventilation duct. I asked if the room had cockroaches. Not nearly as many, he said, but the ventilation duct has bats. I told him to take the apartment and shove it, I'm moving out. I said I'd rather be homeless than live there, but now I realise that's exactly what I'm about to become. God my life is such a failure, it's fallen apart before my eyes. I've failed adulthood for the rest of time."

"Ha! what's that supposed to mean? You're just a kid."

"That's what everybody says, but it's not true. Eighteen is when you become an adult. It's when you have to take your life and show that it can become something of value. That's why I moved to the city, to find the opportunity to prove myself. Two years later and all I've found is my cockroach infested basement apartment and this crappy labour job. I've completely failed as an adult, and I know the future is bleak, because this is the time that decides it."

"Listen to you, that's quite the theory, but I think you have at least a few more chances left in life. Go tell your creepy boss in the truck I want to talk to him."

Kitty closes the door.

Cecilia says, "What a weird character that guy is. He's obviously going nowhere in life."

"Ugh…you know, it really makes me upset to hear you talk about someone like that. You weren't even listening to him. He doesn't want to go nowhere in life, but he hasn't been given a chance. You don't see that he's been stigmatised as a labourer, you just see a worker, but I see someone who could do something really successful in the world, if only he were given a chance. I also see a kid who's pretty good looking, and that deserves a little faith."

Cecilia roles her eyes. "Blind faith at best. Kitty, this is the same philosophy you follow when you think of Alex, isn't it? You think that ultimately it doesn't matter what happens in school. You think that as long as people are nice to him he'll become something special. Well I have news for you, that labourer out there will always be a labourer, because he's clearly waiting for some chance that hasn't come yet, rather than training himself in a formal way. If you don't want Alex to become the same you better get out of this delusion."

"I think this is where you and I are completely different. I believe people's particular personalities, no matter what the nature of them are, can facilitate their lives."

"You're wrong. There are only certain personalities that do well in this world: organised people, adaptive people, social people…"

"Social? Cecilia you haven't had a friend in years."

"That's because the kids at my school are idiots, and anyway, I do well enough faking a personality that gets me through the days, which is exactly my point. It doesn't matter what kind of personality you have, what matters is how good you are at faking a personality that survives all the idiots in life."

"Ugh…that sounds so horrible. People should be themselves, you know why? Because it shows the best and most important kind of bravery. That's what I hear when you tell me this Cecilia, a complete lack of bravery, a fear of whatever the consequences are of people at school seeing your true self."

"Well what you call a lack of bravery I call skill."

"Oh, here comes the boss of these two guys." Kitty goes to the door. The man stands there with a coffee in one hand, and a folded newspaper in the other. "Well hey, did your worker tell you I want that tree branch down? I think it's obvious which one I'm talking about." The man nods. Kitty waits for him to say more, but he simply takes a sip from his coffee. "So good, because I keep thinking that thing could crush my car any day. And with these storms the less danger we have around here the better." Kitty pauses again. The man glances at his newspaper, takes a sip of coffee, looks at the tree, then at Kitty. "Right, so, when can you get this done?"

"Next week," he says in the most nasally voice Kitty has ever heard.

"Next week?"

"Nghhhhhhh," answers the man.

Kitty looks back at the kitchen, raising her eyebrows, as if asking Cecilia if what she's hearing is real.

She looks back, "Okay good, and listen, I want that kid Coast to go up the tree and do the…whatever…the cut, the hard part." This puts the man into pause as he's sipping from his coffee, and leaves him staring at Kitty, the cup to his lips. "The kid needs a chance, and it's important for labourers to do some skilled work once in a while. So get 'em up there."

"Kidd," says the man.

"What?"

"KIDDnghhhhhhh," he screams behind him at the other worker. The worker approaches the door, shutting off a line trimmer as he does, and the man whispers something into his ear before he walks off. The worker sticks out his hand. "Hi, I'm Kidd." Kitty shakes tentatively. "I'm the one that does the cuts in the tree. See that truck over there? That's my truck, I own it, even though I work for Tess, and in there I've got five different kinds of chainsaws. The hedge trimmers and the line trimmers are Tess's, but I don't care about those, I only care about my truck and my chainsaws. Cutting down branches and trees is my life."

"That's great, your truck is impressive, as I'm sure your chainsaws are, but I'm sick of watching this guy do nothing but the most basic tasks out there. I want him to have a chance to do some of the skilled work I see you doing. He's only twenty, he could probably learn to do anything."

"I'm not sure you know everything you need to know about Coast. He gets hurt anytime he's near something with a blade. I mean look at him, his head's so low he hardly knows what's going on around him. You think that's safe for this kind of work? It's not, that's why we have to yell at him all the time. He's just depressed and there's nothing sending him up a tree is going to do about that."

"Sure it will. It will show him that someone believes in him, it will help him out of his funk…okay? A good looking kid like that shouldn't be depressed."

Kidd looks back at Coast, then says, "If you say so," to Kitty.

Chapter Thirty

2008 – Toronto International Dragonboat Race Festival

We paddle back to the end of the lanes and I pull out my notebook to write about the race, and to look more journalist-like. We see the boats appear from behind the island at the start of the lanes. They're too far to make out the teams, but the announcer broadcasts the team names and which lanes they're in: the Scarborough Buffs are in a centre lane next to the golf shirts.

The start gun goes off, but I can't see who came out in the lead. I look around at the audience. There's lots of people here, right up to where the grass meets the water. I'm trying to write some of what people are saying, but the white noise of voices is so loud I can only hear what's right up close.

"Steve, Steve let's go try for the bleachers," yells a guy on the bridge to a dense crowd surrounding the pub. The booths are scattered around and behind the stadium and up near the pub. It's hard to see what they are through the crowds, but I can see one selling paddles, another footwear, and another with big pictures of somewhere tropical, probably selling tours. Then I notice that same police zodiac parked along the shore, and the cops at a police tent near the stadium. I really don't want those guys taking notice of us; our canoes can not be searched.

Kate, who is intensely energetic about the race, says, "Fuck this is close. Scarborough Buffs are going to take it though."

Cecilia says, "This is kind of exciting, it's so *Last of the Mohicans*."

That was the movie reference I was trying to think of; book reference, except I've never read the book, so movie reference.

Sam says, "Is it over yet? I seriously want to get out of this canoe for a bit. Get something to eat."

Kate says, "The Scarborough Buffs and the golf shirts are really close together, because those handshaking douchebags keep angling into their lane."

Sam says, "Pass me a bottle of something, Coast."

"Let him write," says Kate. "This is intense, it's something exciting for his book."

Cecilia says, "It would be better if it were more like *Last of the Mohicans*. Maybe somebody will get killed."

Kate says, "Maybe the golf shirts should get the fuck away from the Scarborough Buffs, they look like they're going to collide."

They are about three quarters through the course, still the Scarborough Buffs and the golf shirts are tied for first. It looks amazing. I'm scribbling fast to get as many details down as I can. Even the wakes and waves and slosh the two boats are stirring up are impressive for...*goddamnit fly*...impressive for a paddle...*Christ, stop landing on my stupid arm. I don't get why they do that over and over...*It's going to be one hell of a finish. As the boats approach the final sprint the Scarborough Buffs and golf shirts are still really close, but it looks like the Scarborough Buffs...*Holy Christ, screw off. The second this race ends I'm going to fucking kill you. Whatever advantage in life you think you're achieving by landing on my arm over and over really does not outweigh the fact that I'm going to...*

WELL THAT GODDAMN FLY MADE ME MISS THE END OF THE RACE, and something bad happened too. The golf shirts took it, but Kate started flipping out the second they did. Apparently she saw Ronny make a jabbing motion mid-stroke near the end. Their boat was right beside the Scarborough Buffs, who were ahead, but just, so Ronny was only slightly behind Heather. He made his jabbing motion, Heather stopped paddling, and the golf shirts got ahead.

Ronny yells, "GO GO GO, we got to get back to the dock" before anyone in his boat starts celebrating. I can hear the announcer going off, getting the crowd excited over the closeness of the race. Heather isn't saying anything to anyone, but her face looks tense and she's holding her wrist.

Kate says, "They absolutely did that on purpose. Did you guys see that?"

Sam says, "I don't know, they almost collided and then your friends fell back. Why are you getting so involved in all this? It's just a race, it's no big deal."

"Because that asshole Ronny just won by hammering Heather's wrist and how the fuck am I the only one freaking out about this? Drink some liquor and get riled up; you" (pointing at Cecilia) "smoke a joint if you have to."

"I'll do both, can't promise I'll get riled up."

We paddle over to the Scarborough Buffs' dock, where they're unloading. Les motors over and yells, "EMS is on its way. How bad she get hurt?"

Kate immediately starts screaming at him, "You're disqualifying those assholes, right? They did that on purpose. Coast, tell them what you saw. He's reporting this. That's why he's here, he's doing a story for the Montreal Herald. Coast, tell them."

"Yeah, I saw it. They did that on purpose."

Everyone keeps looking at me, waiting for my full account. As the silence I cannot fill stretches on it becomes obvious I missed whatever happened. Cecilia laughs, both Cecilia and Sam laugh.

Kate says, "Coast, you're the worst journalist ever. Anyway, I saw it. That asshole Ronny jabbed at Heather's wrist on purpose. She screamed and stopped and everyone else slowed and they fell back. That team should be disqualified and kicked out of here."

Despite my blunder, Les keeps looking at me nervously. You really don't have to look like much to look like a journalist. It's got to be the easiest profession to fake in the world. As an ambulance pulls up he says, "Let's see what EMS says. Heather, you all right?"

She shrugs as EMS walks her to the back of the ambulance, Spry and Eddie by her side. A few moments later Eddie comes back. "Her wrist is broken."

Kate says, "That settles it, her wrist wouldn't break in an almost collision. That asshole jabbed at her with his paddle."

"All right, both teams race again, in separate heats," says Les. "The last two only have four in them anyway, you guys take the last one. Now let's go, let's get these races going. We have two hours to finish this whole thing." He motors over to the dock where the golf shirts are and tells them. They nod and shrug their shoulders, seeming indifferent.

We tie up to a row of trees and shrubs along a part of the shore near their dock, get out, and push through the shrubs. Martyn and Alemu are sitting on the grass behind the Scarborough Buffs' dock, and behind a wall of vines hanging from two large willow trees. The vines don't quite reach the ground. All that's in view from where they sit is the start-line, hazy and distant, beside the island. We sit down beside them and face the same way.

Alemu says, "Thanks for getting us a rematch, Kate, but it doesn't matter anyway. Without Heather we're toast, she's the engine."

"What are you talking about, you've got all these built guys in your boat."

Martyn says, "Yeah, but paddling's technique and core muscles, we're all arm muscles and we don't really train for this like Heather does."

"Heather lifts the boat for everyone else, believe me, we've practised without her and it's just not the same," says Alemu.

Kate jumps to her feet. "Well gear up for your race, because I've got the perfect ringer. Sam here's a fucking hippy paddler like you wouldn't believe. She spends every moment she can paddling for days at a time, she's got to be built in all the right places."

Sam snaps. She gets up and stands face to face with Kate. "Why do you have to call me a hippy all the time? Even when you want me to help you, you still have to talk down to me. You know what, Kate? I give up. I've been trying to get you to take me seriously, to stop with the hippy stuff and everything else you call me, so I can tolerate living with you, but you just don't get it. I'm not moving in with you anymore. I never told you this before, but Beth at the coffee shop wants me to move in with her too. We both love and play music, we're both really artistic, and she thinks I could really thrive living with someone more like me."

"Yeah, good, fucking do it. And you know what? I didn't really need the fucking explanation, you could have just said I'm not moving in with you. I really don't care why."

"You're funny. That's why I like you, Kate, you make me laugh, but I really think you might be holding me back; like I could be doing better in life if it weren't for all the horrible, cynical things I hear from you all the time."

"Fine, don't move in with me. I really don't care. I care about the race, which is why I'm going to paddle for Heather instead. And we're going to win the heat, you know why? Because I don't need you. See ya, hippy."

Sam, infuriated, marches off into the crowds of teams behind us and Cecilia goes after her.

Kate, collapsing to the ground, moans, "Um…that kind of fucking sucks."

Martyn says, "Are you okay? I'm sorry she doesn't want to move in with you anymore."

"Yeah, that's not even what sucks. Sam's never gotten that mad at me before. She's never said anything like that about me holding her back. I don't know, maybe she doesn't want to be close to me anymore. Oh fuck, we're going to end up like Coast and Cecilia."

I say, "Kate, if I can offer a little advice, just try saying some nice things to her."

"And don't worry about us," says Martyn, "that last heat is a really tough one, almost impossible for us to win even with Heather."

Kate falls back onto the grass. "Ugh, I suck, I can't solve anything."

Alemu says, "We understand, Kate, families are tough."

The start gun goes off, and we all watch the five boats launch into the lanes. They look miniature at the far end of them, the yelling like an echo coming from a battle on the other side of a mountain.

Chapter Thirty-One

2013 – Toronto East (last story written by Alex before leaving Toronto, first draft)

Title: To Be Determined

Coast is halfway up the tree. Kidd stands near Tess's truck in the driveway, Tess sitting in the driver's seat with his coffee and newspaper. Kitty, Cecilia and Alex stand near the front door, watching Coast, Kitty hoping their presence might help with his obvious anxiety. He has moved up at a very slow pace, tentatively pulling out the spike of each climbing spur and pushing in only inches higher, then tentatively moving the climbing belt up the same small incremental distance.

He yells down to Kidd, "This belt is frayed. It looks weak. Every time I move it up I can see strands of material breaking. I think I should come down and get a new one."

"There is no other one, and you should feel lucky I even gave you a belt. Now come on, we don't have all day."

"I'm going as fast as I can. It's tough with this gear." His chainsaw hangs from a shoulder strap along with a very large bundle of climbing rope.

He finally reaches the branch. It's a massive thing, forming its own satellite canopy. From the trunk it grows almost straight out before turning up, maintaining a solid two foot diameter from the base to the elbow of the turn. The elbow extends about eight feet out from the trunk and it looms above Coast, who clings to the tree beneath the branch.

"I'm not doing this," he yells; "there's no way." He looks down at Kidd from about thirty feet up, who squints at him, hands on his hips. Tess leans out of the driver's seat window and looks up at him too.

"That crazy looking elbow in the branch is going to come right at me, I can tell; the canopy is leaning all its weight over it. When the cut is made it will swing right at me like a pendulum..." Coast looks more fixedly at the elbow, "I think there's a face in it. In the bark. It looks like the devil."

Kidd starts laughing, laughing and looking back at Tess, who starts laughing with him. "Trust me. I checked this out. Don't worry about the branch; don't even look at it. Take the climbing rope off your shoulder and throw it around the branch. Oh man, 'devil in the wood', you've got an imagination alright. Now throw that rope, but keep one hand holding the slack. You drop that thing and you'll have to climb all the way back down here; either that or you'll just have to deal with that branch yourself. Don't look at it, just throw the rope on three: one, two, three. Okay good, keep feeding it around the branch. There's lots. You could go around that branch three or four times with that pile of rope. Ha—ha, that's my rope. I always keep good rope in my truck. See, Tess takes care of all the hedge trimmers and lawnmowers, but I've got the tree gear. Just keep feeding that rope around the branch; let the end pile up on the ground. Okay good, try to throw the loop down the branch, away from where I told you to cut. You see, you see what's going on here? This isn't my first tree, not my biggest, definitely not the hardest. I don't even need my really good rope for this tree. I haven't even shown you that rope."

Kidd ties the ends of the rope to a spot beneath the front end of the truck, slaps the hood, then walks his hand along the slack rope, while Tess, newspaper still sprawled in his lap, coffee still in his hand, hears Kidd slap on the hood, turns the ignition, shifts into reverse, and lets the truck idle backwards. Eventually the loop around the branch makes it to the elbow and the rope goes taut with enough strength to hold the truck from idling back. The truck is now poised to jump backward as soon as Coast finishes the cut, pulling the branch away from him and the tree.

Kidd says, "Now remember what I said, cut a wedge in the branch on your side, then finish the cut on the truck side. And start that chainsaw the way I showed you."

He pulls the choke then cranks on the chainsaw's pull-string. The engine turns then stops with a puff of black smoke. He smacks the choke back in then cranks on the pull-string again. This time the engine roars on. He presses the trigger a few times spinning the teeth into a blur. He looks down at Kidd. Kidd looks up at him, waves him on, then turns and walks towards the truck.

Leaning back on the strap, his spurs wedged into either side of the tree, Coast reves the engine and moves the blur of teeth towards the branch above him. As the teeth cut into the wood a loud, penetrating squeal sounds out and a shower of saw dust pours down on him. Kidd walks underneath and inspects the wedge cut out of the side of the branch. He signals Tess to give the truck a little gas, thus increasing the tension on the rope, and its pull on the elbow of the branch, then he signals Coast with a slicing motion: *finish the cut*. Coast steals one more glance at the satellite canopy the branch opens up into, the maze of twigs bursting out of the Black Oak's massive arm.

Crack! The sound of wood splitting. The crack is deafening. The branch has split right down its centre. The split begins where Coast cut the wedge halfway in, then runs all the way to the elbow, then a few feet up towards the canopy, where the split finally ends at the side of the branch facing the truck. It leaves the truck-facing-side still attached to the tree, but the side that Coast has cut through – the side that still includes the entire canopy above the split – completely severed from the tree, save for whatever strands of wood remain attached between the split halves.

Coast drops the chainsaw, but it's halted by the shoulder strap. Then, staring in horror at the split branch, he drops a couple feet down the trunk, barely controlling the climbing spurs.

The next sound is something between crackling, fibre ripping and Velcro. It's the remaining strands of wood peeling away from their respective halves. The branch is separating like a pair of scissors. Coast looks at Kidd below. Kidd is screaming and signalling 'step on the gas' at Tess, but the rope is powerless to pull the dislodged-half of the branch and canopy away while the remaining attached-half blocks the efforts of the truck. While the end of the dislodged branch that Coast cut with his chainsaw scissors upward, the elbow sinks beneath the weight of the canopy. The separation forces the rope to the centre of the x-shaped halves. The engine in the chainsaw stalls. The wood strands are all ripped. The pendulum canopy and devil-faced elbow swings towards him quickly, yet silently, through the air.

Thud, "Oof", snap are the sounds of the elbow making contact with his gut, winding him and breaking the harness (though not his back, most likely because the frayed, weakened harness strap snaps first).

The chainsaw-cut end of the scissored branch slides through the loop of the climbing rope, still pointlessly held taut by the truck. Coast and the branch free-fall. His body forms a V at the base of the V that is the branch, with his feet pointing towards the canopy, his head towards the opposite end, and his torso beneath the elbow. The Blinds close their eyes and hold their breath just before the elbow drives his torso into the ground. With his last breath, Coast sees the canopy explode into splinters.

Chapter Thirty-Two

2008 – Toronto International Dragonboat Race Festival

Damiond and Rory show up. They both put the butt-ends of their paddles on the ground and lean against the blades for much needed support. Rory asks after Sam, which makes Kate groan: "She hates me now, so she took off somewhere."

"Got in a fight? That's too bad, you guys are good eggs."

Kate shoots up. "Rory, go talk to her. She loves your weird accent for some reason. Go talk to her and tell her Kate's all right and she should totally live with me still. No, forget me, just go tell her she's awesome and talented and there's really nothing wrong with her at all. Fuck, why am I such a prick?"

Damiond sits down beside me. I ask him if he's still feeling confident about the race. "I was feeling confident. The three other teams in our heat are worse than us. I thought we scored the jackpot. Then those broker assholes from last night got put in our heat. That's the last team I want to lose to, and I hate to admit it, but I don't think we can beat them."

Kate says, "Wait, what heat are you in?"

"Second from last, we're queuing up soon."

Kate scans the parkland behind the docks. "Where's Eddie? There he is." She runs over to him.

Rory sits down beside Damiond, and it's just the guys left sitting around on the grass. A heat finishes. We listen to the announcer list the placement of the teams. Down the shore teams are standing at the docks with the pit crews, but nobody needs the Scarborough Buffs' dock, so it remains empty.

Martyn looks at me quietly for a moment, I suppose thinking of what he's about to say. "You seem like you've got it figured out, Coast. You've got work figured out; I bet you're a good fisherman, and have no problem getting a job when you need one."

"I suppose you could say that."

"So you can spend all your free time adrift – Spry told us all about it, how you spend days at a time around bonfires, talking to strangers, and how you quit your job and gave up your place out West. I bet she'd give up every opportunity she has just to drift around with you."

"I'm not so sure."

"She would. But you have to remember, she doesn't have a good way of making a living like you. She needs to go to school." He pauses. When I go to say something, he says, "Alemu, wouldn't you agree?"

Alemu smiles his put-everyone-at-ease smile. "My friend, Spry is going to do exactly what she wants. If she wants to live a drifter lifestyle with Coast, even he won't be able to stop her." He laughs and I laugh.

Martyn says, "He could leave now, so she doesn't have the option." There's an awkward silence. "Well you could. You could walk away. I'm just saying it's a possibility."

It's a weird moment. Something about his expression, his tone of voice, gives away that Martyn is in love with Spry. But that isn't working for him, so now he's attempting to satisfy his desire with an overdeveloped sense of protection for his friend. Christ, this is awkward. And I can't think of anything to say to diffuse the situation. Fortunately Sam and Cecilia come back and sit down with us.

Sam says, "Hey, Cecilia got me really stoned and now I feel better."

Rory says to Sam, "Kate told us you won't move in with her."

"Ugh, I don't know. I love Kate, but you guys see how different she is from me, it's tough."

"My cousin moved in with his best friend," says Rory, kneeling beside her. "They're exactly alike. Everything they watch, listen to, do, is exactly the same. And you know what? It took a month for them to hate each other."

"I get that. The truth is I don't really want to live with Beth. She would be so boring to live with. She's so pretentious about music, always talking smack about other musicians we know. And how am I supposed to know she doesn't say the same stuff about me behind my back?"

Cecilia says, "That's right. With Kate you know what you get. She seems about as honest as anyone can be."

"Kate's great, we're just so different. I know that's a good thing, like we should hang out with people completely different from ourselves, but it's so hard sometimes."

Damiond and Rory leave to queue up for their heat. Kate comes back and she looks thrilled. "Guys, guess what, guess what! I got Eddie to talk to Les and put you in the Bastard's heat. You guys can kick ass now."

Alemu says, "Thanks, Kate, but we told you we can't beat anybody without Heather."

Kate sits down, remembering where that conversation leads to. Without looking at her, she says, "Sam, do you still hate me? Or are you going to get over whatever this is and paddle with these guys?"

Cecilia answers for her: "Kate, Sam's a little busy right now contemplating how much of a cunt you are, so unfortunately she can't."

Kate sits between them, squeezing in and leaning against Sam. "You're better than me."

"Go away."

"No, I'm serious, you're better than me. You have a brighter future than me. Look at what you're into and what it means. You love to paddle and go on canoe trips. Everybody respects that. It's a useful skill. You could get a job leading outdoor education trips and you'd be awesome at it. But you're also a musician, and everybody respects you for that too. You could make it big, or play in pubs your whole life and be happy with just that. I know you. You could be happy off so little because you love those two things so much.

"Me, I'm a dirt biker. I ride bikes in the summer and sleds in the winter. Who respects that aside from the guys who do it? What am I going to do with my skills, which are epic for sure, but what am I going to do with them? You're better than me, Sam, and that's why I give you such a hard time."

She pauses to let that sink in. Sam stares ahead.

"You know the one thing I do have going for me? I know how to latch onto good fucking people. That's why I begged you to move in with me, and that's why I want you to race with the Scarborough Buffs. They're good people, just like you, Sam. And you guys make me look good by association."

Sam laughs; everyone laughs.

"It's true! Who would I hang out with if you stopped hanging out with me? Those punks in the kitchen? Those idiots that I dirt bike with? I'd get ten times dumber without you."

"Oh Kate, you're just trying to get me to paddle with the Scarborough Buffs. That's the only reason you're saying all this."

"No, seriously no." Kate says to Alemu and Martyn, "You guys, Sam's not paddling in place of Heather, so stop asking her, okay? Stop it." And back to Sam, leaving Alemu and Martyn laughing with palms up, "See? And you can back out of moving in with me, if that's what you really want, just please don't stop hanging out with me all the time. Bartender, a bottle for my cousin, no, my friend, please."

I run back to the canoe and return with vodka. Sam takes a big swig, then she hugs Kate and says she's going to paddle in place of Heather.

Chapter Thirty-Three

2013 – Toronto East (last story written by Alex before leaving Toronto, second draft)

Title: Cecilia

The days are rotting. One after another, the days are rotting, and now almost two years of days stand rotting.

Looking back at the last two years is like looking into a bowl of pudding – it doesn't matter where in the pudding Coast looks, it's still the same pudding. The last two years are like drab shades of brown, green and yellow. Looking back on them is like staring at a wall of green, yellow and brown splotches, but with no single point of focus.

He rides through though. He witnesses whatever scraps of life there is to witness. He stares into those scraps, stares and never gives up. The Fear. It's The Fear. He doesn't know how to deal with it in retrospect, in memory. He doesn't know how to deal with the past of it. The Fear is fine in the present, the present he can adapt to, but in the past The Fear is so befuddling to look at.

How does everyone else see the past, how do they so easily see the story in it? They have lives. They go outside the walls of his universe; they go to see, go to experience events in different places. Those events become markers on their past, markers they can focus on.

CECILIA, COAST'S NIECE, WALKS INTO HIS APARTMENT around the same time he's mulling over the pudding and drab colours of the last two years and says, "The last time you left was when?...Three days ago, I can tell by the garbage. It stinks. How's your frozen food supply?...Wow, that's a lot. Three days and your stores are still plentiful. I can't imagine how much you buy at once. I brought an apple. I'm cutting it up for you…Sorry, but you have to eat this. I can barely look at you knowing you've eaten nothing but frozen foods for three days. Here, please, eat this."

Usually she shows up with Alex, Coast's nephew, but today she's alone. There's an awkwardness without Alex. It puts Coast face to face with how little Cecilia thinks of him. Apparently she's irked by Coast's frozen dinners, and she'll often show up just to bring a piece of fruit or a vegetable. Sometimes Coast's apartment irks her as well, and shortly after these visits a housekeeper will appear at the door.

Cecilia walks up to the large living room window, which Coast has blocked out with an old blanket. "Do you know what the valley is like right now? Probably more lush and green than ever before. These thunderstorms we keep having, the heat, the sunshine – it's turning the trees tropical. Aren't you curious? Just behind this blanket is a panoramic view of the valley and the city beyond, a twenty-third floor view you have never seen." She looks closely at the blanket. "Where did you get this thing from?" Coast shrugs; he can't remember the blanket's origin. "Next time I come over I'm bringing blinds and throwing this out."

Coast's apartment has the most minimal of furniture, the most minimal of shadows and corners. The bedroom door is permanently closed, which is why he keeps his mattress on the floor in the living room in front of his TV. The kitchen is equally simplified; there's the microwave to cook his frozen foods, the freezer to store his frozen foods, the fridge to store his juice, the counter where he keeps his supply of disposable plates and utensils, and a large garbage bag with the opening kept tied shut.

Cecilia walks around his apartment, observing the washroom, corners where the floors meet the walls, and the mattress in front of the television, where Coast is presently laying. The floor-length, blue-terry-cloth dress she wears is a staple for Cecilia, and combined with her short steps, which are nearly absent of any vertical bounce, it gives her the appearance of floating across the floor, but he notices something odd today – rather than hanging a perfect millimetre from the floor, the dress drags. He also notices a trail of water and mud at the front door which goes into the kitchen. He looks to where she's walking beside the bed and sees that the trail of water and mud comes from the dragging bottom of her blue-terry-cloth dress. He squints through the shadiness of his apartment and sees mud caked around the bottom, and mud stains up and down it. He also notes that the rain jacket Cecilia wears is covered in mud stains, and even her hair, usually pulled back tight into a ponytail, is loose, tangled and wet.

Cecilia looks at her dress, at the trail behind her, and then at Coast, but her eyes never simply look at something, they snap to their subject, her head snapping in the same direction. "You know what you are? You're a rabbit. You're a rabbit because a rabbit hole would suit you so perfectly. You could sit in your rabbit hole all day and night doing nothing. You'd just have to monitor that one single solitary space where danger could potentially come from. It would make you perfectly content, wouldn't it?" He says nothing. "God," she says, snapping her eyes back to the blanket. "What would you do if I pulled this blanket down right now, just forced the biggest expanse of view you have ever feared on you right this moment?"

He can't imagine, but he knows she wouldn't. He says, "What happened to your clothes?"

She sits on the floor beside the mattress with the wall straight against her back, folds her arms, and looks straight ahead. "Are you even aware of the storm that ended an hour ago? It was the biggest of the summer, probably flooded every basement apartment between here and the lake, and every ravine."

She stares into oblivion, into a universe of nothing a few inches in front of her. "Alex was at the park when it was at its worst. I went to fetch him, but he wasn't there. When I asked some people standing on their stoop if they saw him, they pointed to the stairs…stairs that go from the park down to the Valley, down to Taylor creek. I couldn't believe it, right beside those stairs is a sign that says, in big red letters, *flash flood warning*. What was he thinking? I ran down. When I got to the bottom the water had already flooded over the bridge and the valley floor.

"Alex, the little weirdo, was on the bridge, kneeling down and holding onto the railing. This was in the middle of the flood where the water was running at its fastest. I freaked out and went for a life ring beside the ravine, but of course the water had flooded past the post, so I had to slop through this muddy flood water, falling on the way and getting drenched, before I get the ring. Alex is facing the current, leaning back while the rush crashes into him, nearly covering him. I could barely see his face for the splash; it must have taken all his strength just to hold on. Can you imagine how dangerous that is? He could have died…actually he would have died. That's exactly what would have happened if I didn't grab the life ring."

Cecilia pauses and stares at Coast. He says, "The water pushed him off the bridge?"

"No, he let go. That crazy idiot just let go on purpose and started floating with the flood. I panicked and yelled, 'Alex, grab the ring,' and tossed it to him. He grabbed hold and I pulled him in. He got to shallow water away from the centre, but still had to hold onto the ring until he reached the stairs. We both collapsed on the bottom steps, out of breath. I screamed at him and said, 'You suicidal little freak, what were you doing?' He doesn't say anything. 'You could have died, you must have known that,' and still he says nothing. When his breath comes back he just stands and runs up the stairs and back to the house, without saying a word to me…

"…that kid…God…every single day he spends in Taylor Creek Valley. It's part of what makes him so reclusive, so…weird. Of course you think he's as normal as he thinks you are…well next year he goes to high school…maybe…and I just finished…there his weird, reclusive little personality is really going to…forget it, look who I'm talking to."

And again she stares into oblivion, into the universe of nothing a few inches in front of her. "Kitty, our insane mother, is planning a séance, or some such event, to mark the second year anniversary of the death of your brother…of our father. Apparently this is what we need to start healing." Slowly, almost imperceptibly, she shakes her head. "I disagree. I think we need a catastrophe; not more family tragedy, but something really big, like a plague, a meteor strike, or a tornado that just rips apart the downtown. See what I'm saying? Something close, almost too close. Something that throws everybody into a panic, even us. I don't want anyone to get hurt, I just want the aftermath of panic, when everyone is forced into a massively introspective phase. I don't want chaos, just the calm following chaos. I think that would do us a lot of good, don't you?" And she's really asking, waiting for his answer.

He says, "I don't know what you mean."

"Of course not; what would you even do in an apocalyptic situation? Seriously, just imagine it. Pretend you're over for dinner and all of a sudden the world collapses into a burning chaos. We can't depend on anyone for anything. On top of that, we have to leave the house because of looters. We don't bring anything with us. So there we are in Taylor Creek Valley wondering what to do next: me, Alex, Kitty – our oblivious mother – and you.

"Alex wanders off and is immediately mauled by coyotes. Now there are just three of us. Kitty is so upset over the loss of the house, which is looted and burned to the ground, that she dies of grief. It's just me and you, Coast, so what do you do? You don't know because you're waiting for me to decide. In all these years that you've lived you've always depended on somebody else. You think by shutting yourself into the apartment you've created some kind of independence, but you're as dependent as ever. You don't understand that independence requires relationships.

"I don't have a lot of friends, sure, but I talk to people. Miguel at the fish shop – I've known him for seven years now. His wife just had a baby. His cousin is in jail again. See? I know people. You and Alex don't interact with anyone, you have no connection to the outside world. At high school I at least had acquaintances, I had truces, because I had enough social skills to form that kind of thing. Alex is going to get mauled by those coyotes."

Frustrated, she stands up and walks to the door. She opens it, looks back, says, "Do you know what Alex is asking for now? God knows why, but he's actually impressionable around you. He's asking me to buy him frozen foods. Not because of ads…he wants the ones he sees you eating over here. Do me a favour and grab a piece of fruit next time you're near him," and leaves, slamming the door behind her.

Chapter Thirty-Four

2008 – Toronto International Dragonboat Race Festival

Everyone leaves to queue up. I stay behind to write about Kate and Sam, what Martyn said, and the race. The next heat starts. It's cool watching the paddling from the side rather than having the boats coming towards me. It's less war-like and more...*goddamnit fly, are you the same one?* I hate flies so much right now, Christ. Just calm down. If the fly lands on you don't even notice...Jesus, it's so annoying though. I'm going to kill it.

I didn't kill it, I tried really hard for ten minutes.

Cecilia comes back. "Well that was interesting. Sam's in the boat, Heather and Spry are thrilled. Not only that, Kate's in now too. Eddie said she should sit in the pacing drummer's seat and help yell motivational statements. I think it was her yelling qualifications that got her the job. They're queuing up after the next race. Smoke a joint with me?"

"Sure."

Cecilia lights up a joint without looking to see who's around us. There's no one close, but still…

She passes it to me without taking any herself. I drag on it, pass it back, then fall back on the grass. "Martyn thinks I should leave, so Spry doesn't have a chance to live some bohemian lifestyle with me, so she goes to school."

Cecilia, after a moment's meditation, says, "He's in love with her."

"Definitely."

"That makes life a little difficult for you."

"Yes, just a little. I can't tell if he wants me to go because he really believes I'm bad for her, or if he's just hurt because she likes me."

"That's a tough one. On the one hand, you'll most certainly ruin her life – she'll probably fall in love with you, give up her own opportunities to embrace your drifter lifestyle, find out you really have nothing else to talk about except bonfires and fishing, and subsequently throw herself into the lake; on the other hand, for a sensible, caring and attractive man to see his heart's desire fall for the most ridiculous guy who ever wandered into this town, well that's gotta hurt."

"Yeah, I guess."

Cecilia sucks on the joint and passes it to me. "Brother, you're rolling over so easy. I thought you had thicker skin than this, it was the one thing that made you fun to be around."

I take only one more drag then pass it back to Cecilia. I hold the notebook above me, in front of the awning of vines hanging from the shoreline willow trees, the pot smoke from Cecilia passing between them, and reread some of what I've written. "I'm so depressed."

Cecilia says, "Me too. It's because we don't make friends. Isn't that nuts? Neither of us makes friends, unless they're forced on us somehow. I don't know what it is. We both gravitate towards people. You and your bonfires, which are obviously just a passive way to have people in your life; me living in a city, only so I can meet people whose lives I can just as easily disappear from. But we never make friends. That's what makes me depressed at least."

"So are you going to start making friends then?"

"Oh fuck no. People are shit. And I just can't handle talking to any one person for too long. I can keep a friend for…um…two weeks; I can handle someone for two weeks before I start to *tromper* them, but that's it. Haven't you noticed how often people repeat themselves? That's one nice thing about you. You don't say much, but at least you don't repeat the same boring stories over and over. I guess that's why you're so quiet. Why are you depressed?"

"I don't know, I don't know what the possible reasons are. Biological chemistry I suppose. This weed is making me feel better. I should smoke weed all the time."

"Yeah, you should, in your case it would make you more interesting. Maybe it would help you find something to be depressed about."

The Scarborough Buffs and the Bastard's heat start. They're close enough to see, but I still can't tell who's in the lead. The sun's angled so that it's beaming off the splash from the paddles and boats. Then the yelling comes through the ambient noise of the crowd. I can hear Kate above all of them, "Push it! Beat the Bastards!", and I start to write.

Cecilia says, "Don't try to describe the action, Alex, you'll just make the race sound boring. I'll sports announce this for you." (I stop writing notes on the race and scribble along with Cecilia instead) "The start gun goes off and the race from shame begins. Who will escape finishing as the most laughable team of the festival? The Bastards, powered by the sheer excitement of not coming in last for once, are in the lead, but the Scarborough Buffs, powered by the yelling of the psychopathic girl who has latched onto them today, are not far behind, and a boat with a tipsy looking steerer is a close third. The other two boats aren't even in the race. The Bastards keep their lead, but, oh no, the steerer of the third place boat is in the water. It's just the Scarborough Buffs and the Bastards in the race now. The Bastards are burning out and slowing a bit as of the halfway mark, but the excitement of actually not being last is still in their eyes. The Scarborough Buffs are closing the gap, but not quite fast enough. Kate screams 'Push it guys, this is your last race and your chance to take it. Sam, lift the boat for them.' And the gap is closing, closing, and Eddie is yelling 'TAKE IT, TAKE IT, TAKE IT.' And they do, they get their nose in front right at the end. The Scarborough Buffs have won and the Bastards have returned to the place in life they were destined for. Poor Kelly, ha—ha."

The boats paddle back to the docks. The Scarborough Buffs holler at the Bastards. The Bastard's boat is an eruption of Irish expletives, from Rory too, but his eyes smile in awe every time they lock with Sam's.

The Scarborough Buffs get out of the boat and huddle around Eddie and Heather, who has a temporary cast on. The buzz of the moment is palpable. "Scarborough Buffs kick ass," yells one of the girls from the team huddle, and her words ignite a long round of chants and screams. Kate looks at Sam, then throws her arm around her shoulders. Sam just laughs, they both laugh huddled together while the Scarborough Buffs erupt into shouts and high-fives.

Cecilia says, "They're really quite the pair. I doubt that anyone in our entire family history has gotten along as well as those two do. And look, they're actually accomplishing stuff with their togetherness."

We watch the last heat of the round. At first nobody wanted to.

Alemu said, "The golf shirts are going to take it, I don't even want to watch."

Eddie said, "Don't be so sure."

The start gun goes off, but it's hard to see who's in the lead – the sun's still glittering off the water – but it's definitely two teams leaving the rest behind right away. When they get closer I'm blown away by what I see. One boat is easily overtaking the other, and the golf shirts are the overtaken. Jonathan, Mary and the Sunset Masters are the overtakers. They're machines; they're pistons. They're cylinders of form and muscle calmly focused on the easy victory before them. Their drummer isn't yelling. Their steerer isn't yelling. The boat is a silent torpedo.

At the end of the race we all see the golf shirts swearing and acting like the biggest sore losers. The Sunset Masters paddle over and Jonathan and Mary offer their hands, an amused smile overcoming both of them. At first Ronny yells, "Let's go," but the stadium applauds in expectation of a good show of sportsmanship, and he and everyone on their team has to shake the winners' hands.

Kate says, "Well that was satisfying. I think I love dragonboating now. No, scratch that, I just love paddling, in all forms, and I love everyone that paddles. You're my hero today, Sam."

Alemu says, "I really don't want to race that old crew, they'll wipe us out, even with Sam."

"Guys, we're going to give the spot to the Bastards," says Eddie. "They'll appreciate the opportunity to paddle in the next round, and I think Sam and Kate have helped us enough today. So congratulations, you paddled well and persevered through an unexpected challenge, earning yourselves a placement ahead of your rivals – the RH Customs team." They erupt into cheers. "Okay, okay, I just want to say one more thing. It was a real pleasure coaching you guys, and I'm really going to miss you next year."

Spry says, "Oh no, this is the last time we're going to see Eddie."

Heather says, "Are you even going to miss me?"

"Oh, especially you, Heather, ha—ha. Okay guys, get some food in the athletes' area and make sure to watch the last round of heats before you go. Diego, Priscilla and Joy – you guys help me clean up and prepare the boat to put on the trailer. Fists everyone."

Everyone knocks fists with Eddie as they leave.

Chapter Thirty-Five

2013 – Toronto East (last story written by Alex before leaving Toronto, second draft)

Title: Cecilia

Alex rarely makes eye contact. His eyes are usually too focused on whatever is in his hands – a patch of moss, section of root, bushel of rhizomes, chunk of bark, piece of quartz, nest, feather or egg; often insects, usually dead. It's a compulsive habit, and the habit doesn't quit when nature finds are unavailable. In a grocery store he'll grab cans from the shelves or roots from the produce stand. He'll grab merchandise of any hand-sized kind from any store he walks through and examine it in just the same way, turning it in his hands, never raising his eyes, until he eventually returns it to a passing section of shelf.

A large selection of picture books sits on the bookshelf in Alex's room, and he traces their images with his fingers and eyes in just the same way as he does objects. He has a particular fascination with black and white photography, an obsession with the contrasting lines of light and dark that moves his fingers just as the bends and groves in physical objects do. The walls in his room feature black and white prints of his absolute favourite subjects – old, wrinkly people. "Wrinkles," he once said to Coast, "are my favourite thing in the world."

Alex walks into Coast's apartment and, before he even says a word, fits himself between the pinned up blanket and the living room window (Alex's perch, as Cecilia describes it), experiencing the 23rd floor view in the most complete way possible. It gives Coast shivers up his spine just to think about it.

When he reappears, he sits on the mattress next to Coast and places the leather satchel he uses to collect his nature finds from Taylor Creek Park in front of them. He looks at Coast and says, "There are five finds I want to show you today, and I'm going to save the best for last."

The main pouch of the satchel is separated into three large pockets, and additional pockets are sewn into the side and cover flap, all held closed by buckles. A small pocket holds the first find Alex shows Coast – a stone. "It's quartz, which is no big deal, I have lots. This one I grabbed just because nobody would have noticed it except me. It was glittering beneath a boulder sized rock in the middle of the creek where I was looking for fossils, and since I didn't find any I just took this." Coast holds it in his hands for a moment then gives it back to Alex. Alex takes a while with the quartz, which he's already familiar with, turning it in his hands, staring at it in meditative silence, before returning it to the satchel.

From one of the main pockets Alex pulls out a long, black feather. "I have plenty of these too, but this feather fell at my feet while I was walking through the woods. I saw the bird that it fell from, a vulture, flying above the canopy and heard it land way up on a tree along the valley ridge. What are the chances? I made up a rule right there: Anytime a feather lands at your feet you have to take it, even if you already have a bunch, even if it's a seagull feather, but not if it's a pigeon feather, they don't count. You never see pigeons in the woods anyway; they stay in the city streets with the rats."

Alex pulls out an old and worn field guide from one of the centre pockets, a field guide he carries in the satchel always, even though it's outdated and not for the region. "You know how I press flowers in this book? It's fun, but I kept pressing the same ones, the same three, so I made up another rule: Only one of each kind of flower can get pressed each day. It became a game because I kept trying to beat the record, but when I got to ten I figured that was the most I'd ever find. Then I was up the valley wall in this part of the forest where there's a clearing with lots of tall grasses. I was just sort of walking circles, not expecting to find any more flowers because I had ten. All of a sudden I see a patch of red flowers, bright red, like they were from Hawaii or some place and that was eleven. Look at them, I don't even think they're from here; someone threw some seeds maybe."

Next Alex hands Coast a piece of gnarled wood from the flap pocket. "It's root, actually." The piece is elbow shaped and smaller than hand-size. It has the shade of driftwood.

"Guess why I picked that up?" The piece doesn't look like anything special, but Coast turns it in his hand anyway, and looks at it thoughtfully. "Come on, look," says Alex, "look at this side," and he traces the grove lines in the wood. "Don't you see?"

"Ha," says Coast, recognizing a now obvious face in profile, the bend in the elbow making the nose and a tiny knot surrounded by swirling groves making the eye. It looks like a very sad, very old man with a very large nose.

"Are you ready to see my ultimate find Coast?" ("Yes.") From his satchel he carefully pulls out a stick. He holds it with both hands, his eyes wide, monitoring the progress of the stick from satchel to mattress. The stick is delicately placed on the surface, and his hands are slowly removed. Coast is confused. Alex blows on the stick, breathes in, blows on it again, and the stick starts to move. All of a sudden Coast is staring at a very large insect. "It's a stick insect," says Alex.

"Incredible."

"Just watch him, watch how slow he is. Seriously, it's so funny because it's hard for us to watch him too long, to watch something move that slowly, it can drive you crazy. But it's like a game: just keep watching as long as you can. Well he's going to escape, but we'll play again when I get him into an aquarium. I'm going to try and feed him leaves." The insect, walking around the mattress with the most tentative of footsteps, calmly goes back to his mimicry when Alex scoops him back up for the satchel.

Heading for the door, Alex says, "Cecilia and Kitty want you to come for dinner…" pausing, he says, "…um…Saturday."

Coast says, "Okay".

"They say it's been too long."

"Ah…Okay," says Coast. Alex closes the door.

ALEX SPENDS EVERY DAYLIGHT HOUR HE CAN IN TAYLOR CREEK, which he likes to describe in detail to Coast. The valley is heavily forested, and in the summer the Birches, Maples, Willows, and Oaks form such a full canopy that it's impossible to see the houses lining the ridge or any of the city beyond. An activity trail winds along the valley floor, sometimes crossing the creek via small wooden bridges; and the valley itself curves, opens, and thins along its jagged route. At Coast's apartment complex, where the valley opens into a park, it's wide enough to contain fields and parking lots, but near the house it becomes quite thin, the walls so steep they are almost like forested cliffs.

Whenever Alex arrives back at the house, Cecilia asks him where in the valley he was, as it's rarely the same place two days in a row. On the hottest days he spends most of his time in the shaded forest. If he gets out early in the mornings he'll go to the field at

Coast's apartment where a thick mist always hangs just above the ground. He'll spend some days just wading through the creek, and when he tells this to Cecilia she cringes and sends him to the shower. "Disgusting," she'll say, "that creek is linked to hundreds of storm drains, most of them industrial; there's no telling what gets dumped in there."

Alex isn't supposed to go too far west along Taylor Creek trail, though he has told Coast in secret of day hikes he has taken all the way to the Don Valley, where Taylor Creek joins with the Don River. Coast is not unfamiliar with the Don Valley, the largest landscape feature in the region. In his mental projection he sees the valley, like an obvious and brutal dent in the landscape, running across the top of the Danforth-Taylor-Creek-Y. While Taylor Creek empties into the Don River at the northern tip of the Y, the southern tip turns into a black steel viaduct which carries the Danforth and the subway across the kilometre wide floor to the city's West.

Kitty works in one of the highest towers of the West side, and she spends a substantial bulk of her waking hours working. She describes so little about the downtown, except to say how busy it always is, and so little about her work days, except to say how busy they always are, that Alex and Cecilia have learned to see this half of the city as just some void that swallows their mother up for most of the day. This disinterest in the city at large has become so ingrained in Cecilia and Alex, and is so passively accepted by Kitty in her reluctance to describe where she disappears to for so much of the week, that Coast can't even remember the last time any of them spoke the city's name.

Ironically, Coast spends more time exploring the downtown centre than Alex or Cecilia. Coast strolls in what's called the PATH, an underground network of corridors lined with shops and offices, interspersed with food courts and subway stations, and all interconnected like a labyrinth burrowed beneath the city's office towers, condos, and busiest streets. It always amazes him how much the people he observes in this submerged world can accomplish, with its dentist offices and clinics, government service centres and libraries, bars and restaurants, gyms, and fountains for the public to lounge beside.

Coast loves walking there at 5pm when the bank and office towers flood the corridors with rivers of commuters, sometimes seven wide, curving with the turns, splitting where the corridors split, merging into slow moving lakes through the larger spaces. Coast has observed the 8am rivers as well, when the condos flood the corridors instead, and he has walked the labyrinth for hours and hours in those middle times when the lives of the PATH's shop workers are much the same as those of any above ground row of store owners, chatting and trading with locals in the middle of the day.

Standing at the window, staring at his stained blanket, Coast realises he's never once mentioned his walks in the PATH to his in-laws.

Chapter Thirty-Six

2008 – Toronto International Dragonboat Race Festival

We watched the Bastards race in the next heat. They didn't win, but they didn't lose either. They got fourth, which at least made their placement legitimate. We stayed for the final heat too. The Sunset Masters were in it. They got second, only half a second behind the Japanese team. "The Japanese team is from a very historic club," Eddie said, "Me and Les were thrilled that they flew here for the race, so we can call this a good win. Too bad for the Sunset Masters though, it would have been a good win for Jonathan and Mary."

The Japanese team were precise in their movements and exact in their synchronisation. The drummer screamed war cries and it was the most intimidating yelling in all the races that I heard. The Sunset Masters ended side by side with those warriors, and that thunderous voice. I bet it was the voice that kept them back.

After that Cecilia and I go to the beer gardens. Everyone else trails behind with the Scarborough Buffs who are not old enough to get in. We get stopped at the gates – "Athletes only." Cecilia gives the journalist story. Les sits with some other race officials near the gate. He watches us and lets us flounder for a bit. "Let them in, Steve, it's okay. Better be a damn good story."

"It will make you cry," says Cecilia as we walk away.

"Christ, Cecilia, did you see the way he looked at you? It will make you cry?"

"They're more passionate in Montreal, Alec Le-Loc, remember that. Your dry, pathos-less writing wouldn't actually fly there."

I look back as we move through the groups of teams and see Les still looking at us through eyebrows bushy-grey with suspicion.

We come first to the food in the line. It's catered by a Portuguese Restaurant. I've never seen Portuguese food before. It's all chicken, rice, fish and potatoes. The potatoes are cut into golf-ball sized spheres, and whole chickens roast on a spit above them so that the potatoes bake in the juices.

I say, "It looks good, but I don't think I can eat."

"Because your stomach is rotting from twenty-four hours straight of sipping liquor?"

"You know, I think I actually, really, actually have to sleep before I do anything. How do my eyes look?"

"Oh, here." Cecilia hands me Visine, then uses some on herself. Before we get to the beer spouts we pass a woman in an apron standing at a table of greasy pastry cups filled with custard, and she's blow torching the surface of each. "Portuguese Custard Tarts," she says, passing each of us one without asking.

The crowd is steadily building. There are groups bulging between picnic tables. We walk through them, towards the end where there are less people. The people bulge with movement and cheers. I'm happy for the Visine; my slowness stands out, I can feel it, but nobody takes notice.

We get to the fence opposite the beer and food – a rent-a-fence running between two large Kentucky Coffee trees. I watch the sun flash through the trees' long leaves of mini-leaves, and see that the shadows of all the trees in the savannah-parkland are getting longer. I look around the whole athletes' area and consider if I would ever get involved in dragonboating. But then I think that the real question is could I ever commit dependably to a team. If they paid me then sure, I would never let a job down, but something that's just for fun, I can't see it. And then I question what Spry is. Is she just for fun, or someone I can dependably commit to? I look at the gates expecting to see her. Instead I see Ronny with a package of golf shirts behind him. He looks at me with angry disgust, and I think I would never join a team, no matter how much I was paid, if a guy like that were on it. He's probably never done anything oddball or that carried the risk of embarrassment in his life – just kept it straight and narrow for ever and ever, only so he can lead a package of golf shirts in rounds of group-snickering over anyone they felt superior to.

They sit at Les's table, or at least Ronny does, and Les doesn't look all that welcoming. Kate, Sam, Martyn, Alemu and Spry follow them in and when Ronny catches sight of Kate his face turns red. He starts talking with Les, who's looking around the crowds, trying to be disinterested in whatever Ronny is saying.

Spry comes up to me and I ask if she wants the last bite of custard tart. She takes it and I offer the beer. She drinks it and looks brilliant. I want to give her potatoes baked in chicken drippings, but I don't have any. I ask how Heather is. She says they're trying to get her to go to the hospital for x-rays, but she's arguing with them. Her eyes are so sad when she talks about Heather that it pains me to think about how close her group is. I look at Martyn, and remind myself that I cannot fathom the connection these card players have with each other, and I should respect that.

I give Spry my whole beer because she's thirsty for one, and I don't need it. After a big gulp she says, "This is amazing. We've always wanted to have a drink in here after the races and now we can!" When she drinks from the beer she wraps both hands around the rim like it's the Holy Grail.

Heather shows up: "nobody and no broken bone is stopping me from having my first post-race beer in the athletes' beer garden."

Kate, holding her beer out, says, "You sure? If you need a ringer for that too I'm still available."

Heather elbows her in the ribs. "Hey, why don't we start a team for next year – a Hamilton-Scarborough team."

"Are you fucking serious? I would love that."

"All right, you're the new Eddie – that means you steer and yell a lot."

"And keep you fuckers from playing cards so much, I'm on it."

Cecilia says, "I have to say you chaps paddle with something fierce on your faces. Must be a thrill."

Spry says, "It is! You've got to try it. You should join a team in Montreal."

"I'm not much the team type, and I don't typically join…um…anything, really. You people and your interests, it's like your whole lives are dedicated to extracurricular activities."

Spry erupts into affectionate convulsions of laughter and drops her forehead onto my shoulder – Cecilia really gets her laughing easily, trying or not.

Rory and Damiond find us. They cheers everyone and give the Scarborough Buffs a sincere congratulations. Rory stands next to Sam. "You are paddling in our boat next year. Damiond, you're off the team."

Sam says, "Perfect! That means I can race against Kate, it's like I'll get one weekend a year to get my frustrations out by kicking her butt in a race."

We laugh, Kate shyly, so Sam hugs her.

"Where's Kelly?" I ask Damiond.

"Drinking caesars with the other girls near the water."

I notice Ronny speaking to Les through the crowd. He's complaining, I can tell by the way he's throwing his arms around.

I turn my attention back to Spry, who's talking about the last heat Damiond and Rory raced in. "Fourth place is amazing, and at least you didn't get fifth, this way your placement is legitimate and not just because we let you take that win." She elbows Damiond when she says this.

"Ha—ha. Kelly's sure inspired by our placement. The moment we got out of the boat she started talking about winter training schedules, for us and the Irish half."

Rory says, "Good, that's just great. I'll message her from the pub to say we're keeping up."

Spry finishes her beer and I say let's get another. We walk between the picnic tables and trees. The atmosphere is brilliant, mostly because the tables are alive with chatter and the chatterers glow with post-athletic effort and the kind of satisfaction that comes with accomplishing something that is difficult, but all for fun.

The sun is beautiful at this hour. It has descended to an angle that no longer treats the surface of the earth like a toaster oven, but it's still bright. Its brightness has simply aged, ripened. We stop at the back of the line and I look at Spry. The sun, sitting above my head, is reflecting off her dark eyes. I tell her so and she says she can't see me. So we change places and she says she can see the sun in my eyes now. She bounces in the rays and I grab her hips to keep her still. We move closer, slowly, and I don't remember moving my feet, but I remember her lips, the top one in particular. For a moment her top lip curved between mine, the touch felt faintly.

Chapter Thirty-Seven

2013 – Toronto East (last story written by Alex before leaving Toronto, second draft)

Title: Cecilia

Coast takes the subway to the underground PATH, to one of the many places where the subway intersects with its corridors, to where exiting the subway requires no stairs, just a pass through the doors. Moving briskly, he walks through a number of polished silver doors that separate the webs-of-walkways particular to each office and bank tower, and the webs-of-walkways that connect them. One set of doors leads to a large space where a tailor shop has racks of suites out front, and a suitcase shop has suitcase sets out front, and where there's a bar-lounge and a coffee shop with corridor side patios. The doors at the end lead to another subway station, through which the polished and artistically lit surfaces of the PATH would, if he were to walk through, change back to stained, rusted floors, and walls of a dingy tile in some 70s shade.

Before the station, where Coast first thought there was simply an entrance to the bar lounge, he catches a glimpse of an opening to another space. He turns, walks the thin space, climbs a set of five stairs, and enters another wide corridor. This space almost mirrors the previous one exactly, with the bar-lounge facing here as well, and another coffee shop further on, and a handbag store on the other side, neighbouring a men's shoe store. There's one big difference though – at the centre is a raised fountain made of white marble and framed in limestone rocks. It's not just a fountain, but a long artificial stream. The rocks are interspersed with a beautiful foliage of fake plants and fake moss. It even contains two taxidermized flamencos. Coast circles the fountain a couple times before he walks from the large space into a food court.

The food court is longer than it is wide, more tile and fibreglass than marble and granite, but still glossy and mostly white. It's declared natural by the fake plants hanging from pillars throughout. Usually the food courts are a little difficult for him, as the expanded field of vision and added details, corners, and shadows will raise some slight fear and send him rushing through looking down at the floor. This food court, at least today, raises no fear in him. He attributes this to the social equilibrium. There are twice as many people eating as there are people serving, a reasonable balance. The people behind the counters don't look busy; in fact most are conversing freely with their customers. Those without customers are still occupied enough to fend off boredom, meditatively wiping counters, refilling containers, and monitoring the spaces around them.

At the other end of the food court, Coast turns left and enters an immaculately designed foyer-like expansion. There's a ridiculously long row of bank machines and a ticker screen that lines the wall opposite running stock prices. Although there's no shops or places to eat in this prime PATH real estate, there are security guards standing on the floor, making their presence known. He must be in the central sub-ground section of a bank tower.

He sits on a bench and appreciates the décor: the light fixtures are not just stainless steel, but steel and crystal. The marble and granite, of which there are both, are not faux, but inches thicker than necessary, as is clear by the coldness of the stone to the touch; although the lobby is filled with people, he can't smell a single organic cell, such is the power of the ventilation system. And the décor extends to the people as well, not just the suits, ties, and shoes of the bank employees, who could only be described as shiny, but the clothes of the security guards too.

Coast enters the next subway station he comes to. He sits on a bench in the centre of the platform, contented and drowsy. Some time passes before he notices that no other faces are with him on the platform, or even on the platform across the tracks, and no trains for that matter. Another length of time passes and it's clear there's a delay, but usually that results in a pile-up of people waiting. The complete absence of others has him feeling like there's some piece of information he's unaware of.

The waiting makes Coast feel tired. He leans his head against the tile wall and closes his eyes. For a long while he continues to hear no subway or footsteps, just the sound and echos of the escalators as they hum and occasionally squeak. Unsure of how much time has past, he feels compelled to open his eyes. Immediately he notices something to his left, the direction which the subway should approach from, but it's not the movement of a train. Instead, a bird passes from the darkness of the subway tunnel into the fluorescent lighting of the station.

Her wingspan is the width of a subway car, and the flapping has a deep muffled sound, like a blanket thrown flat over a bed. Even from half a subway platform away, he can see her beak curving down into a large and threatening spike. The bird flaps her wings three times, echoing a deep muffled sound off the tiled walls, and goes into a glide above the tracks. When Coast sees the body, huge and muscular looking, and the stability with which she glides, he knows he's staring at a hawk, but no kind of hawk that he's ever seen. Her feathers are marbled red, brown, black and white, and this look of marbled colouring, and this mass of muscle, is so unlike any city bird he can imagine – pigeon, seagull, crow – that he wonders if he's seeing an escaped bird from the zoo.

The hawk glides by, and Coast looks directly into her black and yellow eye. The eye is so large that for a moment he sees his reflection staring back at him. He becomes completely transfixed by this beautiful bird of prey as she starts flapping again, flying away, the wings inverting and reverting through as much space as a subway train would fill, Coast watching and becoming relaxed like he's in a dream, inverting and reverting, feeling drowsy and trance-like, inverting and reverting, when the metallic rumble and squeals of a breaking train startles him out of his trance by appearing directly in front of him. He flattens his back and arms against the tiled wall, watches the train whip by, and feels the rush of air drawn with it. How did he not hear it approach, did the hawk have him in that much of a trance?

The subway comes to a stop and the doors part. An operator's window in front of Coast slides open and a transit employee leans his head out. He looks both ways along the empty platform, then looks at Coast and says, "Need a lift?" Coast looks to his right, wondering what happened to the hawk, but sees nothing. He is so shocked and confused that he wants to say something to the transit employee, but all he can manage is, "You're late". The man slams the window shut. Before he closes the doors and leaves, Coast boards.

Chapter Thirty-Eight

2008 – Toronto Harbour's West Shore

When we get back to the circle, Damiond's telling the story of how their team started. He and Rory went to school together, George Brown College to be chefs, both of them, and it was there that they first joined a dragonboat team and paddled together. They didn't want it to end, so they recruited enough people from the team to form half of one of their own, and Rory said he'd return with the other half from Ireland. Damiond didn't think he was serious: "I just kept telling Kelly and my friends that this Irish guy was coming to visit and might have some friends with him. I made sure the guys from the school team were still available, and I registered for the race and found out how to rent a boat, just in case, but I didn't expect that he would actually show up with half a dragonboat team. Sure enough they all show up, half a team, each one with a bag and a paddle."

"And you know what Damiond says, the Canuck bastard, just when I'm expecting him to drop to his knees, thrilled that I actually did this? He looks at our paddles and says, Those aren't carbon fibre. Go home!'"

We all laugh.

Martyn cuts in on the laughter and says, "Spry, we shouldn't stay too long, we should hang out with the team."

Spry crouches and screams, "What? It's the beer gardens, we've wanted to come in here after the race for years, it's the dream my friend." She stands stolidly and holds her beer out for a cheers with a rigid arm.

It's agonising to watch him. Martyn hesitates before he cheerses her and releases her back into vibrations of movement and joy, and in that moment I could read his thoughts – he was taking inventory of what Spry is aware of, what she isn't aware of, and how often his reason for suggesting something like not spending too much time in the beer gardens is misunderstood. It's painful to watch because he's the type to take advantage of someone's unawareness to indulge his self-pity. He says, "I'd just feel a lot more comfortable if we were out there…with the rest of the team."

Spry squints at him in confusion, then laughs as she turns her attention back to me.

I believe Martyn could have gone on like that. I could have married Spry and as a courtesy asked him to be my best man (I wouldn't have anyone else to fill the role anyway) and throughout our marriage he would come over to play cards – insisting on bridge of course, finding a way to make some small wins – and still he would have gone on like that, indulging his self-pity in the face of Spry's unawareness of his love. But Cecilia smells that stuff out, and she has her own way of taking advantage of people's blind spots.

She materialises beside Martyn and shakes his hand, "I don't believe we've formally met: I'm Alex's sister, Cecilia. Bravo on today, you were the stars of the show for us."

"It was a good last day of paddling."

"It was particularly a pleasure watching Spry, she's such a lively little thing. They should call you *esprit*."

Spry laughs and paws Cecilia's arm.

Martyn says, "She's a special one," and he even said it like a spotlight staged him and everyone else fell out of earshot for that one sad line. (You fool, a shark just appeared beside you and you're swirling clouds of your own blood around the water for amusement.)

Cecilia says, "And so good she has this team, this group; a gem of a girl like this, with all her adventurous energy. I bet she needs a solid group to keep her out of trouble."

Martyn laughs a laugh of philosophical understanding.

"I mean, backpacking through warehouses and all." Cecilia looks straight into Spry's eyes, which are, for reasons beyond my understanding of how woman see each other, looking back at someone powerful, but benevolent.

Spry says, "Yes, oh yes, for five days." She puts her hand up and splays her fingers; Cecilia high-fives her.

"SP, not the warehouse camping idea," says Martyn.

Cecilia says, "Oh don't worry, Alex is going to go with her."

Martyn looks at me. Cecilia looks at me. "But you're not quite the best at looking out for others, are you, Alex?"

Martyn, now with more disappointment, says, "Spry, don't go to the warehouses. I know what you're going to do, you're going to look for abandoned places to break into and graffiti."

Spry smacks his elbow. "Stop making me sound so petty."

"That's the way your 'street art' will always sound if you don't go to school in September. You've got to settle down."

"Like you?"

"Yes, like me."

"Not like Alex," says Cecilia. "He's what you might call the bad boy in this trio."

Spry, looking at Cecilia with furrowed eyebrows, says, "What trio?"

"She's just saying you should stick with me and not go all bohemian with warehouse trips."

Spry looks at Martyn hard, shocked. She looks at him the way someone who depends an awful lot on their friends looks at one who has just become something else entirely. "Martyn, no."

Him, he smiles, pleasantly, a tinge of fear in his eyes, "No? No what? I'm being annoying. Please, I'm sorry. I'm nagging you. I shouldn't. It's your life, of course, of course. It's just that today's it. This is the end. The finale. And it was good. I pictured this a bit differently. The beer gardens, I pictured the beer gardens differently."

Cecilia says, "We've encroached on your party, maybe."

I rebuke her by pressing down on her toe with mine, hard, but she takes no notice.

Spry says, "Is that true, Martyn? Are they here, and they're not supposed to be?"

Martyn looks down at his shoes. Spry looks angry. She looks like she wants to round house kick him. She turns her back to him, then faces him, then turns her back. I wanted to make this easier somehow, help it end in a not-so-bad way. Is that what I did? Why is it so hard to figure out if your actions come from good intentions or selfishness? "Maybe you should get it out, then it's done, what needs to be said can be said."

I knew Martyn didn't dislike me, it's just complicated stuff. He nods slightly, accepting sage advice from an enemy. "I'm in love with you."

Spry pushes him lightly, "You can't love me. You have to be my friend."

"And I was, for all of high school, right up until the last day."

I can see the weight of Martyn's words fall through Spry like lead. It's heartbreaking. It's heartbreaking even for those of our group that go quiet at the last moment, and don't really know what it's about. It must be heartbreaking even for people too far to hear, their hearts breaking at the mere sight of such a spirited disposition cracking down its centre.

It's quiet, and because it's quiet I'm able to hear Ronny yell at Les "Journalist? The Montreal what? Les, they're not even here for the races, they drifted in last night looking for a bonfire party; they're from Hamilton! They lied to you so they could help out their friends, look, they're with them right now."

Martyn and Spry are still in a heavy silence, hearing nothing, but I'm watching an enraged Les coming towards us with Ronny and another golf shirt right behind them.

Les yells, "You four, you're out of here."

As they walk up to us, Ronny keeps yelling that we fooled Les into thinking we were journalists just to help the Scarborough Buffs.

Cecilia says, "Don't get your haircuts in such a ruffle, it was only a joke."

Kate says, "Yeah, I saw what I saw."

We three stand face to face with them, Cecilia beside me and Ronny in front of her.

Les, coming to a stand-still in front of us, says, "Well that's bad enough, playing me like a fool. I want you guys out of the athletes' area, and you better not come back in that contraption next year."

Ronny yells in Les's ear, "What the hell? Tell them to pay my team our race fee back and kick them out of the whole festival."

Les yells back at him, "Give it a rest, Ronny, you give me a goddamn ulcer for every race you lose, they're leaving, that's it."

Ronny sees a joint that's sitting in Cecilia's ear behind her hair, too hard to see from far, but he's up close. "What the hell is that? Drugs? That's some real trash you let in here, Les."

I say, "Shut your mouth and go to hell."

"Forget this, I'm taking you to the police tent." Ronny grabs Cecilia by the arm, and in his fury he grabs her hard and fast enough to make her yelp. I grab his shirt and slam my forehead into his nose. He stumbles backward. In a shocked moment of silence he brings his hand up to his face and feels the blood spouting from the bridge of his nose. His friend moves toward me, but Rory immediately grabs his shoulders and shoves him into the crowd. Les whistles a screech to the other race officials at his table and waves them over. He points at me and Rory. "You two, you're coming with me, like it or not."

Martyn, only loud enough for us to hear, says, "Over the fence, go!" He pushes me and Rory behind him and gets himself, Alemu and Damiond to the front. "You too, Spry."

"Martyn?"

Alemu, his big arms held up like he's about to ask everyone to take their seats, says, "Fellow athletes, let's discuss this civilly."

Martyn says, "You were a good friend, the best, but I can't…Go with Coast, go!"

Spry turns, squeezing her eyes tight. She grabs her bag and sheathed paddle and tosses them over the fence, then jumps on the fence just as Rory and I, and a little farther down, Kate, Sam and Cecilia, already have. Counter to the impression her light, zealous movements make, it turns out Spry's dense as concrete. I feel the fence reverberate from the shock of her landing and climbing, and see the ends break away from their wedge between the trees. It's a wild clang and crash we make. We all land flat on our faces, and only the absurdness of our buffoonery keeps the athletes too shocked to pile on top of us right there. In the strangest silence of my life, we hop to our feet and get a head start.

Les, the raspy old bulldog – "Get'em!"

Ronny, the golf shirts, Les and Les's crew of officials start the run, but hordes of half-buzzed paddlers spring to foot right behind them.

Kate yells, "Oh my shit, whatdowedo—whatdowedo?"

I keep position beside Spry. Cecilia's just ahead and on the other side of her, closer to Kate, Sam and Rory.

Cecilia says, "You're our resident trespassing expert, don't you have any ideas?"

Spry glances back a couple times, but I'm sure it isn't Martyn she sees behind her, just an angry wave of rowdy athletes. They aren't gaining on us, but…I say, "Guys, we can't get in the canoes and out without them catching up."

Spry collapses into herself, as if breaking as she's running. I want to say something.

Cecilia says, "Kate, seriously, ideas."

Kate says, "Why don't you try your kidnapping story."

They convulse into breathless laughter as we run, and it almost turns to hopeless laughter, but Spry, after a final glance back, speeds ahead and yells, "Scatter! Break right or left and when you reach the shore hard turn back to the canoes – they don't know they're behind those trees."

We scatter and it creates confusion in the mob. They think we'll run along the shore in the directions we've angled at it, and our hard turns back toward the canoes leaves them standing, thinking they have us surrounded. We squeeze between the trees and the water and regroup at the canoe-catamaran.

Kate says, "Spry, you're a goddamn genius."

She unties the rope and we jump in, Spry in the bow seat of my and Sam's canoe, unsheathing her paddle, Rory in Kate and Cecilia's, sitting sideways because of the hammock bed.

Kate says, "Spry, seriously, you are so on our team."

She starts paddling immediately. Our eyes linger on her. Spry doesn't want to talk about teams. She paddles hard. She paddles like someone in very desperate need of a distraction. She puts her right foot forward and her left foot under her seat and paddles on the inside of the canoes. Her back's straight, but she bends at the waist to lean forward and over the gunwales, so the paddle enters and leaves the water far from the canoe. She looks remarkably taller when the blade catches the water. She twists and extends her back and shoulders in an expansive stretch, then it all contracts as she pulls what seems like the whole great lake with her stroke.

Nobody chases us in boats. The mob turns to a deflated audience along the shore. But when we are far from them, clearly in safety, nobody speaks. We all watch Spry, expanding and contracting her whole body, propelling us forward.

From the centre of the canoe I glance at Sam, Kate, Rory, then Cecilia. Their faces are bright with excitement. Laughter and cheers sit below the surface, but they're focused on Spry, on her stroke, which in this moment is a ritual, so we're all quiet for it. I take the opportunity to pull my notebook out and write a few lines about the beer gardens, and to describe Spry's ritualistic paddling.

We leave the islands. We exit through a channel that leads us direct to the edge of the airport's runway. The sun is low, low enough that it's partly behind the control tower and modestly-sized terminal. I look east across the harbour and see a plane descending over the black-tarp mountains. The harbour is full and alive with ferries, freighters, sailboats, boat-taxis and day-cruises. The lights of all the buildings along the skyline are coming on, just barely pushing through the still vibrant light of the sun.

The plane flies above us and the roar draws cheers out of even Spry, breaking our silence. The plane's landing gears screech on the runway and a loud acceleration of the propellers brings it to a halt. Spry spins around with a did-you-see-that expression and Kate and Sam stop paddling. Spry's expression turns apprehensively to something behind us. I turn to look and see the police zodiac speeding towards us from the island.

Cecilia says, "Goddamnit, they actually got the cops to come after us."

Kate says, "Fucking assholes."

They stop beside us and an old cop with an angry face screams, "What the hell do you think you're doing here?"

Sam, after a moment's confusion, answers: "we're paddling to the other side of the harbour."

"You're paddling through the restricted zone, didn't you see the big red signs on those white buoys? You can't be this close to the runway, are you guys drunk?"

"No, no, sorry, it's our first time in this harbour and we didn't see them."

"Well hell, now I'm supposed to tow you to the station and charge you a five thousand dollar fine, this is serious business."

Kate says, "You're not actually going to do that, are you?"

"Do I look like a goddamn trespass cop?" He waits for her to answer, but Kate has nothing but an eruption of laughter in her, and she can barely keep it from bursting out. "Do I? A trespass cop? I've got more important things to do than deal with you. Now get the hell out of the zone, fast!"

Sam, teeth clenched to keep her laugh in, says, "Yeah, okay, we're going."

Chapter Thirty-Nine

2013 – Toronto East (last story written by Alex before leaving Toronto, second draft)

Title: Cecilia

Coast pictures this scene: a metamorphosis and he becomes the hawk, perched just outside the apartment window. Nothing is visible, just rain and white. Dropping off the ledge, keeping his wings tucked in, he dives down twenty-three floors plus the valley wall to the wide open field below. The blur of apartment windows passing fades quickly into the thick rain, and the field appears only just as it's about to meet with his beak. He pushes out his wings, their ridges catching the air, and glides above the field. The field is flooded – a lake, rather than grass; a broad sheet of glass perpetually shattering beneath the downpour.

Where the field meets the creek, the creek bleeds into the field, so it's difficult to see the creek itself. Coast flaps heavy rain soaked wings to the end of the field. Rows of trees reveal the now submerged banks of the creek. He flies between them and above the creek going with the current. The valley walls close in, making the trees of the forested banks visible through the rain. A wall of trees appears ahead, too, and he sees that it's a sharp turn in the valley. He banks with it.

Despite the heaviness of his rain soaked wings, Coast flies with a speed that blurs the trees into a mosaic of grey, green and brown, while staying just above the rushing current. The smell of muddy water is overpowering.

Brown lines ahead…wood two-by-fours crossing the creek…a bridge. A person to the side…a girl, wearing a long, blue terry-cloth dress. Red and white…a lifeguard ring, attached to a rope, held by the girl. Splashing in the centre of the rush…desperate, grabbing, brown hair bobbing at the surface. A miss, and Alex rushes away from the ring and Cecilia.

Coast quickly gains some height then pulls in his wings and bullets towards the desperate splashing at twice the speed of the current, aiming the curved hook of his beak at Alex's neck. He throws out his wings and slows to a hover just above him. The point of his beak jabs down at the skin, but only close enough to pierce his t-shirt from the inside.

Hard, desperate, straining flaps force more air onto the river than rain, making the muddy water push out in ripples. It takes a mountain of effort, but Alex is lifted from the flood. As soon as no part of his body is dragging in the current, Coast banks a turn back to Cecilia, carrying Alex to his distraught sister. Only when he is almost upon the landing at the bottom of the stairs does she see him. She screams at the appearance of Coast the hawk with a body hanging from his beak, but calms when she sees him slowly release Alex to the ground, then disappear into the rain.

COAST WALKS INTO THE HOUSE PERCHED ON A BANK overlooking Taylor Creek Valley and finds Cecilia and Kitty in the kitchen. Kitty's standing near a kettle, waiting for it to boil, and Cecilia's chopping carrots and onions. "Coast, guess what! Guess what!" Kitty yells to him before he even gets in from the front foyer. "The principal just called, Alex is not going to have to repeat grade eight, oh yes!

We're celebrating tonight, I tell you, celebrating with a big meal of, um, Cecilia, what are we eating?"

"Carrots and onions."

Kitty frowns. "Ugh, at least make some rice, and maybe some protein. Cook the chicken fingers in the freezer."

"Frozen food…great," Cecilia says, flashing a look at Coast.

"Not everybody can live off boiled carrots and onions, okay? Anyway; Doug, the principal, said he faced a bitter set of teachers who wanted Alex to stay behind, but he managed to push the trauma argument enough to account for a second academic year."

Cecilia says, "A second year that was academically worse than the first."

"Yes, but the point is he's moving on to high school and in September he will go to class and do, um, do what Alex does."

"…sit at his desk and stare at either a piece of nature crap or some object he picked off a shelf at a store and walked out with. He'll sit there and ignore the teacher. He won't make eye contact with any other kids. He'll freak everyone out by staring continuously at whatever is in his hands."

Kitty throws her hands up at Cecilia and turns away. "Ugh…"

"Dear God Kitty. Listen, I'm happy Alex is moving on; it's great that you pushed the principal to push the teachers. My point is you're not recognizing the real issues…are you listening to me? It's no wonder Doug's battle with the teachers was so bitter, you wouldn't even listen to them on parent teacher night. You drag me along and who ends up keeping the discussions going, asking all the questions? All the while his teachers are trying to explain his absent mindedness to the mother of the child, not me, but you won't even pay attention in those meetings. You're not even paying attention to me…right now."

"You know I don't have time for all this school stuff, okay? Once you and Alex were no longer toddlers I stopped sacrificing the career that supports this family to keep mothering you. If you guys make it to university I'll pay, but that's all I can do, okay?"

"Well that's just it, what if he doesn't make it to university, what if he drops out of high school? Right now all he cares about is that ravine and collecting nature crap to the point of obsessiveness, and an obsessive disorder isn't something you can ignore for the sake of work. We're falling apart here; you may not have noticed it over the last two years, in the two hours you spend away from work to eat dinner with us, but we're falling apart."

Kitty sits on a stool at the kitchen counter which divides the kitchen's sitting area and cooking area. Cecilia stands across the counter from her on the cooking side. Kitty takes a sip of her tea and says, "If there's anything that's fallen apart over the last two years it's this house and our meals. That's what needs fixing, okay? Ugh, how are we supposed to heal when we live in disaster and eat these flavourless dishes? If you want to help us turn a corner I say loosen up, become a little freer with what you do with this house, what you do with our meals. Get some flowers in the gardens and let us, I don't know, sort out ourselves."

"Dear God Kitty, it's always about the house and the meals; what would that really change? Nothing. We would just continue our own downward spirals to...I don't know...you know what I feel like? I feel like everyday this last two years the four of us have drifted further and further from reality. We're all going to become convinced that whatever it is we're collapsing into is normal, and that's when the rest of the world will truly start spinning without us. Do you see this? We are so completely disconnected. It's like we lost what connection we had to a normal life, and that's not something that can heal."

"Um, what we lost had nothing to do with normal. Actually I think what we lost was extraordinarily different, and what made us extraordinarily different. Listen, I agree with you, okay? I have worked more and more this last two years, and Alex has perhaps gotten a little weirder, and Coast you need to start going to your therapist again. But the way you see things, Cecilia, is more to do with this rigid life you expect everyone to live, with this, um, control you want to have over everything.

"Alex will be fine, because now he has the freedom to be who he is and not be stigmatised by being held back a grade. If he hates high school and drops out that's fine, even if he never makes a friend that's fine, because without a stigma put on him, without people determining that he's a failure and abnormal, any decision he makes is at least made of his own free will. And who are we to judge the way Alex wants to live his life?"

"Who are we to judge? You're his mother and I'm the only one that seems worried about what's going to come of this kid. What will he do if he drops out of high school?"

Kitty takes a big slurp of her tea, thinks for a moment, and then says, "He'll become a naturalist. We'll turn the shed in the backyard into a nature hut and he can collect his nature crap and preserve it all in there, maybe he can train in taxidermy and start stuffing animals too. We'll build stairs coming up from the trail by Taylor creek so people can come up to the nature hut and pay to see it by donation. We'll build a second floor so Alex can live above the hut, and if times get tough, he can live off insects and berries, which he may already."

"I don't think naturalist is a profession."

"That's not true. Remember when we rented a cottage up north a few years ago, and there was that shack on the grounds with all the crazy bones and spiders in aquariums and patches of moss and stuffed bats? There was a guy who ran that place – a naturalist. I remember him, he was a professional naturalist and he seemed perfectly at ease with himself. Of course we never paid anything to get inside, and the guy looked old enough to be retired…maybe he was an owner in the cottages."

Cecilia says, "You're not thinking realistically. It's like you think all this nature stuff makes him happy, but he's not happy. What does letting yourself go in a life threatening flood say about your happiness? Suicidal tendencies."

Kitty, shocked, sucks in a breath and plants her fists on the counter, "My baby is not suicidal you cynical little—"

"—Fine, he's just crazy then. Coast: dinner's almost ready, can you call Alex? He should be close."

"I'm right here," comes Alex's voice from just outside the screen door, which is next to the table where Coast sits. He pulls open the door, walks in, and sits beside Coast. Kitty and Cecilia are frozen. He puts a book of black and white photography on the table and starts looking through it, silently. Kitty and Cecilia exchange looks, at a loss as to what to say, and so instead of saying anything, start filling serving dishes with food and doling out the cutlery and plates.

"Kitty," says Alex, not looking up from his book. Kitty quickly comes to the table. "Yes hun?"

"Can I start putting stuff in the nature hut after dinner? I have an insect in my room that would probably prefer it there."

"Of course," says Kitty, flashing a quick look and slight shrug of the shoulders at Cecilia, "and Alex, sorry you heard us talking about you."

After another long silence, Alex, eyes never leaving the book, says, "That's okay, it's not the first time; you guys always talk about me."

Chapter-Forty

2008 – Ireland Park

The cop speeds off and we paddle out of the restricted zone. Spry doesn't paddle. She turns around and looks at me with something like panic in her eyes. She bounces her legs up and down nervously. I move closer to her and put my hands on her knees. She must feel so sad right now, but all I see is fear. Looking deeply into her panicky eyes, I fall in love with her. I've never fallen in love with anyone. But now I understand it, or know why I've never felt it before, it has to come simultaneously with a complete dedication to someone: "Spry, I know how hard losing Martyn as a friend must be. I remember what you said, that you make your own family." I pause, hoping I'm not speaking about this in the wrong moment, that the topic isn't too sensitive, but I want her to know. "Listen, I'm completely here for you. I'm not leaving Toronto, unless you want to, in which case we can both leave and…the point is I'm 100% here for you."

She smiles and covers my hands with hers. There's still fear in her eyes. I realise helping her feel secure again is going to take some time.

Although the airport is detached from the mainland, you have to go to the mainland and take a ferry across the Western Gap to get there (there's no canoe landing, unfortunately). Spry tells us to tie up at Ireland Park.

Rory says, "Is that a joke, you Canuck Bastard?"

"No, you Irish Bastard, look, it's right there."

Ireland park wraps around the narrow south-face and long east-facing side of a complex of abandoned malting towers. The towers stick out from the mainland, so that their east side faces a marina and the rest of the downtown's shoreline, and the north-east corner of the park marks the entrance to the Western Gap.

I say, "We may never have reached the city, but we paddled from gap to gap."

We all climb out and we're immediately confronted with a collection of life-sized sculptures. They're coloured a pukey mix of grey and green. They're emaciated, a child collapsed in a puddle of rags and his own body, and a man reaching bony arms from his rags to the big fucking tower.

Rory says, "A tribute to the famine, of course, that's all anyone here knows about the Irish."

There's a couple walls too, made of grey brick and shaped like walls of a house falling apart, but they look stylish. Beside them is an information screen that nobody bothers to look at.

I say to Rory, as he walks to the east edge of the park, "I know the Irish can paddle a hell of a dragonboat race if you get them drunk enough the night before."

"You know more than most."

Sam gets a call from her dad and she takes it, Kate by her side, listening in. Rory faces away from them, looking out over the harbour. Although there's still daylight to the west, from the east a heavy overcast has closed the sky almost to the city and made the inner harbour darker than night. Swarms of small sailboats are moving towards some point along the city's shoreline, and the lights of the city and the more scattered lights of the East Shore look as if their colour is greying beneath the clouds. Although I can't feel a wind, all the trees along the shorelines of the islands shake beneath the damp grey overcast. The islands do not look like a place you would want to go to.

I walk over to Rory and stand beside him. "Hey, Rory, thanks for intercepting Ronny's friend back there, it was good to have you on my side."

He turns to face me and grabs my shoulders so that I face him. "Say nothing of it."

He turns to face the harbour again. I look back. Sam's finishing up her conversation with her dad. Spry's talking to Cecilia. Their backs are to me, so I only know that Spry is the one talking. She's moving her hands and hanging her head then throwing it back.

I face the harbour with Rory again. This time I can only see the trees, shaking in the wind like they're petrified, the wind that I can't yet feel myself. Kate yells to us and waves us over. As we walk towards them I notice Spry isn't talking to Cecilia anymore; she's staring sadly into the suffering eyes of one of the sculptures.

Sam says, "That was my dad, he's really worried about us. When I told him where we were he said to stay right here, that he's on his way with the boat to grab us and tow the canoes back."

"And isn't that a nice thing for an asshole to do," says Kate.

Sam concedes with a half-smile, then speaks to me and Cecilia, "He didn't have to go to jail, but your folks are long gone. Sounds like this is the last time they'll attempt any reconciliation."

Cecilia looks at me and I shrug my shoulders. She looks away, disappointed, like I should have more of a reaction.

Sam, looking into Rory's eyes, says, "Anyway, time to go to Hamilton." She grabs his hand, like they're already married and she's simply updating her husband on the plan. I'm not sure Rory sees all this so clearly, his eyes are filled with both anticipation and confusion.

Cecilia says to Kate and Sam, "Well kids, it was…a show."

Sam says, "Are you really leaving, Cecilia?"

"Yes, not because I'm not having fun, only because it can't continue."

Kate says, "You never coming back here or what?"

"I wouldn't depend on me for friendly visits, nothing personal, I'm just not the type."

"Cecilia, open your heart," says Sam, "we're your family and we could be your friends."

"Yeah, I'm pretty sure I've seen the worst of you and it's not so fucking bad," says Kate.

"No, you haven't. I like you two, I really do, so I wouldn't put my friendship on you. It only lasts a couple weeks and then it turns to vindictiveness."

Sam says, "But Cecilia—"

"Hey, she's being honest with us. Let's just say goodbye."

Cecilia, after looking into Sam's sad eyes for a moment, says, "You know what, I want you guys to have this."

"Your Paul Brazer DJ shirt, aww," says Sam, taking the shirt from her.

Kate, her face twisted, says, "You can hold on to that, Sam."

Cecilia says, "Okay, well…Oh, awkward hug, thank you Sam, well…Oh, you too Kate, okay, you are an affectionate, um…okay, maybe we'll do a Christmas together sometime."

Sam says, "Yes! Okay, you can go now."

Cecilia says to me, "Walk with me to the ferry?"

A path on the other side of the grey-brick walls leads to the end of a road where taxicabs line up. The terminal for the ferry is on the other side of the road. We stop before we reach it and stand at the edge of the gap. A yacht is passing through to the inner harbour, its lights on, guiding it through the dusk. The sunlight is almost completely gone and the overcast hangs very low and opaque over the inner harbour right up to the malt tower. We say nothing at first. We can't see the runway on the other side of the gap, just the terminal and the control tower, but we hear the twin propellers of a passenger plane roar to life. A moment later the plane takes off to the west, away from the harbour.

Cecilia says, "Well you certainly know how to lead an exciting adventure. Your book may turn out all right after all. I'll keep an eye out for it. May I suggest the pen name Alec Le-Loc. I think it gives you—"

"I want to tell you about something, but first I have to apologise for—"

"No need, your act of valency on my behalf is apology enough for your little stunt, and anyway, like I said, this trip—"

"No, no, no. Not that. For taking off out West when you had to stay behind another year. For not knowing anything about you in Montreal. I worry, Cecilia, and I feel like hell that I let us get so distant."

"I had a feeling your kidnapping stunt had some ambition behind it."

"I guess, I don't know. But yeah, I want to be closer with you."

"And Mum and Dad?"

"Cecilia, come on, it is what it is with them."

"You think I was upset after you left over being the only one there, with them? You're wrong. I was upset, but only because I knew this meant we weren't going to have much of a family from then on. I'm sorry if you thought you could pick me out of your past and make something of us, but it doesn't work that way."

The overcast is above us, the sky completely dark, and I feel the wind, feel the bite of dampness in it.

"You can't decide we need to be closer, that we're going to be a family, that you're going to foster some concern for my well-being, but continue to see our parents as something completely unimportant. If you came here to make peace with all of us, to bring us all closer together, that would be something. Alex, the only reason I came to the reunion was because I thought maybe something like that might happen. But this, the choices you're making, it doesn't work. I don't work in this…"

She stops, frustrated that I'm not getting it. I say, "Cecilia, I don't…but listen: I'm in love with Spry."

"Oh God Alex." She looks away and puts her hand to her eyes.

"It's not foolish, it's real. And maybe up until today I didn't know how to show concern for anyone, but now I do because for the first time I love someone and—"

"Stop it," she says in a choked whisper.

"Starting tonight, I'm spending everyday for the rest of my life with—"

"Put this thing on pause. You're too messed up right now. Go back to Hamilton with Kate and Sam and Rory. Be with them and get some sleep."

"Put this thing on pause? Aren't you listening? I'm in love. Okay, it sounds foolish because it's me, and I'm talking with you, so all the context is there. And yeah, this is the kind of thing we once laughed at as kids, like church, behind Mum's back; we just laugh at all this stuff, right?" I stop, not because I think Cecilia has something to say, but because I'm trying to interpret her expression – sad, maybe nostalgic. Does she miss our childhood, the good parts, as much as I do? Maybe, but we'll work on us, we'll get it back. I move on: "But this is real."

"No, this is messed up. Think of everything we just went through, without a moment of sleep or sobriety. Put this on pause and go back to Hamilton."

"I'll…I'll talk to Spry and see what she thinks about Hamil—"

"No, decide right now that you're putting this on pause and going back to Hamilton with Sam, Kate and Rory."

I watch a sailboat, sail down, putter past us, and another not far behind. To the west I see a plane approaching, its light so bright and wide it looks like liquid. I feel a wave of disorientation, and hope the sleep deprivation isn't completely killing my understanding of what's happening around me.

"You think I'm not concerned about Spry losing Martyn's friendship right now. That's it, you see me excited about her and not aware that she's hurting. But that's not true. I am aware. I'm not going to say any of this to her tonight. I'm just going to comfort her. And Cecilia, I'm going to be good for her. You'll see. You'll see when we come to see you in Montreal."

She's still looking away from me when she says, "How long do you think we've been standing here? My perception of time is completely off."

"Ten minutes, maybe."

Cecilia looks east down the gap towards Ireland Park. With an air of detachment, she says, "That sounds about right." Then she snaps out of something and turns to face me, arms folded. "Goodbye, Alex."

"Yeah, okay, I guess…bye, Cecilia."

She turns and walks to the ferry terminal. I stay at the edge, watching a few more sailboats return to the harbour, watching the ferry cross the gap to our side, watching all the natural light drain from the world. What the hell is wrong with Cecilia? She's left me feeling so cold and chaotic. There must be something going on in Montreal. She's going through something and needs help. I can see it all. This thing I have with Spry, it makes her feel like I'm even less of a possible help to her than ever. But Spry and I are the solution, she'll see. We'll go to Montreal, and then she'll have us to help her through…

I turn and walk away, but not back to Ireland Park, inland until I reach the road that runs behind the malt towers. There's a community centre at the back of the towers with a big and well lit plaza beside it. The plaza has multiple layers connected by stairs and ramps and it all looks nicely made. There's no grass at all, just a couple planters. The bottom layer against the road is a basketball court. I sit down at a bench somewhat distant from it with my notebook and write a description of the game. It's a pick-up game, I can tell because there are guys of all ages, and no one's yelling names, so they must be strangers to each other. There's enough players to form full teams and there's guys on the side lines.

It's also busy on the sidewalk, and along the dedicated bike lanes that run in front of the courts. Cyclists and runners pass regularly, head-lights and tail-lights beaming from the cyclists, and beaming back from reflectors worn by the runners. Many groups, mostly teenagers, are hanging out and talking beneath the lights of the plaza up from the courts. Across the road is a large red brick building of about five stories and with enough satellite dishes on its roof to identify it as a television station. This feels like a big city. I'm getting excited. Spry's going to show me so many amazing places, and we'll find so many amazing places together. I'm overwhelmed by my feelings for her again, and the oddness I felt after saying bye to Cecilia is fading.

The question is what should I do for Spry? She's really hurting, and in a way I can't understand. But somehow I have to make her feel secure, something I've never done for anyone.

Beside the road with all the taxis there's a tree that's dropped a large branch. The branch is cut up into small pieces, but nobody has taken the pieces away yet. I'll go grab an armful of wood and we'll have a bonfire all night in Ireland Park. We'll talk things through and fall asleep. It might rain, but if it does we'll break into the malt towers, maybe take the fire inside them. No, that would burn them down.

My thinking's not great right now, but I'll still grab some logs for a fire and hey, it's a start. I don't know why Cecilia thinks I should go back to Hamilton with Sam, Kate and Rory, she's simply not making any sense. So I forget about Cecilia, grab some wood, and go to help Spry.

Chapter Forty-One

2013 – Toronto East (last story written by Alex before leaving Toronto, second draft)

Title: Cecilia

Corridors and corridors, retailers and restaurants, travel agents and dentists, granite and marble, benches and fountains, kiosks and coffee, corridors, corridors, corridors. Corridors, Coast realises, are his rabbit hole. With only two directions anything could come from, they never raise The Fear in him, even when flooded with people. Here crowds are a comfortable buffer around him, and he likes to people-watch, likes to sit on a bench or stand in the centre of a floor and watch the river of people pass him. He imagines what their universes are like, what the confines are, where their walls are built. Over time, in a collective kind of way, he has built a conceptual understanding of the landscapes beyond his own universe in the faces of the underground crowds. He has built it by reading what they must have seen – the contours, slopes and depressions of the world's places in the contours, slopes and depressions of their faces.

Coast is in the PATH at that moment when the office towers flood the pathways to condos and subway stations with home-bound commuters. He stands in the centre of a dense population that moves like a river, observing something in the faces that pass him: a lady in her fifties, blonde, has lines on her forehead from a day of furrowing her eyebrows; a man, young, early twenties, has an intimidating look on his face, but one that seems intended for somebody in his memory rather than anyone here; another man is speaking on the phone as if he's angry, his voice wanting to rise, but his words are kind, are words that don't want the voice that's expressing them; and a woman, mid-thirties, beautiful, dressed elegantly, has a look like she's sick of people noticing, eyes that seem to search for the most distant place possible.

Coast deduces precisely what's causing every one of these bad moods, the one thing that can bring distance to the face of an entire city – a day of gloom and rain. He walks to a set of escalators and, sure enough, sees crowds descend from the surface with wet shoulders, umbrellas in their hands, and soggy hair sticking to their foreheads. Then he sees something else descend from the rainy surface, but above the heads of the rain soaked crowds.

"The hawk," he whispers. As soaked from the rain outside as the pedestrians, the hawk dives down towards him and banks around the back of his head. He spins around, keeping his eyes on the mass of feathers, and sees the same pattern of marbled red, brown, black and white he saw at the subway platform. He follows, hustling through the crowds, catching glimpses of her as she rounds corners in the corridors, until she gets further ahead than he can see.

After hustling through a number of crowded turns and straight stretches, devoid of the hawk, he steps into a corridor empty of commuters, one that's not joined with the main commuter paths. The corridor dips and curves so that as he walks deeper in he can only see a short distance ahead. The pink granite wall to his left is embedded with display cases. With each successive case – displaying jewellery, then shoes, then watches, then wallets, then bags, then ties – the corridor descends three steps, curves slightly, descends three steps, curves slightly, and so on until Coast can no longer see the commuter crowd behind him; the sounds of their footsteps replaced by silence.

In the emptiness he feels he has lost the hawk for good, so he stops and stares into a case filled with ties, considering which he would wear if he were to ever wear a collared shirt. There's a sound, an echo of a flap like a blanket thrown flat, and the hawk appears from the direction he came from. She glides down and banks towards him around the bend in the corridor. As the heavy wings beat out a series of flaps directly in front of Coast, he gets another perfect view of the marbled red, brown, black and white pattern on top, the colours zigzagging through the feathers in the strangest mix of lines.

The hawk flies to where the corridor straightens out and exits into a high traffic walkway bordering a half-moon food court. He follows and joins the walkway, and as the movement of the crowd carries him towards an exit at the opposite end, he sees that the hawk is following the circumference of the half moon space. She's in a slow glide, flapping only once every few seconds above the heads of people waiting in long lines at the restaurants. Her flight is so slow and silent, and her red and white blends in so well with the lights, tiles and multi-coloured plastics that make up the landscape, that no one seems to notice. The hawk's head shifts and her eyes wander around the space looking for the exit, until they look directly at Coast, just as he reaches the doors. With a few hard flaps the hawk flies over his head at a speed that has him twisting, almost falling, as he attempts to keep his eyes with the blur.

The blur tucks in her wings and bullets through the gap in the doors above the heads of the crowds passing through. He moves through the doors and finds himself in the familiar corridor with the luggage store, bar-lounge, and long fountain-river with fake plants, moss and flamingos down the centre. The corridor that mirrors this one on the other side of the bar lounge is clearly the commuter path, because this space is sparsely populated.

He walks slowly, thinking he has lost the hawk again, but after walking a short distance along the fountain he sees her perched on a branch of a fake tree. He just stands for a moment, transfixed by the hawk. She looks at him curiously, opens her beak, and then closes it again. Tentatively, he walks right to the tree, with the hawk perched only just above his head. He looks closely at her, the pattern of red, brown, black and white in her feathers, the reptilian skin around her talons, the sharpness of the beak at its point, and the yellow and black eyes, which Coast again sees himself in.

He slowly reaches his hand towards the hawk. The hawk again opens her beak, so he pauses, but continues when the beak closes. He opens his hand and reaches for the marbled feathers, but just as he reaches only a few inches away the hawk opens her beak and lets out a piercing cry. He startles backward, then notices a mother with a toddler close by, and hears the toddler begin to cry. The mother looks at Coast with a terrified expression. "Oh…I…that wasn't…." he mutters, but they rush off down the pathway before he can point out the hawk.

Coast hears a shaking of the entire fake tree and the heavy flap of the hawk's wings. She flies away, towards the doors, and bullets through to the other side just as an unsuspecting pedestrian walks through them. He pursues, but, in the wide corridor of retail spaces on the opposite side of the doors, he is confronted by a river of commuters moving in the opposite direction of the hawk's flight.

He tries to move against the river of people, but there's just too many flooding the corridor from escalators and pathways adjoining at the sides. The movement of commuters is slower at the edges where they merge, but heavy and quick in the centre where he attempts to walk against the current. He's a boulder slowly rolling down-river during an up-river salmon swim. He relents. Now he's a pillar that does not move, the commuters separating only just as they reach him, their footsteps echoing quietly, but so numerously they sound like a rainstorm.

The hawk flies above their heads, red and white tail feathers shrinking into the tiny space at the end of the corridor. Once the hawk disappears from his vision, Coast lets go and floats with the current to the subway station.

Chapter Forty-Two

2008 – Back to Hamilton

I get back to the park with an arm full of wood. Rory, Kate and Sam are standing near the edge of the gap waiting for Jake's boat to appear. I put the wood down in the centre of the pile. Nobody comments; my building a bonfire is not extraordinary to see anymore. "Hey, where's Spry?" I walk to the other side of the towers and look down the park, then I walk back to them. "Did she break into the malt towers or something?"

Sam's about to say something, but she stops when Rory steps ahead of her. "She's gone, Coast."

"What? Is she coming back, or am I supposed to—"

"She left, brother, she's gone now."

"Did she say…" I don't bother finishing the question. It doesn't matter what she said. I run to the pile of logs and kick them hard into the fence. They ricochet off and leave it rattling.

I stare up at the sand coloured concrete of the malt towers for a long while. There's many sections broken away leaving concrete holes. They expose criss-crosses of rebar that look like criss-crosses of exposed bone and ligaments in a wounded leg. I hear a motorboat slow to a stop behind me. When I turn around Jake is out tying the boat to the wall. He doesn't say anything at all, and he doesn't acknowledge anyone around him. It's like he's just doing a job, and Kate, Sam and Rory have not stopped paying attention to me.

I walk up to them. "Well, it was a good trip."

Kate says, "Shut-up and get in the boat, Coast."

I look along the shoreline, the city shoreline, this massive downtown I've never been to, even though I've circled its perimeter from the water. I could easily be homeless here, living on the shores, around fires, and whatever happens happens.

I say, "Guys, thanks, but I…"

Sam says, "Coast, just get in."

Jake's finished tying the canoes to a tow rope and he's getting back in the boat. He never took notice of anything anyone said. I look back at the airport and think about what Cecilia said – *how long have we been standing here?…that sounds about right*. It turns out between the two of us she's the only one that was able to help Spry. *Decide now to put this on pause*…and save yourself the rejection. I'm not mad at her, embarrassed mostly.

I look at Rory. "I've got to go, budd—"

"Not now, not ever, hop in, brother." He says that while firmly grabbing my shoulder where it attaches to my neck.

Kate says, "Come on, Coast, get in."

What's the difference if I wander off into Hamilton instead of Toronto? None, I get in the boat. We all climb in. Sam stands next to Jake at the cockpit, her hands braced on the dash. She tells him to go out of the Eastern Gap so she can show him the way we came in. He doesn't respond, but powers up the boat and heads east along the downtown's shore.

Kate sits in the shotgun seat beside Sam, and I sit behind her on a bench seat running along the starboard side. Rory sits down last. He sits directly across from me, and rests his elbows on his knees. "You'll be alright, brother."

I can't speak, so I try to focus on the shoreline passing behind him. Funny thing is, I can't. Jake isn't driving all that fast, either, but I can't focus on any of it. There's lights and lots of people walking along a promenade. I can't focus on any individual, but I can see the blurred patterns of shirts and hair in the streaks of lights. At one point a big thick streak of yellow waves goes by, and I guess that the waves are a collection of beach umbrellas. There's cars farther back and I see streams of light that must have come from cyclists' head-lights and tail-lights. When we pass another marina the sailboats' masts fill the background like a crazy scribble. I can see the raised highway when there aren't any buildings in front of it, a thick green steel line with streaks of white and red lights from the cars on top. When we get to the centre of the skyline I see the tower and look up. The overcast hides most of it, the upper-lights illuminating a glowing circle through the clouds.

Rory says, "You're going to pull through, brother."

My thoughts are erratic. I just want to feel sad, that seems the right thing to feel, but my mind won't let me focus on any one state of being. Spry's gone. Your mother and father don't know anything about you. Sooke is a better place for fires than Victoria – less people. I picture a bear with its mangled paw in a bear trap. I imagine myself throwing up over the boat. How funny would it be if I sat back and enjoyed the lovely scenery. Spry left. I should punch Rory for saying that. I visualize myself in a great rage, throwing everyone from the boat and stealing it, then speeding to the American border screaming "I'm a bomb" until their coast guard hears me. I'll steer straight for the biggest boat and scream until I fall into the scope of a rifle, beneath the crosshairs. I want to live alone, beneath crosshairs.

I can't focus on the background, but Rory is perfectly clear. He reminds me of those scenes in movies when the patient wakes up slowly and sees an angelic nurse's face, but everything else in the background is still an incomprehensible mess. That's the way Rory is looking at me though, like I'm a patient who could pass out again at any moment, or a drunk who could fall into traffic, or a fool who could throw himself off a boat. Nevertheless, he's all that will come into focus, so I meet and hold his eyes. He keeps turning his head to the back of the boat, then to me, then up front, then to me, and I just hold his sharp image.

I feel myself take a deep breath, and it feels like I've been holding my breath this whole time and just now letting air in again. Rory is watching me less, and he seems relieved, as if the patient can now be moved out of ER at least.

We come to the East Shore and the sounds around me start to come into focus. I realise Sam has not stopped talking to Jake this entire time. Jake doesn't say a word, and he doesn't turn his head when Sam points to where the night market was, or when she points to the black-tarp mountains, but he nods, a slow, heavy nod. Then he pulls out a pack of rolling tobacco and Sam immediately grabs it from his hand and rolls a cigarette for him.

Kate has put her foot up on the side of the boat. Her head is leaning back over the chair and her eyes are closed, but she isn't sleeping; every time her name is mentioned by Sam she turns her head.

I try to focus on the East Shore. It's brighter than it was last night, the lights reflecting back down from the heavy overcast. But still they are greyed, blurry and greyed. I don't want to think of her. Embarrassment and loneliness are such a horrible combination.

We pass through the gap and it begins to rain, lightly. None of the passengers care, but a drop puts Jake's cigarette out. He says "Ah fuck" and throws it into the lake. Sam gives him an earful over it and he smiles for the first time.

Then it's quiet.

Rory says, "It's not good to isolate yourself when you're hurting. You think it is, because nobody else has to be bothered by it. But everyone's hurting sometime or another, usually once a day, and when you're off by yourself there's always people, your people, picturing you out there" (he turns his head to the black, muted lake) "alone."

I still can't talk, but I think of Cecilia, how worried I always am about her, even though I know nothing about her. Sam looks back at Rory and smiles. He seems to want to say something to her, but can't find the words. Jake keeps a relatively slow pace. I want my mind off Spry, I can't think about people that are no longer here, that can only leave a gap in my mind. Even dead people can't do that. Someone dies and you know what they were like when they died so they hold a perfectly comfortable and real place in your mind from then on. But when someone leaves your life, but goes on living, they immediately become someone different, and someone you will never know, and that leaves a gap in your mind – that's loneliness, the worst kind.

So I focus on Rory, who's having a stream of thoughts rushing through his head, I can tell, all related to the people very present in his life, newly present. He sits with his elbows on his knees and his hands folded together. He looks between his legs, to the back of the boat, then to Sam with a big smile, then to me where the smile releases, and he repeats that sequence over and over, until he pushes himself up high by planting his hands on his knees. "Sam, I want to tell you something, or ask you something, um, too, I think. I want to ask what you think of, if I cancelled my flight back to Ireland, um, for you. Or, I mean, don't worry, I've got a work visa here. I didn't know if I'd use it, if I'd want to stay in Toronto, I'm not even sure why I got it, maybe because I get laid-off every other week in Ireland, and because I could and my friend…anyway, I like you Sam! A lot. I hope you don't mind me saying that in front of your father, but it's important. You know, that I want to stay, for you! So it's out of respect, or—"

Kate, her head still leaning back over the seat and her eyes still closed, says, "Shut the fuck up, Rory. We're taking you back to Hamilton with us, you're obviously not flying back anywhere."

"Oh." (Sam never stops staring straight ahead, but I can see the corners of her lips and eyes shining.) "Okay then."

Rory sits back, elated, arms stretched along the sides of the boat. He smiles at me. "Hey, Coast."

I wait for him to continue, then finally ask, "Yeah Rory?"

He looks to the back of the boat, then back to me, beaming his smile. I don't know how, but the joy that this guy's feeling, so completely opposite to the emptiness I'm feeling, is floating across the boat from him to me. I don't like it. "Rory, what?"

He looks to the back of the boat again, then to me and he shakes his head, pointing his palms up, as if he doesn't know the answer to the question. In spite of myself, I laugh. Rory's confusion and elation make me laugh. I hate it. "Rory, please, what's on your mind?"

He finally calms himself down. He leans forward on his knees and folds his hands. "It's just…it's funny how we come to know our people, don't you think?"

He holds my gaze. Kate and Sam look back at me, expectantly. Jake, acknowledging any of us for the first time, looks back too, interested as everyone else in my response.

My eyes turn to the back of the boat. We're passing the lighthouse. The skyline is dim and grey beneath the very low overcast that has enveloped the tower. A light appears from behind the island, from a twin-propeller passenger plane, then disappears into the clouds.

I blink at Rory through dried tears. "Rory, you're funny…you're alright. Hey Kate, what do you think of this guy?"

Kate, incredulous, says, "If you're okay with him, Coast, then we're all fucked."

Chapter Forty-Three

2013 – Toronto East (last story written by Alex before leaving Toronto, second draft)

Title: Cecilia

Over the last two years most of the space in the house has degraded to somewhat of an organised disaster. All the non-essential rooms are covered in piles: piles of books, magazines and piles of newspaper; piles of gardening equipment, art pieces and piles of craft supplies; piles of floor mats, baskets and piles of pots; piles of pillows, sheet sets and piles of blankets. There are many piles of shoeboxes: some are filled with screws, piping and old burnt out light bulbs and batteries; some are filled entirely with recipes on cards. There are piles leaning against the walls: paddles, skis, ski poles, camping equipment, exercise equipment, inflatable pool things (though strangely there's no pool in the backyard) and unused furniture. Some of the furniture still has the plastic and Styrofoam packaging from the store, never removed, as the furniture was purchased by Kitty, but not actually placed somewhere by Cecilia on the ever shrinking floor space.

The piles fill all rooms except the ones Cecilia fights them back from: the kitchen, laundry room, bathrooms and bedrooms. The dining room, living room and hallways are all a maze of piles. The attic is Kitty's private office. Nobody but her knows what state the piles are in up there, but it's presumed critical. Kitty has purchased shelving for Cecilia to put together, but Cecilia refuses, preferring to maintain only her chosen rooms. Even the old shelving, through spontaneous deconstruction, has begun to form its own piles.

The pile rooms are a good example of why Coast's diagnosed phobia is not quite accurate; nothing in the house can count as an open space, yet the details, corners and figure eight paths that are littered through the pile rooms feel equivalent to some panoramic views.

Coast is standing outside a pile room with Kitty, listening to Cecilia toss objects onto piles. Cecilia had called Coast earlier: "Come over. It's Alex. He's…I've asked Kitty to come home from work too. You guys need to…just come over."

Kitty walks into the room. "Okay, we're here; I don't know what you're freaking out about, but I had to cancel two meetings this afternoon. So what is it, and what are you doing in this decrepit space?"

"I'll show you." Cecilia leads Coast and Kitty to the backyard. "Remember your great idea about Alex becoming a naturalist, the one he overheard?" Kitty shrugs. The grass is littered with objects from the shed. "He's emptied the entire thing" – Cecilia snaps her eyes to Kitty – "to make way for his nature hut."

Kitty laughs. "Wow, he's really serious about this."

Cecilia doesn't laugh. "Come on, this is too much. Talk to him."

Alex appears from the shed with an aquarium and walks to the border of the forest. He walks along the edge, inspects small branches and leaves, then breaks one off and puts it in the aquarium.

Kitty says, "Hey kiddo."

"Hi."

"I hope you're not taking what I said about becoming a naturalist too seriously, you can't actually spend the rest of your life in the shed."

"I know, but I'm still going to use it as a nature hut, not to show people from the trail like you said, but just for fun."

While Alex adjusts the sticks and leaves in the aquarium, Kitty shrugs at Cecilia, silently communicating a *why not, what's the big deal?* Cecilia, in response, widens her eyes, drops her jaw, and with her hands motions a *can you please keep talking to him.* Kitty points her palms upward and, through furrowed lips and eyebrows, expresses, *what do you want me to say to him?* Cecilia throws her hands out in an *I can't believe you,* points at him, then circles her finger next to her temple. Kitty sucks in a breath and covers her mouth in shock, then puts her fists on her hips and scowls a *he is not crazy.* Alex suddenly turns away from the forest, and just as suddenly both Cecilia and Kitty drop their hands to their sides and look casually away from each other.

After Alex walks back into the shed, Cecilia whispers, "You know we'll never see him now. He'll either be down in the creek or in the shed. Basically you've told him he can become as reclusive and weird as he wants, and that that's okay."

"You have such a narrow perspective on everything. Alex is just trying to be comfortable and enjoy the places he spends time in. If that house wasn't such a disaster he probably wouldn't need the shed."

"Dear God Kitty, please stop complaining about the house. The house is just a house, let it be; I'm talking about a living breathing person who you should, according to evolutionary theory, have more interest in."

"I'm not telling him he can't have his nature shed, okay? You know I can't be mean to Alex, and anyway it will be easier to talk about him if he's out here all the time."

"Fine! But since this was your idea in the first place, you have to help move all this stuff on the lawn…Don't look at me like that. I'm not doing this by myself. You're helping me move this stuff into the house and onto the piles."

"Me? Ugh…you can't be serious, those pile rooms drive me nuts."

"Those pile rooms are necessary for all the meaningless, useless, unusable crap that accumulates around here, most of which comes from you or your ideas, case in point," says Cecilia, picking up a load of items littering the backyard. The shed is no small structure, and it was full of items. Almost every object was purchased at auctions, some for use, but many as decorative antiques. So along with a lawn mower there's a scythe; along with tool boxes full of bolts and screws there are old jars full of hardware unrecognisable to Coast; along with spring loaded hedge clippers and pruners there's an array of curved knives wrapped in oak handles; and along with the paint cans, gas canisters, and clay pots are old pop bottles, rusted signs, and out-dated garden sculptures.

After Cecilia and Kitty walk into the house with their arms full, Coast walks into the shed to see what now fills it. The inside has changed dramatically. There are only a few things he recognizes from before: work tables at the back and to his left, benches in front of both, the large stump cut to be a circular table to his right, and a pull string light hanging in the centre. The work tables, window sills above them, and stump are all covered in rocks, oddly shaped roots, bones, pressed flowers, dead butterflies, dead beetles, and aquariums filled with living plants, mosses and insects.

There's even more hanging from the rafters: a collection of skulls and bones, which has Coast pausing at the door until Alex grabs his hand and leads him to the table. "Look at this. There has to be fifty different kinds of mosses here. Get close, then you can see all the different kinds. You have to get right down and look at all the tiny stems sticking up from the green parts, or look right at the green stuff and see how many parts there are to each tiny piece. See how different they all are? You don't, that's okay, but if we could shrink to microscopic size the differences would be so obvious because it would be like looking at trees."

They move along. "Look in this aquarium. See all those cocoons? Each one is going to become a different kind of butterfly. Each time I found a different caterpillar I put him in a container with some leaves and a branch and waited for him to cocoon. Who knows what they'll think when they turn into butterflies and find themselves in a tank with a bunch of strange species, but it will be interesting to watch.

"These eggs were still in this robin's nest when I found it, but the eggs are completely empty. They all have tiny holes in them, so something came and sucked the yoke right out."

Then Alex draws Coast's attention to the mobiles. This is the spookiest part of the shed, as most of the mobiles are skulls.

Alex says, "I don't know how to identify most of this stuff, but I don't think it matters. What matters is noticing the particular details to each one. I like this one because of the fangs, it must have been a killer. All the small ones on that string are flat, so I think they must be salamanders or snakes, and these are either chipmunks or squirrels, or muskrats. It's easy to tell which skulls are birds, and there's one that I can identify because it's just so obvious. See the really big bird skull hanging above the stump? It's a hawk, you can tell by how the beak turns down into that point; that's how it rips open prey. Anyway, it's not just a hawk, it's a red tail. You know it's a red tail just by how big it is. They're the biggest anywhere in the city, but I bet most people have never noticed one."

Coast is mesmerised by the skull. "I've seen one."

"What? Where have you seen one?"

But he's suddenly self-conscious about saying the PATH. Thinking about the hawk, a bird that spends most of its time high above the city, while standing with Alex, who spends every day outdoors, he starts to wonder whether what he saw was even real. "It's hard to explain exactly where," says Coast, "but Alex, why are all these skulls hanging from the ceiling?"

"Oh, let me show you." Alex drops the wood board shutters for each of the windows latched up inside the shed so that the inside goes completely dark. Coast hears him stand on a chair, then hears the jingle of the pull chain light. The light turns on and casts shadows of the skulls across the walls and table. Even the insects seem to pause for a moment at the sight.

Seeing the shadows of bird skulls all over the walls, most notably of the red tail hawk's, motivates Coast to ask about the flood. He tries to think of the best way to approach the subject with Alex, which in itself is hard, because he's never approached a difficult subject with him before. He decides to take the direct route. "Cecilia told me about the flood."

Some silence follows, then much silence follows. Alex picks up a piece of slate and starts turning it in his hands, and Coast understands that he didn't exactly ask a question. "Maybe you want to tell me what happened…just because Cecilia…um…seems upset."

Alex walks over to the aquarium with the stick insect inside and tries to feed him leaves. "The water was brown, really dark like mud, and it moved so fast there were whirlpools, big ones and small ones, appearing and disappearing everywhere. They kept appearing and disappearing all over the creek, which was really more like a river at that point. The whole park and valley was like some fantasy water world. We've never had rain like that before, and so, well, I'll tell you what happened:

"I walked onto the bridge, leaned on the railing facing upstream, and watched the rush come towards me. When the water reached the top of the banks it started coming in these wide sheets, sheets that covered grass on the sides, sheets that flooded between the trees. The sheets hit the bridge and splashed up in a big wall. It's crazy to look back on now, but for some reason, at the time, I wasn't scared at all. I crouched down, grabbed the handrail, closed my eyes, and let it all flood around me; the water felt so warm and so fast. Then it got higher, more powerful, and I had to hold on stronger to keep from going with it. But then this thought hit me, where does the water go?

"It joins with the Don River, then it joins with the lake, then it drifts out to the islands. I saw myself floating to the Don, then to the lake, then to the islands, and for some reason felt like, 'Yeah, that's exactly what I should do.' It was like the creek convinced me to go with it, so I let go.

"When Cecilia yelled and I saw her throw the life ring, I got scared all of a sudden, like she suddenly woke me up to the real world, so I swam for it and got out."

Coast walks up to the skull of the red tail hawk, spins the mobile with his finger, and says, "I can't believe you weren't scared to let go."

Alex, still holding a leaf near the stick insect, says, "There's an encounter I've never told anyone about: an encounter with a wolf in the city. It happened one time when I walked Taylor Creek to the Don Valley, so I'd get in trouble if Cecilia or Kitty knew. No one believes there's wolves in the city anyway. They'd think it was just a coyote, but I know the difference.

"It was right where Taylor Creek joins the Don River. She was as tall as me, and she was panting so I could see her fangs. I was scared, but I just kept sitting where I was, frozen. She walked to the edge of the stream, right across from me, and sipped from the water. Then she sat down and just stared at me, just sat and stared for probably an hour.

"I never moved, at first because I was frozen, but slowly that went away. She never looked at me aggressively, but always with drowsy eyes, like animals do when they feel comfortable with you. Slowly I started to feel comfortable too." Alex drops the leaf and raises his eyes to Coast.

"That was the same day as dad's funeral, after we got back. It was dusk. It's strange when you lose your fear of something that could so easily kill you, when you become calm in a situation that is supposed to make you afraid. I haven't been scared of much since then. That's what animal encounters do, they change people."

"You can say all this to Coast, but you can't tell me anything," says Cecilia, appearing at the door.

Alex startles at her voice, but quickly looks away from her; he walks to a table with some larger rocks on top and inspects them with his eyes and fingers, turning his back to Cecilia.

Cecilia shakes her head. "I should've let you go."

"You don't mean that," says Kitty, appearing behind Cecilia. "Listen, I have to go back to work. Those pile rooms are driving me nuts, okay?...I have to go." She turns and walks away from the shed. "You're going to have to finish this on your own, I have to go. I'll see you at dinner."

Chapter Forty-Four

2013 – Leaving Toronto (segments from Alex's present-tense-journal, final entry)

I'm on the subway, returning from the warehouse wastelands of Kipling (the furthest stop west), where I picked up my new phone, but I can't switch it on because I need a charged phone today.

I grabbed all I wanted from my apartment (nothing more than what I'm carrying), called junk-removal for the rest, and now I'm back on the subway, heading to Union to catch a train out of the city, out of the province. What a crazy day. Hope I remembered everything. Beside me is my wheeled-luggage-bag with a duffle bag strapped on top, and I'm wearing my backpack.

I'm excited, but my head is spinning, and I'm feeling vulnerable to absent minded travel errors. An infinitely delayed reconstruction plan has made Union Station the largest, craziest construction zone ever for running around, trying to find the elevators to platform twenty-four. But Chad VanGaalen is the perfect soundtrack for watching television screens report on clean-up and emergency power restoration, and crowds of winter ice storm survivors move through the station: "I can see it in your eyes / peace was on the rise."

The damage from the ice storm is catastrophic. So many trees down. It looks beautiful, the centimetres of ice encasing branches, twigs and winter berries, but the death of the trees, so sad.

I'm on the train, leaving the station. Leaving the city for good. My window faces south towards the lake. I don't see the lake, but I see the Gardiner Expressway, raised like the train yard we're traversing, and the upper levels of Red Path sugar, Loblaws, warehouses, and now they're blocked by other trains. It's getting dark; still light, but when I see the expressway again its lights are on, and so are the Lakeshore boulevard's lights running beneath the expressway.

Now I'm seeing the expressway, packed with tail-lights, sink and disappear beneath me. The tracks turn the train north into the city. I see a snow-covered park with guys playing shinny in a lit outdoor hockey rink. And now a red brick factory with dim lights behind icy windows...getting darker...row houses with porch lights illuminating shovelled walkways...darker and darker...darker until all I can see is the reflection of the train's interior. Strangely, I'm not in it.

Permanence Reviewed

Part 1
Remembered-Thinking-Theory

Abstract

This investigation isolates remembered-thoughts as a means of contemplating the structure of thought, specifically by interweaving the concept of certainty into the concept of remembered-thinking, and representing each logical argument mathematically as well as in verbal-form. The paper contemplates mental methods for predicting the accuracy of a memory of an external observation at varying points in the future, in terms of evidence the theory hypothesizes the mind has evolved to perceive, and theorizes about how those same methods must carry-out when turned to memories of internal observations. The theory concludes that introspective contemplation drives perception to perceive concepts as perfectly-persistent in time and perfectly-relatable to other concepts, often to a degree of infinite (timeless) existence and infinite-relatability, and demonstrates a correlation between this phenomenon and the establishment of perfect belief in concepts. The paper presents a comparison between the reality of this perfection and the inherent imperfections that exists in the universe described by special relativity, and based on this comparison defines knowledge as an entity that oscillates between conceptual perfection and real-world imperfection.

Introduction

How can conscious minds really know that they had the thoughts they remember having? What they have is the memory of the observation of the thought itself, either a stable object, like a colour or a familiar face remembered to have been brought to mind time and again, or a one-off thinking event remembered as a sudden insight, a final decision, or some other newly mix-and-matched set of concepts. Memories-of-thoughts are all the evidence conscious minds have of thought objects and events. Unlike memories of observations of external-objects, there's no way to return to the object and reconfirm the remembered-features, and unlike memories of observations of external-events, there's no residual event-effects reverberating into the future that offer evidence substantiating or unsubstantiating the remembered-details.

Axiom

The evidence substantiating or unsubstantiating the accuracy of a memory-of-a-thought is finite the moment the memory is created, and sourced solely from the thinker themselves. Remembered-thinking-theory is built entirely off this axiom.

Values

An internally experienced memory is a unit defined by the beginning and end of the reflecting mind's attention, which creates temporal boundaries around the unit. Conscious minds build their picture of the external world through units-of-memory that are like windows along a hallway that minds walk whenever they are reflecting on their memories and memory-built-knowledge. If that picture is of a forested landscape, then those windows may present one tree here, a collection of trees there, and an assortment of undergrowth and animals. Each window provides only a segment of the forest, but the knowledge gained is not segmented itself. The mind recognizes that in between each window are many unseen trees, animals and undergrowth. The mind's picture of the forest is built from familiarity and previous knowledge that allows the mind to quickly form hypotheses and conclusions: when three successive windows present birch trees the mind will hypothesize-and-conclude that out there is a stand of birch trees; when each passing window presents a squirrel in an oak tree ever focused on an opening in the trunk, while occasionally looking suspiciously from side to side, the mind will hypothesize-and-conclude that the squirrel has a stash of acorns in the opening; when the mind sees moving water with each window representing a glance to the left, and each window relaying a left-sourced-sound of moving water, it will hypothesize-and-conclude that to the left is a river, that between each left-glancing-and-listening-window is an unbroken continuity. The most important categories of hypotheses the mind makes for building its picture of the world is of repetitions in events and continuities in objects.

Every conscious mind comes to understand the benefits of their capacity to hypothesize and conclude about connections between objects and events observed through the windows and those that are unseen, but at the same time they inevitably come to understand the fallibility in what they conclude. A picture of the world is easiest to manifest when it consists of repetitions that repeat perfectly, when it exists in a completely knowable environmental context, and when it consists of continuities that are never deformed at any point in space or time. When three birch trees guarantee the presence of a stand of only birch trees, when squirrels that are focused and suspicious are always squirrels preoccupied by acorns, and when rivers are always rivers, and never slow to a lake or wetland, minds can indulge in what's possibly their favourite emotional state, a feeling of perfect certainty. Unfortunately, this is not the universe the mind ever experiences. What the mind comes to understand is that the connections between what's seen in the windows, and what's unseen between them, are too numerous, imperfect and deformable to ever truly present perfection.

Often a conscious mind will go ahead and assume perfect repetitions and continuities to exist anyway, sometimes just to indulge in the false-sense-of-perfect-certainty, but the difficulty with the external world is that their observations are never the only source of evidence substantiating or unsubstantiating a conclusion. First, those unseen objects and events may become seen in the future, so that a later-seen map showing that a river does in fact slow to a lake falsifies a belief in the river's perfect continuity, or a stand of birch trees experienced many years later exhibits the occasional alder, so that now the mind must be suspicious of whether that presumed purely-birch-tree-stand experienced long ago was really that. Second, other conscious minds are forever available to provide new evidence, so that perhaps one day a mind meets an ecologist specializing in squirrel-tree-interactions, who informs the mind that squirrels have object-interests that go well beyond just acorns, and now the mind must acknowledge that maybe there was some other kind of food, or something else entirely, in that hole in the tree. And third, minds come to recognize that those windows to the external world eventually crack, fog, and become opaque if the mind does not refresh their observation of that part of the universe, and so their certainty in their conclusions too cracks, fogs and becomes opaque.

With every step forward in time, the more unseen events and objects have the chance to come into view, the more other conscious minds have a chance to present evidence that challenges, and the more distant and opaque becomes the initial memories that originally gave a sense of certainty in a mind's conclusions; eventually all knowledge gained from observations of external events and objects becomes just as likely to be true as untrue. This gives the theory its first value: $P_{external}(t) = 0.5$

where $P_{external}$ represents the probability that a memory is accurately representing an observation of an external event or object, and t is a value of time that is big enough to account for the eventual degradation of certainty.

Imagine that on the other side of the hallway are a similar row of windows, but this time the windows represent memories of observations of a conscious mind's own thoughts. These thoughts might also be of a forest, but in this case the forest would be an imagined happy-place that a mind manifests every time they feel they need a little escapism. In this forest are stands of only birch trees, squirrels forever obsessed with acorns, and rivers that run exactly as expected all the way to the ocean. On one imagining, a mind may realize that they visualized a waterfall downriver from the birch stand when last they imagined it upriver, but this kind of discrepancy only ever happens for recently remembered thoughts. The more distant the window a mind hypothesizes to match the presently seen window, the easier it is to believe with perfect certainty that the two windows match perfectly. This point is worth a deep exploration, and, when contextualized under the axiom, will ultimately lead to the final equations of remembered-thinking-theory, but for now it will simply provide another value: $P_{internal}(t) = 1$ where $P_{internal}$ represents the probability that a memory of an internally observed event or object is accurately represented, and t represents a value for time large enough for a mind to feel perfectly-certain in the memory.

Equalities and inequalities

There are two types of certainty that thinkers experience: subjective-certainty and objective-certainty. An example of each has already been presented, but without the terminology. When the forest walker manifested perfect-certainty in a stand of purely birch trees, a population of acorn-only obsessed squirrels, and a river that remains perfectly river-like all the way to the ocean, they exercised their subjective-certainty, a certainty in the accuracy of their memories and conclusions that relies on nothing but their own subjective-opinion. It was shown in the example that the thinker can never fully escape objective-certainty, that certainty of the accuracy of their memories and conclusions that takes into account all available evidence, past, present and future. Objective-certainty takes into account a probability that unseen objects and events, other conscious minds, and the degradation of observation-memories will substantiate or unsubstantiate the accuracy of memories and conclusions to various degrees at various points in time. A conscious mind can turn a blind-eye to objective-certainty temporarily, but inevitably objective-certainty will break the sometimes indulged feeling of perfect-certainty that subjective-certainty can manifest.

Consider once again the windows that represent memories of observations of a mind's own thinking-in-action. As an experience that this theory assumes comes later in cognitive evolution, and later in cognitive development, it also assumes that a first-awareness of a memory-of-a-thought would incite a similar response as an awareness of a memory of an external event or object: the mind would recognize that the longer-ago the observation of a thought that's being remembered, such as the first imagining of the happy-place-forest, the less likely that the memory would be accurate, a recognition that would feel to awareness like a vagueness or faintness inherent to conclusions about the remembered-thought. Was the fantasy-forest really imagined for the first time for escapism, or was some other emotional state, forgotten because it was only relevant to that time, driving the fantasy? Was the initial fantasy, imagined so very long ago, even of a forest, or did the forest evolve from something else entirely? The lack of accuracy would also initially affect certainty in what connections the thought has to other internal information processing. A sense of hunger may be concluded to have arrived with the imagining of dinner, but as time goes on a mind could sensibly question whether the imagining of dinner was brought on by a sense of hunger. This phenomenon, however, turns on its head at that point when objective-certainty comes into consideration.

There is no chance of those unseen, subconscious-processings from long ago to reappear and break a mind's certainty, and there is no other conscious mind who may one day bring unknown evidence to challenge that certainty, as long as the thoughts were never externally expressed. The only real challenge to a mind's certainty is that self-imposed question of whether a long ago thought is still remembered accurately. If a thinker decides yes, their memories are perfectly accurate; in other words, if they manifest perfect subjective-certainty, that subjective-certainty immediately becomes the measure of objective-certainty. At this point in the arguments an important mathematical symbol must be put in the spotlight: the $=$ sign, because in the case of the two types of certainty, when the question is about the accuracy of a memory of observed thinking-in-action, subjective-certainty $=$ objective-certainty.

The $=$ sign is important to highlight because in the case of the accuracy of a memory of observed external events and objects, it's always the case that objective-certainty puts subjective-certainty into question, that subjective-certainty $\neq$ objective-certainty, which is a quality indicated by $P_{external}(t) = 0.5$ – the quality that is the inevitable decline in likeliness that memories are accurate, to the point where they are no longer worth remembering. Theoretically, subjective-certainty could equal objective-certainty in a single instance, but this capacity is insignificant for this comparison to the opposing equality within the internal which has persistence in time. This is the first but not the last time that the signs $=$ and $\neq$ come to differentiate the internal and the external. Once remembered-thinking-theory is fully explained, it will be clear that this is always the case, and that it contains a deeply significant meaning.

Because a thinker's subjective-certainty in the accuracy of their memories-of-thinking is equivalent to the objective-certainty of that accuracy, they are free, at the point following initial awareness, to manifest perfect-certainty in their analysis of the accuracy. This fact does not dismiss the significance of the initial awareness, which was argued earlier to begin with the same questions of accuracy as for external events and objects, resulting in a vagueness or faintness to the analysis. Presuming the happy-place-forest thinker does come to have perfect-certainty in their memory of that long-ago inception of the fantasy, that greater uncertainty, or vagueness, present in the initial awareness, retrospectively becomes nothing more than the presentation of a greater list of options for what memory the thinker will have subsequently remembered with perfect-certainty. In the case of the happy-place-forest-fantasy, a likely forerunner option is a memory that matches perfectly with the most recently-remembered-fantasy. The conclusion of that argument is that if the happy-place-forest-thinker wants to believe that they are imagining a forest perfectly the same as in a previous imagining, they will find the task easier the longer ago was the inception of the compared-to-imagining. This conclusion about remembered-thinking is significant, because just as a mind is free to manifest any level of subjective-certainty in the accuracy of their memories-of-thinking, they are equally free to manifest any sense of age that a recurring thought may have had, since that knowledge is itself a potentially unexpressed thought with an objective-certainty in its accuracy that is equivalent to the subjective-certainty in its accuracy. This final point is one basis for the final equations presented in the theory, but before it's explored more deeply and mathematically, a second point about equivalencies must be made.

The second reason that the $=$ sign and the $\neq$ sign represent the internal and external is because of the inevitable imperfectness of repetitions and deformableness of continuities over spacetime, in all of both common and scientific observation. This fact about the external universe is held true by Einstein's historic defense. Einstein's experience with physics gave him the wisdom to know that there are no rigid bodies in space, that everything is deformable and alters with temperature, and that there's no truth to the idea that two objects can have surfaces that touch, (Einstein, 1916). Einstein pointed out that it's easy to believe that the forces acting on an object like a rigid rod will affect the whole rod at once, but this perspective is only sustainable for rods that exist on the spatial scale that humans occupy. Imagine a rod that is a light-year long, one that is as rigid as anything in the universe could be, perfectly rigid if that's possible. But is it? If a force where to act on one end of the rod, instantaneously moving the other end, one light year away, that would constitute the transmission of force, and information about the force acting on the rod, at a speed faster than the speed of light, and that is impossible, (Einstein, 1905, 1907, 1911).

What this means is that in the universe there is no continuity in any object in space or time. So any identity a conscious mind gives to an object, given that that identity is meant to be the same here and there, now and later, is a simplification of what they're really looking at: a piece of the universe evolving, changing, unpredictably manifesting new forms of never-seen-before being. This fact provides supporting evidence for Einstein's belief that events as he understood events, as all those connections between things, are only conceptual interpretations of something more complex and unpredictable; because if the objects exhibiting the relationships themselves are not stable enough to be identified as a persistent thing, then the relationships between them are even less able to be identified as a persistent thing (Einstein, 1917).

What about perfect iterations of the same event, is that never possible even in the case of subatomic or interstellar observations, where events appear to simplify into perfectly cyclic phenomenon? Science seems to forever discover glitches and wabbles in whatever it first presumed to cycle perfectly, but Einstein introduced a more fundamental problem in presuming the possibility of a perfectly repeating event. To conclude that an event repeats perfectly, with objective-certainty, would require agreement between observers, but Einstein disproved this possibility. First, it's objectively impossible for an event to appear perfectly the same for multiple observers, in other words, for the concept of simultaneity to exist in the universe, which is a foundational proof presented in that paper that introduced special relativity. Second, because special relativity proved that objects interact dynamically with time the same way they do with space, it also proved that there is no such thing as a present-moment objectively-confirmable by multiple-observers (Einstein, 1905). This is why Einstein states, "Since there exist in this four-dimensional structure no longer any sections which represent 'now' objectively, the concepts of happening and becoming are indeed not completely suspended, but yet complicated. It appears therefore more natural to think of physical reality as a four-dimensional existence, instead of, as hitherto, the evolution of a three-dimensional existence," (Einstein, 1916). It's only in the evolution of a three-dimensional existence that perfect repetition has even a theoretical possibility, but that three-dimensional existence is a fantasy established for the human animal because, "The earth's crust plays such a dominant rôle in our daily life in judging the relative positions of bodies that it has led to an abstract conception of space which certainly cannot be defended," (Einstein, 1921b).

The relevance of the imperfectness of Einstein's universe to remembered-thinking-theory is that it shows how wondrously peculiar it is that perfection is manifested in the mind, in a universe where no such thing should exist. This capacity is what the theory explores deeply and mathematically in the following sections, but this section simply needs to end by mathematically defining these equalities and inequalities. The expression $ME_1 \neq$

ME_n – where ME represents memories of observations of the external and n represents any number other than 1 – states the impossibility of an equality between two or more memories of external events or objects because of the steady decline in the probability of accuracy of memories of external observations; as well as by the fact of the imperfectness of the universe relativity-theory describes, in other words, by the impossibility of the universe even offering up such material to begin with. That wondrously peculiar capacity of the mind to remember a most recently remembered-thought as perfectly matching a previously remembered-thought, or any number of iterations of the same thought, with objective-certainty is represented mathematically as $MI_1 = MI_n$ – where MI represents memories of observations of thinking and n represents any number other than 1. Remembered-thinking-theory also proposes that this equation represents a definition of what a concept is, a point that is thoroughly explored in the next section.

A mathematical definition of concepts

No concept exists as internally perceived in the external universe, and here are the reasons why: observed external events never repeat perfectly, and observed external objects never exhibit perfect continuity. Conscious minds are capable of perceiving perfect repetition and undeformable continuity for a time, but eventually all minds must face the objective reality that challenging-evidence will reveal itself in the form of unseen-objects-and-events becoming observable, and other conscious minds revealing their own observations, so that perfection becomes imperfect once again. Despite this frustrating reality, conscious minds have a reprieve: the conceptual landscape.

In the internal world there exists a special kind of object and a special kind of event. Events that are internal revelations or life-changing decisions don't dissolve into atmospheric and electromagnetic substrates like lightening strikes, but are perfectly-recollectable for a life-span, and may even represent to the mind an infinitely-applicable truth. The objects, although they don't exist in the external, often draw their identity from the external. All the observed individual trees in the world have fed the concept of tree, all the observed squirrels in the world have fed the concept of animal, and all the experienced rivers in the world have fed the concept of a hydrological system. In conceptual form, these objects are no different than any abstract, like honor, faith or Euclidean Geometry. In conceptual form, tree far exceeds the known life of any species of tree; the concept has no recognizable beginning or end for a conscious mind. In conceptual form, animal is not bound to the parameters of a particular branch of life, or to life at all, because in metaphorical form it can embody animalistic behaviour, an animated drawing, or a mythical beast. In conceptual form, a river can not only run all the way to the ocean without ever slowing to a lake or wetland, but it can run all the way to the end of the universe. But why? If such perfection does not exist in the universe, if all things have connections to other things that are limited to contextual parameters, and if nothing has the luxury of experiencing unbounded-time, then how is it concepts even exist?

Remembered-thinking-theory does not answer this question, the question of the origin of concepts, or why conscious minds are granted such a special power. This investigation conforms only to the theory of evolution and the universe described by special relativity theory, but while evolution and relativity can model the reformation of material and energy that already exists, they're not necessarily adequate for explaining the manifestation of something that seems to go against the very nature of the universe. Remembered-thinking-theory leaves unanswered the question of why a mind is capable of manifesting perfection, eternal existence, and infinite-relatability, but what the theory does offer is a proposed explication of exactly how this manifestation tool works from a logical and mathematical point of view.

Remembered-thinking-theory states that the fundamental element of a concept is $MI_1 = MI_n$, and now introduces $M_x I$, where moving the subscript to the M is introduced as a convention for representing a concept legitimized by its perfect-persistence across at least two remembered-thinking experiences. The character and feel of a concept are explained by how the mind comes to perceive this perfection.

The longer ago the inception of the concept compared to the most recent recollection of the concept, the easier it is to perceive the two memories as perfect replications of each other. What is the connection between a visceral feeling of certainty and the perception or knowledge of persistence? If conscious minds perceive an object or the recollectability of an event as persisting perfectly from the past to the present, they will predict that that object or knowledge of that event will similarly persist into the future. This is an acknowledgement of reliability, and the quality of reliability is deeply connected to the visceral feeling of certainty. But the connection goes further once a second layer, a far more often perceived layer, of the conceptual landscape is taken into account.

Consider this phenomenon in terms of a conscious mind's complete conceptual landscape. A conceptual landscape is a picture of all the different thought-units that a mind has at some time, and will at some time again, recall as a concept that is perfectly-persistent, that has an undeformable-continuity. For language speaking animals this landscape is vast and diverse, filled with conceptual representations for many observed external species of things and for many examples of iterating events, as well as many unobservable abstracts. This landscape is also filled with emotions, not those emotions deduced to have existed because they explain some self-observed-behaviour, but those that a conscious mind can manifest as a unit-of-experience for the sake of internal contemplation. The landscape is similarly filled with experiences-of-awareness, not the awareness that absorbs event reverberations into the neurology so that the subconscious can navigate behaviour regardless of how much conscious awareness an animal is experiencing, but the awareness that results in conscious minds seeing what they're seeing as a unit-of-experience, hearing what they're hearing as a unit-of-experience, or perceiving a particular identity in the external through their senses, but as a unitized person, object or event, stabilized through conceptualization, so that they can contemplate the unit in relation to unitized feelings, thoughts or other experiences-of-awareness.

With a landscape of $M_x I$'s established, a conscious mind can now recall an $M_1 I$ and consider its relationship to an $M_2 I$. If an $M_1 I$ and an $M_2 I$ are established as perfectly-persistent through an equivalency with their own iterations, then they also have the capacity to not only exhibit a relationship, but to exhibit a relationship that is itself perfectly-persistent, and representative of an undeformable-continuity.

If a lightening-strike is always perceived to be a destructive, fire-starting force, and a forest is always perceived to be a dry, fire-vulnerable forest, then the perceived relationship between the concept of a lightening-strike and the concept of a forest is that the one will always annihilate the other. The important distinction between these conceptual relationships, and their external equivalents, is that in conception they really do represent a perfect equivalency, whereas in the external they only represent a mostly-true-statement, at least in terms of objective-certainty. Here remembered-thinking-theory intersects with a most famous epistemological statement made in Einstein's *Geometry and Experience*, which in part presents a sum-total of his thoughts and statements against perfect-rigidity, undeformable-continuity, and totally-comprehensible external-relationships: "At this point an enigma presents itself which in all ages has agitated inquiring minds. How can it be that mathematics, being after all a product of human thought which is independent of experience, is so admirably appropriate to the objects of reality? Is human reason, then, without experience, merely by taking thought, able to fathom the properties of real things?

"In my opinion the answer to this question is, briefly, this: as far as the propositions of mathematics refer to reality, they are not certain; and as far as they are certain, they do not refer to reality." (Einstein, 1921a).

What if the lightening strike in question is no ordinary lightning strike, but that all powerful weapon held by Zeus? In this case the mind could perceive a perfect causal relationship between the concept of lightening and the conceptual annihilation of a home, a city, or an entire continent. A logical argument was introduced previously to defend the idea that the longer ago the inception of a remembered-thought, the easier it is for a mind to perceive a perfect replication in the most recently remembered iteration of the thought. This same logic is applicable to the relatability of a most recently remembered concept, say that of Zeus's lightning, and a set of concepts successively analysed for their relationship to that initial concept: the less objective-certainty, or more vagueness, the related-to concept has upon first-awareness, the more versions of the concept, the more capabilities to relate, the mind can ultimately come to perceive with perfect-certainty. Awareness will perceive more vagueness the longer-ago the compared to concept was last remembered, such as the vulnerability of a not-often-thought-about-country to Zeus's lightening strike, or for concepts that are further down the imagined list of potentially-relatable-concepts. At the point when objective-certainty comes to equal subjective-certainty, the more in-frequently-remembered and further-down-the-list related-to concepts are, the easier it will be to perceive the relationship precisely as hypothesized.

Just as a concept comes to be perceived as a continuity, that relationship, such as the destructive power of Zeus's lightening, will come to be seen as a continuity independent of the lightening or annihilated objects themselves. At this point, when pondering what objects Zeus's lightening is capable of destroying, a conscious mind can comfortably decide, "anything and everything". A concept, therefore, has a second means of exhibiting perfect-persistence and undeformable-continuity, in addition to its persistence through time: its capacity to relate to a set of other concepts, or even just its capacity to relate.

This gives a new way to understand the relationship between the visceral feeling of certainty and the perception or knowledge of persistence: in addition to a concept exhibiting reliability by nature of its capacity to persist with perfection into the future, it now also exhibits a reliability in its capacity to relate perfectly to other concepts, either causally or through some other type of relationship, a relationship which itself is capable of an independent existence that is perfectly-persistent and undeformably-continuous. Together, these two reliable qualities – a concept's perfect-persistence in time and perfect-relatability to other concepts – are so powerfully connected to certainty that remembered-thinking-theory defines this experience of certainty as an experience of a concept's truth and value. Because of the finiteness and sole-sourcing of evidence that substantiates this conceptual landscape, the truth and value identified here is completely embodied in the conceiving mind, in that visceral sense of certainty, and therefore is further identified as the nature of belief. Perfect-belief, according to this definition, is what the probability value truly represents in the summarizing equation $P_{internal}(t) = 1$, and is synonymous with the idea of perfect-certainty in a concept.

The following section will unpack $P_{internal}(t) = 1$ by thoroughly analyzing the compounded relationship that was just introduced, using a new term: conceptual-expanse. Conceptual-expanse compounds the measure of a concept's capacity to persist perfectly through some quantity of time and relate perfectly to some number of other concepts into a single value. Because a concept's expanse equates to greater persistence, which equates to reliability, which equates to a visceral sense of certainty hypothesized to represent truth and value to such a degree that the theory defines belief by this sense of certainty, the theory here uncovers its most significant discovery: a correlative relationship between a concept's perceived expanse and the capacity of that concept to inspire belief. This is the correlation that is described by the final equations of remembered-thinking-theory.

The Theory

The first mathematical statement made was that $P_{external}(t) = 0.5$ where $P_{external}$ represents the probability that a memory is accurately representing an observation of an external event or object, and t is a value of time that is big enough to account for the eventual degradation of certainty. What is missing is an expression that shows just what happens as t approaches a value big enough for $P_{external}$ to equal 0.5 . The expression $P_{external}(t) = 0.5 + 0.5 \times e^{-\lambda t}$ gives the opportunity to set a rate at which $P_{external}$ degrades from 1 to 0.5 using the common decay function $e^{-\lambda t}$. In this function e is the constant known as Euler's number, t is a value for time where an increase in 1 can represent an increase in one day, one week, one year, or any other unit of time, and λ (lambda) is a value that will either have the function decay quickly or slowly. The value of λ is what's important to focus on because this value is what represents the probability that a memory of an external event or object will be accurate at a particular point in time, or particular value of t . It reflects the measure of what challenging evidence is predicted to be faced at that time because of the appearance of previously connected but unseen objects and events, new evidence from other conscious minds, and the degradation of memory and knowledge that will have to be accounted for at that point.

As an example, consider the forest-walker's capacity to remember details about the forest as time progresses away from their experience. The possibilities for degradation discussed were the later appearance of maps or iterations of similar tree stands that present challenges to the walker's conclusions, other conscious minds with more specialized knowledge that could challenge their assumptions, and the reality that their own memory of the forest would degrade unless the forest was revisited. Assume that an analysis of these factors results in a value for λ of 0.8 , given that a value of 1 for t is equivalent to one year. The results will predict that after one year the walker's knowledge of the forest will have a 72% chance of accuracy, after two years, a 60% chance, after three years, a 55% chance, and ten years following the experience of the forest, a 50% chance of accuracy, meaning the prediction is that the knowledge the walker will have is just as likely to be true as untrue.

A similar equation can represent the argument that memories-of-thinking eventually achieve a 100% chance of being accurate: $P_{internal}(t) = 1 - e^{-\lambda t}$, or $P_{M_x I}(t) = 1 - e^{-\lambda t}$, where $M_x I$ not only indicates a concept legitimized by its persistence, but where x could represent a group of concepts embodied by a set-of-knowledge. If the same values are used, the results are one year equals 55% accuracy, two years equals 80% accuracy, three years equals 91% accuracy, and ten years equals a number very close to 100% accuracy. These values clearly don't reflect actual outcomes of conceptual thought, but that's because the value of λ is not the significant factor in describing a conscious mind's movement towards belief. With $P_{external}(t)$, the λ value represented the measure of objective-certainty, which was the most significant factor in a conscious mind's perspective of the probability of the accuracy of their memories and conclusions about external objects and events. With $P_{internal}(t)$, or $P_{M_x I}(t)$, t is the most important factor, because it determines the measure of time during which the concept is believed to have persisted perfectly. In other words, it's not objective-certainty that affects belief in a concept, but a visceral sense of familiarity, a sense of familiarity that makes concepts feel known.

If t is allowed to initiate at a value higher than a starter value of 1 , then it can also model how a mind recalls a perfectly persistent concept in an isolated thinking-event. Afterall, a mind that has no attention on memories-of-thinking, or that is simply asleep, is wholly part of the imperfect universe, evolving through an infinite-heterogeneity of new states. So the subconscious elements that seed a consciously-aware, introspective thinking-event can't possibly be the exact same as those that seeded previous thinking-events that the mind will nevertheless come to believe contained perfect replications of currently-conceived objects and events. However, what those elements can arrive with is a visceral sense of conceptual-familiarity that instructs the consciously-aware mind to reverse-engineer from those elements, to a degree consistent with the sense of familiarity, or value of t , concepts that have *that* length of existence in time and *that* capacity to relate to a set of other concepts. From there the mind manifests a sense of certainty, or belief, in the capacity of those concepts to persist perfectly across remembered-thinking-events.

So, in the case of $P_{M_x I}(t)$, λ is left as an arbitrary gauge determining to what degree an increase in familiarity with a concept increases belief in that concept. Instead of being arbitrary, this value could represent a measure of a mind's sense of confidence in their own capacity for conceptualization, and that measure could cross over to $P_{external}(t)$ for that same mind as an additional factor for determining their objective-certainty, or λ, in the accuracy of their memories of external observations. This level of modelling is more nuanced than the foundational elements this paper intends to represent mathematically, and less one-to-one representative of the theory, but the concluding section of the paper will make clear that a conduit such as this between $P_{M_xI}(t)$ and $P_{external}(t)$ is important for deriving from the theory a complete picture of human knowledge.

Returning to the foundational elements, there is one more pertinent quality of $P_{M_xI}(t) = 1 - e^{-\lambda t}$ that the theory proposes is illuminating: no matter how large the value of t , whether it represents hours, days or years, P never quite reaches 100% accuracy. In mathematics, the 100% , or a P value of 1 , that is never quite reached, despite values that get very close, is described as a limit. The same equation presented above in limit notation looks like this: $P_{M_xI}(t) = \lim_{t \to \infty}(1 - e^{-\lambda t})$. Translated into verbal form, this says that perfect belief in the truth and value of a concept is achieved only when the concept is perceived to have an infinite-existence in time, and infinite-relatability to an infinite-set of other concepts. This statement happens to agree perfectly with remembered-thinking-theory's proposed idea that concepts, like "tree" or "honor", have no temporal beginning or end, and that concepts like Zeus's lightning can relate to an infinite-set of other concepts, like Zeus's lightning's capacity to annihilate anything and everything. Going forward, in the case of mathematically describing concepts, limit notation is applied because of its value in accurately describing the phenomenon.

A problem with the single equation above is that it describes a unidirectional correlation, which says that conscious minds that allow themselves to perceive a concept as having a greater and greater expanse will feel a greater and greater level of certainty and belief in the concept, but the theory proposes that the correlation goes equally both ways. Here is a second equation that shows how a new perception of a concept's expanse can result from the first equation's ratcheting up of a conscious mind's level of belief: $\left(T_{new} \circ P_{M_xI}(t)\right) = \lim\limits_{P_{M_xI}(t) \to 1} \left(\frac{1}{1 - P_{M_xI}(t)}\right)$. Translated into verbal form, this says that as conscious minds achieve greater belief in a concept by perceiving the concept to have a greater expanse, that greater belief in the concept itself fosters a perspective of the concept's expanse as shooting towards infinity. This mathematical exploration indicates a positive feedback loop that is completed by a third equation which simply says $t = T_{new}$, so that the equations can run again with the increased value in t. The positive feedback loop results in an exponential increase in the perception of a concept's expanse, and a sprint towards its capacity to inspire perfect-belief.

Conclusion

The final equation of remembered-thinking-theory says concepts that manifest perfect-belief and inspire a perception of timelessness and infinite-relatability are a comfortable and self-fulfilling outcome of conceptual-thinking. They're a force that drives towards perfection those knowledge-sets that conscious minds reflect on, and that affect their states-of-perception. This force-of-conceptual-thinking is opposed by experiences of external events and objects that keep a reality check on the hypotheses and conclusions embodied by a set of knowledge.

Consider these forces in terms of the window analogy. While the conceptualized continuities on the memories-of-internal-observations side fill in the gaps between the windows on the memories-of-external-observations side, external observations of individual iterations of events and individual appearances of objects forever call into question the continuities uniformly reappearing in the windows on the memories-of-internal-observations side. Therefor the final conclusion of remembered-thinking-theory is that knowledge-sets that conscious minds reflect on, and that affect their states of perception, are less-so definable as a static mix of abstractness and concreteness, and more-so definable as an oscillation, where they ascend towards perfection, then disintegrate into uncertainty, forcing minds to either rebuild or abandon that knowledge to the infinite-heterogeneity of the universe.

References

Einstein, A. (1905). On The Electrodynamics Of Moving Bodies. Annalen der Physik 17 (1905): 891-921.

Einstein, A. (1907). On The Inertai Of Energy Required By The Relativity Principle. Annalen der Physik 23 (1907): 371-384.

Einstein, A. (1911). 'Discussion' Following the Lecture Version of 'The Theory of Relativity'. Naturforschende Gesellschaft in Zürich. Sitzungsberichte (1911): II-IX. Published in vol. 4 of Vierteljahrschrift der Naturforschenden Gesellschaft in Zürich 56 (1911). Minutes of the meeting of 16 January 1911.

Einstein, A. (1916). On The Special and General Theory of Relativity (A Popular Account). Translated by Robert W. Lawson for Relativity: The Special and the General Theory (Crown, 1961; The Estate of Albert Einstein).

Einstein, A. (1917). Letter to Moritz Schlick, 21 May 1917...via The Hebrew University of Jerusalem and Princeton University Press. (1998). The Collected Papers of Albert Einstein, Volume 8, Part A: The Berlin Years: Correspondence 1914-1917. Edited by Robert Schulmann, A. J. Kox, Michel Janssen, and József Illy.

Einstein, A. (1921a). Geometry and Experience. Lecture before the Prussian Academy of Sciences...via The Hebrew University of

Jerusalem and Princeton University Press. (1998). The Collected Papers of Albert Einstein, Volume 7: The Berlin Years: Writings, 1918-1921 (English translation supplement). Translation by Sonja Bargmann (New York: Crown, 1982).

Einstein, A. (1921b) via The Hebrew University of Jerusalem and Princeton University Press. (1998). The Collected Papers of Albert Einstein, Volume 7: The Berlin Years: Writings, 1918-1921 (English translation supplement). Four Lectures on the Theory of Relativity, Held at Princeton University May 1921. Published 1922 by Vieweg (Braunschweig) English translation by Edwin Plimpton Adams (London: Methuen, 1922; Princeton: Princeton University Press, 1923; later editions in English: 2nd: 1945; 3rd: 1950; 4th: 1953; 5th: 1956).

Part 2
Hedi's Friend Diogenes

In 1944 Einstein read a letter from his old friend Hedwig (Hedi) Born. In it she begins, "I have read [your letter] several times and once again had that feeling of liberation I used to get from our talks during the war." Later in the letter she touches on a philosophical vein that had existed in those talks ever since they first became friends: "I, too, am unable to believe in a 'dice-playing' God, nor am I able to imagine that you believe – as Max has just told me when we were discussing it – that your 'complete rule of law' means that everything is predetermined, for example, whether I am going to have my child inoculated against diphtheriae or not, etc...

"Things would then be as in Omar the tentmaker:

"'That I would drink during my lifetime

"'God has known for all eternity....'

"I have forgotten what follows, but it must have been: where then is ethics, the consciousness of striving?

"You could probably explain this to me with just a few of those vigorous words of yours."[1]

As it happens, in 1919 Einstein had written to her exactly how he would have responded to Omar the Tentmaker's sentiment: "What you call 'Max's materialism' is simply the causal way of looking at things. This way of looking at things always answers only the question 'Why?', but never the question 'To what end?'. No utility principle and no natural selection will make us get over that. However, if someone asks 'To what purpose should we help one another, make life easier for each other, make beautiful music or have inspired thoughts?', he would have to be told: 'If you don't feel it, no-one can explain it to you.' Without this primary feeling we are nothing and had better not live at all."[2] But Einstein was a much different person before 1920 than after, more irreligious and anti-nationalist than Zionist, more pacifist than advocate for nuclear weapons development, and more defeater of absolutes in the intellectual tradition he began than proponent of any 'complete rule of law' in science or philosophy. It's perhaps this story of his friendship with Max and Hedi Born that offers the most illuminating window into his transformation.

Max and Hedi became friends with Einstein when he moved to Berlin during the First World War. They would visit each other frequently and help each other stay sane with music, poetry and conversation. With Max, Einstein found a comfortable conversation partner on, not only the sciences in which they were life-long colleagues, but in politics and human-relationships, particularly during the complex and tumultuous times of the Great War. With Hedi, he found an intellect quite different than his own, fueled by literature, philosophy and theology, so that he himself could delve into subjects that typically sat outside his mind, and find conversational-companionship that otherwise eluded him: "I have no need to assure you how found I am of you both and how glad I am to have you as friends and kindred spirits in this…desert," he wrote in February of 1918.[3]

For someone like Einstein, kindred spirits were crucial for keeping him, at least sometimes, interested in the world outside his mind. Later that year, in April, he delivered what Hedi will later reference as his "talk to Plank". In the talk, *motives for research*, Einstein hypothesizes about the motives of those who occupy the temple of science, highlighting Planck as a special breed. What Hedi references is a segment about what drives scientist like Planck (and, more importantly for Hedi, Einstein) into the temple in the first place: "I believe with Schopenhauer that one of the strongest motives that leads men to art and science is escape from everyday life with its painful crudity and hopeless dreariness, from the fetters of one's own ever shifting desires. A finely tempered nature longs to escape from personal life into the world of objective perception and thought; this desire may be compared with the townsman's irresistible longing to escape from his noisy, cramped surroundings into the silence of high mountains, where the eye ranges freely through the still, pure air and fondly traces out the restful contours apparently built for eternity.

"With this negative motive there goes a positive one. Man tries to make for himself in the fashion that suits him best a simplified and intelligible picture of the world; he then tries to some extent to substitute this cosmos of his for the world of experience, and thus to overcome it. This is what the painter, the poet, the speculative philosopher, and the natural scientist do, each in his own fashion. Each makes this cosmos and its construction the pivot of his emotional life, in order to find in this way the peace and security which he cannot find in the narrow whirlpool of personal experience."[4]

As the war came to a close, and the completion of general relativity, along with the final fallouts of Einstein's divorce, and a most likely not unrelated stomach ulcer that debilitated him, he began to withdraw from society. In the summer of 1918, while on vacation in Ahrenshoop, he wrote to Max: "It is wonderful here, no telephone, no duties, absolute peace. I simply can't imagine now how you can bear life in the big city. And the weather is wonderful too. I lie on the beach like a crocodile and let myself be roasted by the sun, I never see a newspaper and don't give a damn for what is called the world."[5]

But in those days his human spirit was too alive to ever withdraw completely. Later, in a 1926 letter to Einstein, Hedi reflected on words he spoke most likely during this particularly difficult period: "But what interests me most in people is their *spiritual attitude* to life, rather than just their fate; most of the so-called tragic destinies are nothing more than the brutal vicissitudes of life, which are linked by pure chance to one particular individual. When I think of you, for example, I do not think of individual talents and achievements, but I marvel at your supreme mastery of life itself. I remember something you once said, which for me is the key to your personality and way of thinking: when you lay gravely ill you said: 'I have such a feeling of solidarity with every living being, that it does not matter to me where the individual begins and ends'. You probably put it much more beautifully, but this is what you meant. Individual *acts* mean nothing to me: they are just a momentary flash of light."[6]

A second letter from Ahrenshoop indicated Einstein's desire to return to societal life: "Brilliant landscape and satisfied citizens, who have nothing to fear. This is how it looks. But God knows, I prefer people with anxieties, whose tomorrow is threatened by uncertainty. How will it all end? One cannot tear one's thoughts away from Berlin…"[7] At that time both Einstein and Max retained optimism for the future of post-war Germany. Max became slightly more fearful about Germany's reaction to punishments from the allies, but Einstein retained his optimism, "Eventually Germany's dangerousness will go up in smoke…"[8]

In 1919 Einstein and his relativity theory rose to a fame never achieved by a scientist before. By the end of the year it was clear that Einstein was not equipped to navigate such an inflated public persona, in particular the fact that newspapers were so quick to grab any comment that could indicate a drama amongst scientific colleagues, a phenomenon that would continue in many ways, including by portraying collegial debates on quantum physics between him and Max as representing some kind of scientific spike between them, when in fact their philosophical disagreements only ever grew their friendship stronger. By the end of the year he was also losing his optimism for Germany, seeing now that the allies would not pull back from the harshness of retribution against her, and that Germany would be unable to recover from the hurt to her pride. But neither Max nor Einstein at that point new just how bad things would become, and still spoke and thought frequently about Germany's future.

In January of 1920 Einstein's mother became ill. She was in a "hopeless condition and suffering unspeakably". She would remain in that condition until her death in March. It was an unbearably difficult time for Einstein, but from his friend Hedi he did not want sympathy, "Mrs. Born, make yourself interesting in a most reprehensible way. (Whimsical poems and witty letters only are permitted.)"[9]

But in that same sad spring Hedi would bare witness to her own mother's death from the flu pandemic that followed the war. That deeply philosophical relationship between Einstein and Hedi would help guide them both. In April, Einstein wrote, "The news of the bitter experience you had to go through has touched me deeply. I know what it means to see one's mother suffer the agony of death and be unable to help. There is no consolation. All of us have this heavy burden to bear, for it is inseparably bound up with life. However, there is one thing: to unite in friendship, and to help one another to carry the burden. We do, after all, share so many happy experiences that we have no need to give way to pointless brooding. The old, who have died, live on in the young ones. Don't you feel this now in your bereavement when you look at your children?"[10] Hedi would not weather the storm as well as Einstein. Max reported that she had "collapsed in the end, as a result of all the excitement, pain and overexertion".[11]

Hedi slowly recovered over the summer and eventually wrote back to Einstein: "We are very happy that you will be coming to Nauheim, and I hope that you will stay with us for a few days. I am now – after my mother's death – so much in need of these true relationships of the spirit which are left to me. The further the hour of her death lies behind us, the stronger is my longing for the departed; the darker and more incomprehensible seems the enigma of death. The ending of such a strong personality and the sudden extinction of life is such a tormenting problem that one wonders how one is able to live without being constantly troubled by it…One lives under the illusion that it is forever May, and that the whole world is constantly filled with young, juicy and delicious greenery, put there just for one's own use, and then all of a sudden and incredibly fast it happens, and one finds oneself lame and weary of life in the mud of a rain-soaked road. So I thought, well, I am now in the mud, but I can see that it is still May, after all, and I must not allow myself to be pulled down." From their exchange it would seem that Einstein's trip to Nauheim would let them both rediscover young, juicy and delicious greenery of May, but instead events would pass that would bring dark times to even Hedi and Einstein's bond.[12]

On the 24th of August, 1920, Paul Weyland and Ernst Gehrcke presented lectures against relativity at the Philharmonic theatre in Berlin, with Einstein in attendance. The lectures were not just against relativity, but were an attack against Einstein himself as a propagandist who confused scientist and the general public using "mass suggestion".[13] It was in the opinion of most at that time that the lectures were a despicable and shameful attack that Einstein should not have had to respond to. He had already spent his career enthusiastically meeting challenges to relativity from every corner of science and philosophy, and could have easily allowed his success in meeting every previous challenge, combined with the ever accumulating experimental evidence confirming his predictions, to simply speak for itself. In fact it was a time far more apt for exploring the value of relativity theory. Following the lecture, a self-described laymen, Ina Dickmann, wrote to Einstein: "The theory of relativity opened up for me a philosophical world of infinite breadth. In my mind's eye the constraints and boundaries of philosophical systems collapsed, and, for now, my thoughts wander about in the new world (—that is what it is to me) without a horizon in sight. Viewing relativity means to me the toppling of the absolute and the rise of another epistemological world."[14]

But Einstein was drawn into conflict rather than the celebration of relativity. He published an article titled, *My Response*, which defended relativity and himself against the attacks.[15] For his participation in the conflict he was admonished by his colleagues, who expressed great displeasure at seeing a side of Einstein they did not think existed, and pleaded with him to not make anymore public statements.[16, 17, 18, 19]

Einstein was never equipped to navigate a life of fame, but nobody then could possibly know how to navigate a public image that put them at the centre of something as barbaric as an absolute-dehumanization within what was for many the most sacred part of modern society: the temple of science. Only Hedi could understand exactly what turmoil would exist within Einstein's soul during that time, and she wrote to him with a desire to pull him back from the depths she knew he would sink into:

"We are extremely sorry to hear about the unpleasant rows that are worrying you. You must have suffered very much from them, for otherwise you would not have allowed yourself to be goaded into that rather unfortunate reply in the newspapers. Those who know you are sad and suffer with you, because they can see that you have taken this infamous mischief-making very much to heart. Those who do not know you get a false picture of you. That hurts too. In the meanwhile I hope you are like old Diogenes again and smile about the beasts thrashing about in your barrel. That people can still disappoint and irritate you to the point where it affects your peace of mind just does not fit my image of you, which I keep on the private altar of my heart. You could not have withdrawn from the rough and tumble of ordinary life to the 'secluded temple of science' (see your talk to Planck) had you been able to find *the same* illusions, *the same* happiness and peace in your fellow-man as in your temple. So if the filthy waters of the world are now lapping at the steps of your temple, shut the door and laugh. Just say, 'After all, I have not entered the temple in vain.' Don't get angry. Go on being the holy one in the temple – and stay in Germany! There is filth everywhere – but not another female preacher as enthusiastic and *self-opinionated* as your affectionate friend

"Hedi Born"[20]

Hedi understands fully what Einstein finds in scientific-contemplation. When the walls go up to protect that landscape where Einstein once bent time to conform to otherwise misunderstood phenomenon, so that in an instance special relativity had manifested itself, where he once saw the equivalency between gravity felt on earth and acceleration felt in a train, so that in an instance general relativity had manifested itself, where he had no need to declare his philosophical allegiances, to contextualize the sciences he loved in terms of some aspect of his personal life, where he could simply appreciate the beauty of every "flash of light" on his own terms, she understood that Einstein found peace and tranquility. But just because she understood did not mean she believed such isolated thinking was forever good. In fact it worried her, and that's why she wished that Einstein could, "find *the same* illusions, *the same* happiness and peace in your fellow-man as in your temple."

Einstein never heeded Hedi's advice. In *My Response* he challenged his opponents to further debate in Bad Nauheim, debates which were carried out in September. Rather than putting an end to the despicableness of the anti-relativists, the debates brought the antisemitic undertones straight to the surface, as well as Einstein and Max's anger in their in-person response. About the fallout of the debates, Max later wrote: "From then on Lenard carried out a systematic persecution of Einstein. He invented the difference between 'German' and 'Jewish' physics. He and another important physicist, Johannes Stark, who both later received the Nobel Prize, became leading scientific administrators under the Nazis and were responsible for the removal of all Jewish scholars. It was in Nauheim on this occasion that the outlines of the great danger of antisemitism to German science first appeared."[21]

Hedi was not one to suffer alone, which was why she wished for Einstein that he could "find *the same* illusions, *the same* happiness and peace in your fellow-man as in your temple." Of course she would want him to heal in company because she would still be healing herself, still in need of "true relationships of the spirit". But Einstein left the Borns behind in Bad Nauheim to retreat within himself, and Hedi simply offered her understanding: "To judge by your card, Hechingen must be a charming, sleepy little place; just right to calm down the agitation which, to our regret, you were forced to endure here and in Nauheim. We do not want to disturb your slumbering consciousness with effusive letters; sometimes it is a good thing if one's friends are removed from one's consciousness, and I have the feeling that now is the time for us to disappear. After all, there is really nothing more obtrusive than 'suffering with someone'; it is an encroachment on a friend's life, a baring of the soul, of which one is ashamed afterwards," she wrote in October of 1920.[22]

It's unlikely Hedi truly believed the words she spoke, and only wanted to show as much understanding as she could to a friend she desperately still needed to keep her own suffering from isolating, simplifying, achieving infinite-life and infinite-relatability. In that fractured time, instead of disappearing from his consciousness, Hedi and Max took up a battle that was in the name of helping Einstein, but was really more to do with Max's ego, and perhaps Hedi's disappointment in losing an important friend. They learned that Einstein had given his permission for a philosopher to publish a book of his conversations with the great physicist, as a way for people to get to know Einstein the person. At that time, this was a very odd thing in the world of scientists, who went to great lengths to take their personal selves out of their work, both in practice and in publishing. When Max Born published a photograph and one page biography of Einstein the previous year in his book on relativity, his colleagues condemned him for the very unscientific act to a point where Max redacted the biography and photo for the next edition. He admitted later in life that this embarrassment likely led to a resentment over the permission given to this philosopher.[23]

Hedi became so emotional about the issue that she turned her sharp tongue on Einstein's second wife, blaming her for allowing the debacle to happen. When the book published it caused none of the problems the Borns predicted it would, but Einstein's reaction every step of the way was flat and unaffected. His friends and the world were losing this man to the reverberations of depravity, ego and, in the case of Hedi, the reverberations of an unhealed sadness that left her rudderless in the world outside the temple.

For nearly a year Einstein and Hedi's friendship essentially ceases to exist after Einstein has "a tiff with your wife for the sake of mine", he wrote to Max.[24] He and Max continue to exchange letters, but they focus entirely on academic and administrative matters. Einstein once again turned to optimism regarding politics, believing global politics would alleviate the pains Germany still felt, but in a darkly intuitive foreshadowing, Max wrote in February of 1921: "I cannot share your optimism in political matters, although I do not believe that things are quite as black as they are painted. We are not going to pay as much as is asked for. But I can see the effect of this power politics on the minds of the people; it is a wholly irreversible accumulation of ugly feelings of anger, revenge, and hatred. In small towns such as Gottingen, this is very noticeable. I can, of course, understand it. My reason tells me that it is stupid to react in this way; but my emotional reaction is still the same. It seems to me that new catastrophes will inevitably result from all this. The world is not ruled by reason; even less by love. But I hope that the harmony between us will not be disrupted again."[25]

The universe has an infinite-capacity to surprise conscious minds with turns of events that, despite having no place in a consciously-perceived chain-of-events, completely annihilate the past. In August of that year Max informed Einstein that, "A small boy, Gustav Born, came into the world on July 29th."[26] Later that year, old Diogenes read, for the first time in a long time, a little of that wit and humour from his old friend Hedi: "With this card, Gustav Born begs to introduce himself to you, and begs you (1) for your goodwill and affection and (2) not to bear a grudge to his mother for whom he is, after all, not responsible.

"XXX Signed: Gustav"[27]

References

References to The Born-Einstein Letters with Commentaries by Max Born (1-3, 5-12, 20-27).

The Born Letters. (1971). G.V.R. Born, I. Newton-John, M. Pryce; The Einstein Letters. (1971) Estate of Albert Einstein; Commentaries. (1971) G.V.R. Born; Translation. (1971). Newton-John.

1) Hedwig Born to Albert Einstein, 9 October 1944, Pg. 152.

2) Albert Einstein to Hedwig Born, 1 September 1919, pg. 13.

3) Albert Einstein to Hedwig Born, 8 February 1918, pg. 5.

5) Albert Einstein to Max Born, 1918, pg. 7.

6) Hedwig Born to Albert Einstein, 1927, pg. 93-94.

7) Albert Einstein to Max Born, 19 January 1919, pg. 9.

8) Albert Einstein to Max Born, 4 June 1919, pg. 11.

9) Albert Einstein to Max and Hedwig Born, 27 January 1920, pg. 21.

10) Albert Einstein to Hedwig Born, 18 April 1920, pg. 29.

11) Max Born to Albert Einstein, 21 June 1920, pg. 30.

12) Hedwig Born to Albert Einstein, 31 July 1920, pg. 32.

20) Hedwig Born to Albert Einstein, 8 September 1920, pg. 34.

21) Max's commentary for the letter from Albert Einstein to Max and Hedwig Born, 9 September 1920, pg. 36.

22) Hedwig Born to Albert Einstein, 2 October 1920, pg. 36.

23) Max's commentary for the letter from Albert Einstein to Max Born, October 1920, pg. 42.

24) Albert Einstein to Max Born, 30 January 1921, pg. 50.

25) Max Born to Albert Einstein, 12 February 1921, pg. 54.

26) Max Born to Albert Einstein, 4 August 1921, pg. 56.

27) Gustav Born (via Hedwig Born) to Albert Einstein, 1 November 1921, pg. 60.

References for The Collected Papers of Albert Einstein:
https://einsteinpapers.press.princeton.edu/ (13-14, 16-19, 4)

The Hebrew University of Jerusalem and Princeton University Press. (1998). The Collected Papers of Albert Einstein, Volume 10: The Berlin Years: Correspondence, May-December 1920, and Supplementary Correspondence, 1909-1920 (English translation supplement).

Edited by Diana Kormos Buchwald, Tilman Sauer, Ze'ev Rosenkranz, Josef Illy & Virginia Iris Holmes.

Translated by Ann Hentschel.

13) Footnote 1, Letter 111: From Israel Malkin, 27 August 1920.

14) Letter 113: From Ina Dickmann, 28 August, 1920.

16) Letter 114: From Paul Ehrenfest, 28 August, 1920.

17) Letter 114: From Kurt J. Grau, 29 August 1920.

18) Letter 118: From Helmut Block, 30 August 1920.

19) Letter 127: From Paul Ehrenfest, 2 September 1920.

4) Einstein, A. (1918). Motives for Research. Presented 26 April 1918. Published July 1918.

(Untranslated)

Zu Max Plancks sechzigstem Geburtstag. Ansprachen, gehalten am 26. April 1918 in der Deutschen Physikalischen Gesellschaft von E. Warburg, M. v. Laue, A. Sommerfeld und A. Einstein. Karlsruhe: C.F. Müllersche Hofbuchhandlung, 1918, pp. 29-32.

(Translated)

The Hebrew University of Jerusalem and Princeton University Press. (1998). The Collected Papers of Albert Einstein, Volume 7: The Berlin Years: Writings, 1918-1921 (English translation supplement).

Translation from Einstein, Ideas and Opinions, trans. Sonja Bargmann (New York: Crown, 1982).

15) Einstein, A. (1920). My Response. On the Anti-Relativity Company. Published 27 August 1920 In: Berliner Tageblatt, 27 August 1920, Morgen-Ausgabe, pp. [1–2].

About the Author

Twenty-five years of a Kerouacian novelist's life had the final outcome of Andrew Malcolm's life's work: the novel *Die Coast Bye Cecilia* and the philosophical essay *Permanence Reviewed*. His twenties and thirties were marked with adventures in, not only hitch-hiking, but canoeing and skateboarding, photography and music, and living, working and learning in a great many places between Southern Ontario and Vancouver Island. Combined with a life dedicated to creative writing, his explorations gave him a unique and weathered perspective on the nature of experience. His perspective and explorations are shared through his work with the intention of inspiring others to explore experience through their own comparative contemplations of their internal and external lives.